# QUEEN OF HOPE

EMPIRE OF SHATTERED CROWNS

**3**

MAY FREIGHTER

MARKET

SPOTTED
DOGS INN

# ROAD TO THE MINE
# & BARON BALD LUCY'S MANOR

...ARD'S AND FREID'S
...THY & CARPENTER'S

# DRAGON VILLAGE

Copyright © 2023 May Freighter

All rights reserved.

ISBN: 979 8872495444

# DEDICATION

*To my two little goblins—Damian and Elias.
With your unrelenting efforts in keeping your mummy busy, this series has taken three years longer to release. Hopefully, it will take less time to actually complete it.*

*There's always hope…*

# FOREWORD

This book is written in U.K. English.

Some spelling may be different to the U.S.

Author's website:

**www.authormayfreighter.com**

Interior and Exterior Illustration:

**Cristal Designs**

# CONTENTS

|    | Acknowledgments            | i  |
|----|----------------------------|----|
| 1  | Woes of a Knight           | 1  |
| 2  | Mama's Guidance            | 4  |
| 3  | How to Lose a Lady's Interest | 13 |
| 4  | New Appointment            | 17 |
| 5  | A Royal Plot               | 21 |
| 6  | A Perfect Wall-Slam        | 27 |
| 7  | Guilty Feelings            | 32 |
| 8  | A Harem of Men             | 41 |
| 9  | A Kept Man                 | 43 |
| 10 | The Truth Behind the Shadows | 48 |
| 11 | Matters of the Church      | 57 |
| 12 | The Duke's Defence         | 65 |
| 13 | Gut Feeling                | 73 |
| 14 | Wandering Hands            | 80 |
| 15 | Not a Puppet               | 84 |
| 16 | A Weeping Bear             | 89 |

| | | |
|---|---|---|
| 17 | In the Company of Smugglers | 98 |
| 18 | The Impolite Duck | 106 |
| 19 | Around the Campfire | 115 |
| 20 | One Dreadful Night | 121 |
| 21 | Child of Luminos | 127 |
| 22 | Endangered Chastity | 135 |
| 23 | Suspended Search | 143 |
| 24 | Bald Lucy | 150 |
| 25 | A Token of Love | 158 |
| 26 | The Duke's End | 166 |
| 27 | Love or Duty? | 172 |
| 28 | The Dragon's Heart | 178 |
| 29 | Last of the Smugglers | 187 |
| 30 | Whispers of War | 194 |
| 31 | A Taste of Gravy | 197 |
| 32 | A Prisoner's Life | 203 |
| 33 | Restless | 209 |
| 34 | A Bard at Heart | 219 |
| 35 | A Den of Slavers | 227 |

| | | |
|---|---|---|
| 36 | The Paladin | 235 |
| 37 | Hopeless | 246 |
| 38 | Overcome with Sorrow | 256 |
| 39 | Nameless | 267 |
| 40 | God of the World | 274 |
| | Language of the Beastmen | 280 |
| | Beastmen Dictionary (to date) | 281 |
| | About the Author | 283 |

# ACKNOWLEDGMENTS

I would like to thank my wonderful husband for suffering through this book and the following ones in the series. You have no idea how much I appreciate your feedback and ideas.

Also, a massive thank you to Nancy Zee from Crystal Designs for being my cover designer and proof-reader. Although, you did a lot more than just proofread the novel, ha-ha. You are a great friend, and I cannot thank you enough!

Thanks to my friend, I. Galvez for giving it a beta read. You saved my life.

And lastly, thanks to my editor, J. Wallace for butchering my work.

*"For you see, I always wanted to be a bard"*
― Sir Laurence Oswald

# 1
# WOES OF A KNIGHT

### THESSIAN

**S****ensing imminent intrusion** into his bedchambers, Thessian reached under his pillow and aimed his hidden dagger at the door. As a hurried figure burst unceremoniously into the room, he threw the weapon just above the target's head.

Laurence ignored the throw and continued pacing around the room. "I keep telling you to fix your aim."

Thessian sat up in bed and pointed at the dagger lodged in the door. "It was a warning shot." He assessed his friend's suspicious behaviour. "Out with it."

"I may have made a *tiny* mistake last night."

Pausing in the middle of pulling his shirt down his torso, Thessian eyed Laurence with suspicion. "It better not be another fire."

"No, no. Nothing so grand."

"Then did you fornicate with a palace maid and got her pregnant?"

Laurence's mouth fell open. "Not a maid, and, Gods, I *did not* think about that."

"Who was it?" Thessian finished dressing. He hoped it was not someone from Emilia's inner circle. Their relationship was only recently forged. If Laurence ruined what trust he and Emilia had built in the short amount of time, Thessian may need to ship Laurence in a crate back to Darkgate.

Laurence muttered something inaudible under his breath, making Thessian step closer.

"I did not hear you."

"It was Cali."

"Cali?" The wheels in Thessian's head slowly turned, and his eyes grew wide. "As in Dame Calithea Louberte?"

"I may have spent the night with her…"

Thessian dragged a hand over his face. There was so much wrong with what Laurence did that the prince did not know where to begin. Calithea was a good, loyal to a fault knight. The romantic involvement of his two best soldiers could spell trouble. If they fought or fell madly in love, they could ruin the balance of his elite unit.

Laurence rubbed the back of his neck. "I got a *little* drunk last night. When I woke up this morning, I was in Cali's bed…naked. We were both naked."

"That is a picture I never wanted to envision."

Laurence stepped closer, his eyes almost bulging out of his head. "What should I do?"

"Be a decent man and take responsibility. What else can you do?"

"What should I tell Mother? She will skin me alive when she finds out I married a commoner."

Thessian shrugged one shoulder. "And I will disembowel you if you do not fix your mistake." He sighed and pointed to Laurence's chest. "If Dame Calithea declines your offer of marriage, you can move on with your life."

"You are absolutely right, Your Highness! There is a good chance she will reject me."

Thessian arched a brow. *Is Laurence truly so ignorant of Calithea's feelings?*

It may have been a mistake to his friend, but the prince was certain Cali did not feel the same way about the situation.

Laurence grinned.

With a heavy sigh, Thessian said, "Why do I have a feeling you are plotting something even more foolish?"

With a wink and a wave, a reinvigorated Laurence pranced out of the room.

Thessian rolled his eyes. "Off to get himself into even more trouble."

After letting out a heavy sigh, he secured his sword to his hip and headed out in search of his friend.

# 2
# MAMA'S GUIDANCE

## EMILIA

**E**milia stifled a yawn in bed. She couldn't fall asleep last night due to her worries about the missing dragon. With its ability to shape-shift at will, the beast could be hiding among them. Worst-case scenario, it was hiding as one of her aides.

A knock sounded on the door.

"Permission to enter, Your Majesty." It was Ambrose.

"You may," Emilia called out.

Ambrose walked into the room with a silver tray. She smiled at Emilia and brought the tea set over. Placing it on the small table next to the bed, Ambrose began fussing over making a fresh cup of tea.

A soothing smell of roses and herbs filled the room.

"I have prepared a special restorative blend for Your Majesty this morning. I hope it will relieve some of your fatigue." Ambrose carefully handed the teacup on a saucer to Emilia and began arranging Emilia's attire for the day.

"Thank you, Ambrose. You always know how to cheer me up."

"I wish I could do more. There is simply not enough knowledge in my small head to be of greater support to Your Majesty."

Emilia sipped her tea, letting the warmth of it spread through her body. A smile curved her lips. Ambrose had been an unbending support by her side for many years. She learned more than the noble ladies who only focused on painting and embroidery. Such skills were useful in getting a husband for a meek girl, but their goal was freedom from the palace and its constraints.

Emilia finished her drink and, with Ambrose's help, put on a navy dress with detailed silver embroidery on the sleeves and hem. In her past life, the clothes she wore were simple, to the point of a single-coloured T-shirt and faded jeans. The decorative clothes Ambrose ordered from a famous boutique for Emilia were beautiful and hard to ignore. Not only that, Ambrose's taste matched Emilia's well. There hadn't been a time when Emilia had the urge to utter a single word of complaint.

As the Queen reminisced about how her life had changed from a poor and hopeless princess to a respected monarch, Ambrose began fixing Emilia's hair at the vanity.

Emilia spied a deep frown forming on her maid's face. "What's wrong?"

"Some of your hair has been singed, Your Majesty."

"That must have happened during the dragon's attack last night."

"What would you like for me to do?"

Emilia thought of how nobles were obsessed with long hair. If a noblewoman cut her hair out of the blue, she would lose out on marriage proposals. Emilia let out a chuckle. Witnessing the nobility freaking out because of her new hairstyle would be a sight to see.

"Just cut it."

Ambrose's face paled. "Your Majesty cannot be serious! I could trim it and hide the rest with a different hairstyle."

"Cut it, Ambrose."

The maid ran her fingers gently through the length of the silky black hair and sighed. "What length would you like?"

"Shoulder-length."

Ambrose gave a curt nod and hurried out of the room in search of scissors.

The haircut took longer than Emilia expected. She tried not to laugh at how carefully Ambrose handled her hair. By the end of the process, the Queen was so hungry, that she was ready to take the scissors from Ambrose's hands and finish cutting her hair in one go.

"It is done, Your Majesty," Ambrose announced with a nervous look.

Emilia assessed her new appearance in the mirror.

She had been growing out her hair since she was a child. At the age of seventeen, it reached all the way to her hips. Now, all that weight was gone, much like the suffering she had to endure till now.

She turned her head from side to side and smiled. "You did great, Ambrose. Thank you."

Ambrose visibly relaxed. "It was my pleasure."

"Warn the kitchen to have a meal prepared for me in the dining hall."

"Yes, Your Majesty." Ambrose bowed and left the room once more.

As soon as Ambrose left, two maids came in. When they spotted Emilia's new haircut, their gaping mouths nearly reached the floor.

Emilia turned her attention to them, and the duo cast their gaze downwards before busying themselves with tidying up the discarded hair.

If experience told her anything, she had to prepare for similar reactions from the rest of the palace servants and guards. Not that anyone would be bold enough to comment.

*And, who knows? Perhaps I will set a new trend.*

With a skip in her step, Emilia left her bedchamber and headed for the dining hall. Along the long corridor, she spotted an odd sight that piqued her interest. Picking up the pace and making her steps soundless, she approached Riga and Dame Cali, who were too focused on their conversation to notice her approach.

Emilia heard words such as "wedding", "night", and "Laurence". She peered over Riga's shoulder and tilted her head to one side. "What are you two discussing?"

Riga nearly fell over her feet, and Emilia had to catch the young lady by the arm. "Your Majesty! We were just discussing some personal matters."

They went quiet for a long moment as they kept nervously glancing at Emilia's new hairstyle.

Emilia ignored the obvious question that hung in the air. "Guard Captain Louberte, what could be so important that you would leave your post?"

Dame Cali straightened her posture and lowered her head. "I apologise, Your Majesty. It won't happen again."

Emilia feigned a hurt expression and dropped her shoulders. "You must know that I grew up all alone in a tower. I never had anyone to share my worries and loneliness with." It wasn't a complete lie. Before Ambrose began visiting Emilia's tower, she was alone and with no one to rely on. Even sneaking out was difficult with a weak child's body. "I wish I had friends with whom I could discuss my problems…"

Dame Cali lifted her head. Her shining eyes welled with pity. "Your Majesty, we were merely discussing my love life. If you would be willing to lend an ear and advise me, it would mean a lot to me."

Pleased, Emilia kept up her pitiful act. She grasped Cali's hands and gave them a light squeeze. "I would be glad to be of assistance."

"I did not know Your Majesty had suffered so much in the past," Riga cut in with an equally concerned expression. "Should you need anything, let me know!"

Emilia smiled at the two ladies. "Of course. I am so happy to have Lord Fournier's daughter on my side." She let go of Cali and motioned for them to follow. "Come with me to the dining hall. I am famished, but I wish to hear what concerns you may have."

Cali nodded, and they obediently followed.

On the way to the dining hall, Emilia contemplated how to win them to her side while keeping the conversation light. Cali was Thessian's trusted elite knight and Riga possessed powerful magic that could be useful in the future. With them confiding in Emilia rather than Thessian, she could learn more about the prince and the Dante nobility that supported him. There were no downsides.

Once breakfast and tea were served, Emilia dismissed the servants. She made sure the two ladies sat close to her at the table, so they could talk freely.

"You have mentioned your love life, Dame Cali. What is bothering you so much?" Emilia probed.

Cali's cheeks reddened as she poked the potatoes in her stew with a spoon. "This is regarding Sir Laurence whom I've been infatuated with since he became my sword instructor."

Emilia kept her excitement in check by sustaining her expression blank. In this life, as well as the previous, she didn't have any serious relationships with the opposite sex, but reading romance novels was a pastime she couldn't deny. As a woman, she felt compelled to help Cali in her endeavour despite not being too fond of Sir Laurence. He might be one of the best swordsmen in the Hellion Empire, and a son of a marquess, but his licentious behaviour did not make him one of her favourite characters when she was a reader. However, as she got to know him, she could not deny his loyalty to Thessian or his bravery as a warrior.

Emilia smiled at Dame Cali. "Do go on."

Cali's face turned completely red. "Your Majesty, with Lady Riga's advice, I spent the night with him. However, when he awoke this morn—"

Emilia raised her hand. "Wait, you've slept with him?"

Cali gave a curt nod.

Turning her head to the youngest among them, Emilia studied Riga. "What exactly did you suggest, Lady Riga?"

"I simply spoke the words Mama said to my sisters. 'To capture a man, you must bear his child.'"

The Queen's eyes widened, and she couldn't help but explain, "Young lady, that would only work if the man were honourable and would take responsibility for his actions." Emilia turned to Cali. "What was his reaction?"

"He ran away, Your Majesty," Cali mumbled.

Emilia pursed her lips. *Oh, Laurence... You blithering fool. How could you abandon such a beauty?*

From Emilia's perspective, Cali was good-looking, tall, strong, and loyal. Who wouldn't want to date her? The problem was her taste in men. Laurence was a good man but was also a son of high-ranking nobles in the Hellion Empire. His future was most likely decided for him from birth. That, and he had no idea how to maintain a relationship. Emilia suspected that he feared intimacy altogether. To capture a man like that, one might need more than an offspring.

"He was probably panicked due to sobering up," Riga consoled the dame.

Emilia raised a brow. "He was drunk?"

"Lady Riga said—"

Emilia shook her head. *What a mess...* "No wonder he tucked tail and fled."

Riga frowned. "Mama said that drunk men are easier to manipulate."

*What in heaven's name was Countess Fournier teaching her children?*

"That is not the point," Emilia countered. "Imagine if the situation was reversed. What if he got Dame Cali drunk and had his way with her?"

Cali blushed once more. "I would not mind." She was a hopeless case when it came to Laurence, it seemed.

Riga motioned to Cali. "See, Your Majesty? Everything should have worked out."

"Let me change the scenario then. Imagine it was a strange man who did that to Dame Cali," Emilia said.

Cali gripped the hilt of the dagger at her side, her eyes flashing with spite. "I would skin such a beast alive."

Riga piped in with a flame dancing on her palm, "And I would fry him thereafter."

"Since he was drunk," Emilia cut in, "don't you think he might be under the assumption that he took advantage of Dame Cali?"

The Guard Captain's expression became serious as her hands turned into fists on the table. "I was the one who got him drunk, not the other way around."

"Did you force him to drink?" Emilia asked.

Cali shook her head.

"I am of the belief that Sir Laurence has been under a lot of pressure as of late. In his fragile state of mind, you—" Emilia stopped midsentence and sighed.

The world the Queen lived in was not the Modern Age of her previous life. Instead, she was reborn in a time when the concept of consent was not something people even considered. After all, most women married out of duty or to increase their family's reputation. Those who married for love were few and far between, and often disowned by their noble parents if the groom did not have a higher social standing or equal to that of their own.

Returning her attention to the two expectant faces, Emilia went on, "The main question here is, do you think he recognised you?"

Cali's brows drew together. "Why wouldn't he?"

"He was drunk."

Cali shrugged. "Sir Laurence wasn't too far gone."

Riga joined in, "Papa often drinks with his guests. He says it is the best way to bring merriment to the table."

"Yes, it can be a good way to bring down defences for a conversation and unwind, Lady Riga." The queen quickly added, "You need to promise me that you won't go around getting men drunk just to have your way with them."

Riga pursed her lips. "Papa says I must not squander my youth on fruitless pursuits of love and strive to be a great warrior in His Grace's army. For now, I have no intention of getting married."

The Queen smiled. "It's nice to see that despite all the mess in this world there are still young ladies like yourselves who are ready to give their lives for a greater cause."

Dame Cali curved her brow. "You sounded a lot like His

Highness, Your Majesty. In fact, maybe..."

Emilia tilted her head to one side. "Maybe?"

"We all thought Her Majesty and His Highness were...close."

"What made you think that?"

"Well, the guards reported seeing you entering His Highness' bedchambers while he was taking a bath and leaving quite a while later."

Emilia's mouth nearly hung open. *Well, I did see him naked, but we didn't sleep together...which is what everyone must be thinking. Oh, Gods! Thessian is more of an unreachable idol than a man of mortal flesh and blood to me.*

Feeling her cheeks warm, Emilia countered with, "We are friends and allies, nothing more."

Cali glanced at Riga, and they shared a look of confusion.

Ignoring their puzzlement, she decided to drive the point home. "So have you figured out what went wrong in your situation?"

Riga nodded vigorously. "Dame Cali should have tied him up."

"I do not keep any ropes in my storage chest, my lady," Cali replied.

"That is a pity."1

Emilia rubbed her aching temples. She did not know whether to laugh or cry with the things Riga spouted with such liveliness. That young lady's imagination was beyond comprehension.

"...too soon to know if you are pregnant, Dame Cali," Riga said.

"Let us hope she isn't. If—" She looked at Cali with intent. "There's no if. You shouldn't force a man to be with you against their will. It will only make your life miserable. If you are pregnant, I will help you if Laurence does not want to assume the paternity. If you are not pregnant, I advise you to find a good man who loves you and treats you right, and stay away from Sir Laurence."

"But—"

Emilia cut in, "Yes, you love him. Only a fool is blind to that. But the man you love is a fool. Not just a fool, he's a libertine."

"A what?" Riga asked.

Emilia searched for the right words. "Likes women too much to settle for just one."

Dame Cali slumped in her seat, which made Emilia look around the dining room in search of a solution. The tea had long since gotten cold, and they had barely eaten since the conversation began.

The solution was obvious and simple. Emilia had to help Cali get together with Sir Laurence. After all, she had already messed with the original plot too much.

*What could one more change do?*

Resolute in her decision, the Queen placed her hands on the table. "Dame Cali has done so much for this palace that I feel obliged to help you out."

"Truly, Your Majesty?" Cali failed to hide her excitement.

"Indeed." Emilia turned to Riga. "Please refrain from putting any more strange ideas into Dame Cali's head, Lady Riga. It could create a bigger rift between them."

Riga nodded with much reluctance. "Mama managed to get Father to wed her. I heard that in his youth, Father was quite busy refusing marriage proposals from his admirers."

Emilia smiled kindly. "Your mother won the love of Lord Fournier in her own way. What worked for her may not work for everyone else."

"I think I understand, Your Majesty," Riga said.

"Very good." Emilia gestured to the food. "Let us finish our meal and come up with a new plan to force Laurence to talk to Cali and resolve this misunderstanding. An honest talk among friends may work wonders."

A fire lit in Cali's eyes. "You are so wise, Your Majesty! How do you know so much about men?"

"I read a lot." *Romance novels mainly...* "Let's eat. I am starving."

Riga and Cali nodded and finally returned to the delicacies that the chef had prepared for them.

# 3

# HOW TO LOSE A LADY'S INTEREST

## LAURENCE

**Laurence left the castle and rode on** his horse at full speed to the main camp. Cold wind battered his face and hands as he clutched the reins, which helped with the swirling mess in his head.

*How can someone like me court Dame Calithea?*

She was his student, his friend, and a comrade. Aside from swordsmanship, they had nothing in common. She enjoyed spending her time away from Hellion nobility to not become a target of snide comments about her origins, drank her tea with too much sugar, and enjoyed freshly baked sweets from commoners' bakeries. On the other hand, he spent his time engaging with the nobles, visiting exclusive brothels, and secretly honing his sword-fighting skills when Prince Thessian was not looking.

He swayed his head from side to side, and the horse slowed its pace. Changing his posture to a more relaxed one, he contemplated the possibilities of how to get her to dislike him. He knew Cali had feelings for him. To miss the way she looked at him sometimes, he had to be blind. He was all too used to the affectionate stares of the young ladies at the balls.

"Why? Why did that happen?" he shouted out loud.

Luckily, he was in an open field with no one nearby.

Laurence had given up on marrying for love. To escape the stiff air in the Oswald household, he followed Thessian to the battlefield any chance he got. His parents would eventually choose a suitable wife for him to elevate their reputation among the nobility while his older brother would take over as the Marquess' successor. Laurence was a political pawn, and Calithea would only suffer in such an environment. At most, his mother would suggest making Calithea a concubine, which would tarnish her honour beyond repair. Should that not work, she would find a way to make Calithea disappear.

Laurence urged the horse to speed up. He needed ideas from his men to know how to dissolve Cali's affection for him as soon as possible.

After arriving at his destination, he slipped off his horse and tied it to a tree branch. He gave his body a much-needed stretch before heading towards the tents where the squad leaders resided.

The supplies for the standby army were going to run low soon. While there, he made a mental note to check the reports.

He peeled back the tent door and peered inside. Yeland and Sergey were packing their belongings while discussing something near the back.

Striding towards them, Laurence brought out a wide smile.

"How are you doing, men?"

Sergey and Yeland saluted him, which Laurence found amusing. He was no longer Thessian's second-in-command. "At ease. I came to pick your brains on a serious matter."

"What can we help you with, Sir Laurence?" Sergey asked.

Rubbing the back of his neck, Laurence queried, "How would you go about making a woman hate you?"

Yeland's confusion was evident as he scratched his messy dark locks. "Don't you mean the opposite, sir?"

"I know more than enough on how to woo a lady, Yeland. I need to know how to make them run away."

Sergey chuckled. "Who is the unlucky lady that you must go so far as to make her hate you? Did she stalk you or steal your underwear?"

Laurence blanched at the thought of Cali keeping his undergarments like some kind of prize. "No, nothing so vile."

"Is she old or grotesque in appearance?" Sergey probed.

"Well, no..."

Yeland piped in, "Then could she be an evil schemer or a witch?"

Laurence groaned. "Gentlemen, this is a serious matter! I need your opinions, not your guesses."

Sergey crossed his arms over his chest. "Why not tell the lady that you hate her?"

"That would be too cruel. I do not wish to hurt her feelings..."

Yeland and Sergey shared a look.

"Sir," Yeland began with a hint of caution to his tone, "is she someone we are acquainted with?"

"No!" Laurence shouted and quickly lowered his voice. "She is from the Marquess' territory. Regardless of who the lady is, what would be the best way to make her dislike me?"

Sergey rubbed his blond stubble in thought. "You could send her a terrible gift or endlessly talk about yourself during a conversation."

Yeland added, "My older sister told me that any man who gambles or comes home drunk is a fustilarian and should be castrated."

"Isn't your sister married to a baron?" Sergey asked.

"She is…well, was. They are getting a divorce because he lost his family's fortune at a gambling den."

Laurence also hated gamblers. They wasted too much time and money on a useless pursuit of momentary luck. As for getting drunk, he was not about to do *that* again. Sending an ugly gift would not faze Cali. She may even like it. Her taste was completely different to that of the noble ladies of the Empire. "I guess all that is left is to talk about myself."

"Worry not, sir." Sergey grinned mischievously. "You are quite proficient."

Laurence was about to punch Sergey in the shoulder but stopped. These men had given up their positions within Thessian's unit to travel with him north in search of the beast-child. He was beyond grateful for their support. The one person he was concerned about was Ian. The elf had not spoken to Laurence since the fire. Last Laurence heard Ian was at the palace's infirmary, getting treated by the royal physician.

"Thank you for the advice, men."

Laurence turned and started for the exit when Yeland called out, "Women also hate men who stink, sir."

He laughed at the idea of Cali leaving him because he smelled bad. They were knights and trained hard. The stench of sweat was unavoidable. She spent years on the battlefield, sleeping in close quarters with other men without a word of complaint.

*Calithea is no ordinary woman.*

# 4
# NEW APPOINTMENT

## EMILIA

The plan was set. Emilia's task was to lure Laurence to a secluded location that evening and have Cali "accidentally" bump into them and corner him. The Queen instructed Ambrose to find a fitting place that had only one way in and out of the palace. As long as the exit was blocked, he would have no choice but to face Cali.

Collapsing onto a sofa in her office, she covered her face with her arm. Love and romance were the least of her worries. Lionhart reported earlier that there were no traces of the dragon left in the catacombs. He suspected that it had escaped through one of the many passageways. He had asked his guild to scour the city for any sightings of the beast or a small child with the description she gave him. All that was left was to wait for any news or for Count Fournier to arrive in Newburn to track the creature.

Aside from that, Duke Malette's trial was soon approaching.

Clayton was in charge as the judge and was busy putting together the evidence to convict him along with his underlings. The death penalty for him and his family was the goal.

The door gently opened to her office, and Sir Rowell ambled inside. "Your Majesty, Count Edmund Baudelaire is asking for a meeting."

Emilia jerked upright. She got off the sofa and fixed her attire. "Escort him in."

Ten minutes later, Count Baudelaire joined her in her office.

He bowed respectfully in greeting. "It is a pleasure to see you once again, Your Majesty."

She stretched out her hand, which he lifted to his lips and kissed the Dante crest of her golden ring. "Have you come to give me an update on the fire?"

The Count lifted his head with a grim expression. "Indeed. Many citizens have lost their homes and businesses. It will take months to rebuild and there is a matter of where to get the funds for the restoration process."

"How much is required?"

"If we were to take all the taxes for the entire year, it would not cover even half of it."

*Oh, Laurence, you owe me SO much money!*

A slow smile spread across her face. Since the mistake was Laurence's, she could ask Thessian to pay for most of the repairs. From Lionhart's report, the duchy of Darkgate was still in the recovery state after the war with the Hellion Empire. As a war hero and prince, Thessian had more than enough money of his own as a reward from the emperor.

"Has Your Majesty devised a solution?" Count Baudelaire asked with an arched brow.

"I will let you know in due time."

Emilia circled her desk and reached into the top drawer before pulling out a sealed envelope. Once she gave him the letter of appointment, there would be no going back. She and Count Baudelaire would be entwined politically to the end. He was a good man who never disrespected her despite her secluded upbringing.

The Lionhart Guild could not uncover anything about him that caused concern. She could have asked Clayton to look into Count Baudelaire also but chose not to. He had been her support and ally for almost three years. This time, she was going to trust her gut.

He opened the letter with care and pulled out a small pair of glasses from the breast pocket of his ash-coloured coat. In silence, he read the contents. With each line, his brows raised more. Once finished, he swallowed nervously.

"Your Majesty, you do not have to go so far as to give me the title of duke nor Duke Malette's territory. I have never once been greedy for what rightfully belongs to the Crown."

Emilia glided to the Count Baudelaire's side and placed a hand on his shoulder. Despite the Count not being considered tall, she was still half a head shorter than him. "I will need counsel from a trustworthy ally in the future—someone who will keep those pesky nobles in check. The new title should give you enough authority to keep them from wagging their tongues needlessly. As I do not have an heir, I would like for you to take the post of Prime Minister."

Count Baudelaire removed his glasses and put them back in his pocket. He went down on one knee, keeping his head lowered. "Your Majesty, I will accept the new title and appointment to aide you, but I must refuse Duke Malette's territory. I am more than happy to remain where I have been raised and lived for my entire life."

"I understand. You may rise." Baudelaire's refusal was something she foresaw. No one would want to rule the land of a traitor while there was a budding uprising in the territory.

Briefly returning to her desk, she retrieved another letter and passed it to him. "This one gives you the title, and the expectations of a future Prime Minister, without the land."

"Thank you, Your Majesty."

With his refusal, the Queen had few options left. She could reach out to other nobles who had a large number of soldiers. Nevertheless, until she had her official coronation, the nobles could refuse to listen. To make matters worse, the temple was actively stalling the ceremony. She needed to wait for a reply from His

Holiness and trade the bishop for the Pope's blessing.

Her other option was asking Thessian to travel South and suppress the uprising. Option two had to be the last resort, because she feared the novel's story would happen as it did in the original, and the prince would die in the process. Thessian was her golden ticket to prevent the downfall of the Hellion Empire and the cull of the mages on the continent. She couldn't lose him.

"Is something worrying you, Your Majesty?" Count Baudelaire's deep voice reached her, and she realised that he was standing in front of her and actively studying her with concern.

Emilia managed a smile. "Nothing of the sort. I was contemplating when to hold your appointment ceremony. It will have to happen after my coronation, of course. In the meantime, I would appreciate it if you could continue working on the city's restoration. As for the funding, I will find the gold needed."

"I will be on my way then," he said with a low bow. "Should you require anything of me, I will be staying in the capital."

"Thank you, Lord Baudelaire."

Emilia returned to her desk when he left her office and buried her face in her hands.

In her past life, she was a disgraced college student. To her, dealing with numbers was always easier than dealing with people. Politics required way too much energy and pretences.

The knock on the door had her raise her head.

Count Baudelaire stuck his head in to say, "Your Majesty, I forgot to add. Your new hairstyle suits you quite well."

Suddenly, Emilia felt her cheeks heating up.

# 5
# A ROYAL PLOT

## THESSIAN

**Laurence was nowhere to be found**. Thessian concluded that his friend had left the castle to initiate whatever idiotic plan he had devised in his peculiar head. Having wasted his morning, he decided to check in on Sir Ian's condition at the infirmary.

He knocked on the door to receive no answer. So, he tested the doorknob.

The door was unlocked.

Striding inside, he found the royal physician sleeping at his desk with his spectacles barely hanging on his nose. Choosing not to wake the weary man, he quietened his steps.

Ian was propped up by a pillow and staring out of the window. Without the headscarf, his straight, white hair ran down his chest. Warm sunlight gave the elf's alabaster skin an ethereal glow which further highlighted how different they were from humans.

When Ian noticed Thessian's approach, he scrambled to stand.

"At ease." Thessian spoke low as he arrived at the patient's bed. "How are your wounds, Ian?"

"I should recover within a week, Your Highness."

"Are you still intent on finding the beast-child?"

The typically expressionless elf gave a weak smile. "She is a child of the land and deserves to find peace and a new home."

"I did not think the elves of Shaeban cared for other kinds to such an extent."

"They do not."

Double-checking that the physician's breathing remained even, Thessian dropped the superior act and lowered his voice further. "I have misspoken. It was thoughtless of me to mention your people when you can never return to your homeland."

"Our deal remains regardless of your words, Your Highness."

Thessian inclined his head. "Yes. For saving my life, Your Highness Iefyr Wysaran, I promised to aid you in restoring your family's reputation."

Ian's light-grey eyes reflected much sadness. "I have not heard that name in years. I am glad someone in this world still remembers."

"It would be a sin to forget the original royal family of Shaeban."

Ian clenched his jaw and spoke through his teeth. "It matters not. Our names were struck from history by the elders. For now, I must remain here and keep them from discovering that I am alive." His attention was drawn to the physician's stirring body at the end of the room. His demeanour changed in an instant. "Your Highness, thank you for visiting."

Resuming the roles of commander and subordinate, Thessian said, "I am pleased you are recovering well, Sir Ian. I must be on my way."

He marched away.

The matter that Iefyr Wysaran was hidden among his soldiers had to remain a secret. Even his father, the emperor, did not know what Thessian had done. After all, Hellion's royalty harbouring a dangerous criminal would cause trade disputes and a possible war with Shaeban. In reality, he knew that the Shaeban elders would demand for the emperor to hand Iefyr over to them all the while spinning lies about the exiled prince.

As Thessian turned the corner, he bumped into Emilia.

On reflex, he caught her by the arms to steady her.

When she looked up with big blue eyes that were framed by a silky curtain of her ebony hair, he once more realised how striking her appearance was. After focusing on the overall frame of her appearance, he came to the realisation that Emilia had boldly changed her hairstyle. The shoulder-length hair suited her.

When he noticed he was still holding on to her, he released her and took a careful step back. "I apologise for touching you, Your Majesty."

She glanced around, noting they were alone, and cleared her throat. "The fault is mine, Your Highness. I was too busy looking for someone."

"Who would that be?"

"Sir Laurence."

For some reason, that answer displeased him. *What has Laurence done now for the Queen to be personally searching for him?*

Her lips quirked into a smile. "I was about to find Your Highness also."

His interest was piqued. "What can I do for you?"

"We should discuss this in private."

He offered her his arm. "Lead the way."

Emilia looped her thin arm through his. He could not help wondering how such a slim lady could put up a fight against grown men. With each graceful step she made, he had to make half of his usual stride.

A few sets of stairs and long corridors later, they exited into the main garden. It must have rained not long ago because the grass was glistening with water droplets under the sun. She led him to a secluded corner, surrounded by tall hedges and part of the castle's wall, and pulled away.

Placing herself in front of him, Emilia raised her head to look at him. "Your Highness, are you aware of what happened between Sir

Laurence and Dame Cali?"

*How did Emilia get wrapped up in this mess?* "I...am."

"As their superior, I believe it is your duty to help resolve this matter!"

He was about to reply when the curve of her lips turned downward, and she sniffled. Reaching into the hidden pocket of her dress, she retrieved a white handkerchief.

The sudden change in her quivering voice made him worry. "When I heard Dame Cali's side of the story, I was heartbroken. How could an honourable man, who serves His Highness, abandon a woman he got drunk and spent a night with?"

Thessian stared at her, unable to move. He had never consoled a crying lady before. Then, her words registered in his brain. "W-wait! What?"

*Did Laurence force himself on Calithea Louberte?*

"I assure you, Emilia, I was not aware Laurence had—" He clenched his jaw hard enough to hear his teeth grinding in his head. "I will—"

Emilia placed a hand on his wide chest and wiped her welling tears with the other.

In a shaky voice, she continued, "We must bring them together to talk. I am positive there had to have been some kind of misunderstanding. As a woman, just thinking of something like this happening to me causes me great distress."

Emilia's tears, her hot hand on his chest, and the idea of someone touching her against her will angered him to no end. So as not to startle her with an outburst of budding rage, he thought of ways to ease her sorrow.

Emilia was right. Dame Cali was under his protection. Even if she was a commoner, her honour was at stake, and he had never failed one of his knights. If it had been Emilia who had suffered such a grievance, he wouldn't hesitate to kill the bastard.

*Have I been too lenient on Laurence and failed to see the wrongdoing my friend caused by tainting Dame Cali's reputation and honour?*

"I—I will punish Laurence for his misdeeds and confine him."

Swallowing nervously, he took a hold of her hand and gently

pulled her against his chest. Awkwardly, the prince patted her on her back. His mother used to hug him when he felt sad as a child. Hopefully, Emilia would not find his actions too disrespectful.

"What would you have me do?" he asked while looking at the top of her head. "Would you have me beat him and expel him from my guard?"

"W-what?" Emilia peeled back enough to wipe her tears and lifted her glistening eyes to meet his. "Your Highness, I think we should listen to both sides of the story before taking action."

"Dame Cali should have confided in me."

"You are a man. I am a woman. It is easier for her to come to me rather than her superior. Surely, you suspect how she feels about Sir Laurence?"

"Laurence using Calithea's feelings to take advantage of her makes this matter even worse," he muttered.

"I cannot fault your logic."

The prince stepped back, suddenly aware of their closeness. "Are you feeling better?"

Emilia gracefully wiped away her stray tears with the handkerchief. The gesture made him pause to appreciate her beauty until she tilted her head to one side and gave him a timid smile.

"Your Highness, all I ask is that you keep Laurence in one piece, for now, and bring him here at nine o'clock. I will do the same with Dame Cali. This way, through conversation, I am certain they will reconcile and find a way to move forward. If Sir Laurence leaves Newburn before they talk, I fear it will cause a great rift within the ranks of your soldiers."

He nodded. "I will bring him here even if I must knock him out."

"Thank you, Your Highness."

Thessian felt his ears heating up and moved farther away from the young queen. He cleared his throat. "Would you like for me to escort you back?"

She smiled meekly. "Please do not mind me. I will return once I have calmed down a little. I do not wish for the servants to believe I am weak because I have shed some tears."

"I understand." He inclined his head and hurried off in search of Laurence.

# 6
# A PERFECT WALL-SLAM

## EMILIA

**E**milia **tucked away her used** handkerchief and smirked. *All according to plan.*

Ambrose jumped down from the nearby tree and came over. She had changed into a pair of trousers and a dark shirt which was mostly hidden by a black coat. "Your Majesty, your acting was sublime."

*Acting during school plays has come in handy, after all.* "I feel bad for deceiving His Highness like this, but he is the only one who can control Laurence. Without Thessian's help, capturing him would be near impossible."

"I could drug Sir Laurence with a sleeping concoction I've developed or have the maids distract him while I knock him unconscious."

"He would undoubtedly avoid drinking anything made by us,

and I would rather not get the maids involved. I know you and Sir Rowell have cleaned out the spies, yet we must not let our guard down."

"I was too short-sighted, Your Majesty."

Emilia patted Ambrose on the shoulder. "For tonight, I need you to prepare something for me in the room with the best view in the palace."

"What would that be?"

"I am considering following Lady Riga's advice."

Ambrose tensed. "Who is the man you wish to spend the night with?"

Emilia let out a musical laugh. "I do not plan to sleep with him. I was thinking of asking Prince Thessian to pay for the city's repairs."

"Oh... By all means, I will acquire the best alcohol for this mission and conduct a survey of the rooms on the upper floors with the best view. I believe Sir Rowell mentioned there is a south-facing room with a balcony that overlooks the city."

"Great!" Emilia clasped her hands together in excitement. "Have the maids get started on Dame Cali's appearance for tonight and have that room cleaned."

The sun set over the horizon as the clock tower struck eight times.

Emilia's heart thumped in her chest with each chime. The time had come for her to move to the garden and hide where she could oversee the action. Too bad her new world did not have popcorn. Seeing a fantasy romance unravelling in front of her eyes was a dream come true. She was so giddy, that she did her best not to skip to the secret meeting place with Riga.

With her hair tied into a ponytail, and dressed in comfortable clothes, she entered the secret passageways that led to the garden with a lantern.

Riga was already waiting for her behind the tall hedges. The young girl, too, almost bounced out of her skin.

"We have a bit of time left," Emilia whispered to her. "Where is Dame Cali?"

"Last I heard, the maids have almost finished dressing her."

"I hope she likes my present."

Lady Riga's eyes grew wide as Cali glided to the meeting place in a silver gown that hugged her curves and exposed her chest in moderation. Pearls and white ribbons were entwined with her golden hair that was tied back into a long braid. Rose gold and sapphire jewellery adorned her ears and neck.

"She looks gorgeous," Emilia muttered under her breath. "I'm glad the dress suits her. It belonged to the previous queen."

"Your Majesty is so kind to lend her your mother's dress!" Riga replied, her face glowing with admiration.

Emilia couldn't tell the girl that she did not remember the deceased queen who had died during labour. It was part of the reason why King Gilebert hated Emilia so much. The evil prophecy by the temple fuelled his hatred even further.

Although Dame Cali seemed to be getting chilled, sacrifices had to be made for beauty. With her current appearance, Sir Laurence had to be the worst trash in the world to turn her down.

Riga poked Emilia's shoulder. "I think they're approaching."

Emilia diverted her attention to the growing argument His Highness was having with Laurence. The closer they got, the louder their voices became until they arrived at the meeting place.

Unnerving silence filled the space when the men saw Cali standing there, all dressed up.

Thessian smacked Laurence on the back, propelling him towards Cali. "This is an order, Laurence. Deal with the consequences of your actions and do not set foot outside this garden until you two have come to an agreement."

With that, the prince walked off.

Emilia quietly snuck around the hedge and grasped Thessian by the hand before he could get too far away. She pulled him down until they were almost kneeling and put her finger against her lips to silence him.

Thessian took the hint, and they soundlessly shuffled to where Riga was observing the most awkward reunion in all of Dante.

"Why aren't they saying anything?" Riga asked in a tiny whisper.

Emilia smiled. "Give it time."

"I did not know Lady Riga was also involved in this," Thessian whispered.

"Half the castle is," Emilia replied.

Thessian looked down, making Emilia do the same. She was still holding his hand.

She jerked her hand back while a blush coloured her face. Good thing they were mostly in the dark. "I apologise, Your Highness."

"Think nothing of it," he said kindly.

From a distance, she could finally hear Laurence's voice. "Dame Calithea, I—I know what I did was wrong. I am a loose man, bound to the pleasures of the flesh. A man such as me, who wastes his coin at places of low repute, should not have the right to be with you."

Emilia could not make out Cali's expression from where she stood. She frowned, inching closer until Riga gently poked her again. It was a warning not to get too close for fear of making unnecessary noise.

Laurence kept on berating himself for the next five minutes to the point where Emilia regretted not buying a recording crystal from the Mage Assembly.

Taking a seat on the grass, Thessian sighed from time to time. "If I was a woman, I would not want to marry him."

Emilia smothered her giggle. "He must be doing it on purpose."

Thessian gave a curt nod. "At least he knows Calithea is too good for him."

"Not wanting to disrespect Your Majesty or Your Grace, but I'm trying to listen," Riga protested beside them. "What did Dame Cali see in him? He's not even that good-looking."

"Cali could do so much better," Emilia agreed. "But if she wants him, we—" She shut up and placed her hand on Thessian's shoulder. "I think he is done with his commiseration."

The prince turned his head to watch.

"Sir Laurence, I—" Cali wiped her palms on her dress and took a step towards him. "I do not mind your shortcomings. I have plenty of them myself."

"How could that be?" Laurence seemed taken aback. "You are beautiful and have no downsides."

Emilia covered her gaping mouth with her hands and peeked at Thessian, who gave a simple nod of agreement. Perhaps the prince, too, was fond of the dame. Emilia did not get that idea from reading the novel. Thessian was too focused on his military strength and conquering more land for the Empire to go on dates. She could not help wondering if there had been a time when he was a smitten young lad, driven by passion.

Her attention returned to the unravelling scene where Cali had backed Laurence against the castle wall and pushed his back against it. She placed her hands on either side of Laurence's body, keeping him trapped in place. Since they were almost the same height when she wore heels, he couldn't move without hurting her.

Emilia clenched her fangirling fists. "A perfect wall-slam! I taught her that!"

Thessian raised a brow. "What is a wall-slam?"

"Shh!" Riga interjected.

Cali muttered an apology and locked her lips with Laurence's in one swift move. Gone was the shy Cali who blushed at the mere mention of Laurence's name.

Emilia held her breath. She counted the seconds that ticked by, waiting for some sort of reaction from Laurence. To her surprise, instead of pushing Cali away, he grasped her by the waist and pulled her closer.

The kiss deepened, and Emilia swiftly covered Riga's eyes.

The awkward couple seemed to drop all inhibition at long last.

"I think we should leave," Thessian suggested.

"Yes, we should," Emilia agreed.

# 7

# GUILTY FEELINGS

## EMILIA

**U**pon returning to the castle's halls, Emilia tugged on Thessian's sleeve. She could no longer keep lying to him. He needed to know the truth regarding Cali's and Laurence's situation. They were his subordinates, and, since she meddled with their future, she did not wish for him to think any less of them. Hopefully, he would not behead her for a small white lie.

*Here goes...*

"I have something I must apologise for, Your Highness. In all honesty, Dame Cali never told me that Sir Laurence got her drunk or took advantage of her. I said that to get you to cooperate with the plan and bring them to talk."

Riga's eyes rounded, and she quickly bowed to them. "I shall retire to my room, Your Majesty, Your Grace."

He was like an immovable mountain—silent and tall. *Is he going to kill me? Is this the end? Do I pray to God? Luminos? Santa Claus?*

Emilia nibbled on her lower lip. "I cannot apologise enough for fooling you into thinking badly about your childhood friend."

With a heavy sigh, he ran a hand through his blond mane. "After I left, I began to suspect that something was amiss. But, as you have said, the two of them needed to talk things out. Worry not, Emilia, I do not blame you for attempting to mend the bond between my people."

*That's one hurdle down...* "There is something else I wish to show you. Could you please follow me?"

"Is this also related to Laurence's mistakes?"

Emilia laughed. "Not exactly."

"I suppose I have no choice but to follow."

Light on her feet, the Queen guided him to the room Ambrose prepared in advance.

When Emilia opened the door, her eyes caught sight of pink rose petals scattered around the carpet and leading to the bed. The bedding was changed to white silk sheets and scented rose candles were lit all around the room. Without delay, she slammed the door shut before he could glimpse the inside.

*What were the maids thinking?*

"I must have gotten the wrong room!" she muttered with her cheeks burning.

"For a second there, I thought you wished to spend a romantic evening with me."

She couldn't look him in the eye. "I-I did not order this. I think the servants misunderstood..."

"Is what you wanted to show me in that room?"

She glanced up. "Well, yes."

His smile reached his eyes, and he pushed the door open. "I will believe your intentions were pure, so there is no reason not to enter."

Emilia pursed her lips and trailed after him. Once again, she felt heat rising all the way to her face at the overly romantic atmosphere.

Somehow, Thessian appeared unaffected. Since he was almost

ten years older than her, there was a good chance he only saw her as a younger sister.

On the bedside table, she spotted two silver goblets and a bottle of expensive wine. Rather than wallowing in awkwardness, she poured their drinks and handed one to Thessian. With confidence, she led him to the balcony.

Sir Rowell's advice was perfect. The night view of Newburn was breathtaking from up high. She could see oil lanterns illuminating the streets and hundreds of lights from houses that had people living in them. Her people — although temporarily.

Thessian placed his goblet on the stone railing and rested his hands on either side of it. "Your capital is quite charming."

She raised a brow. "Don't you mean small?"

"It reminds me of Darkgate. Although not as big and fancy as the Empire's capital, it is still my home."

"This territory also belongs to you, Your Highness." She sipped her drink. The strong fruity taste perfectly covered the strength of the alcohol.

"I guess, it does…"

She couldn't read his expression as he kept looking ahead and admiring the view. Asking him to spend a ridiculous amount of gold on a territory he owned was logical and practical. She was his vassal and was simply reporting the state of affairs. Yet, as her fingers tightened around her goblet, a pang of guilt made her doubt her actions.

"Are you not feeling well, Emilia?"

His warm words and expression reminded her that he was a person and not a few lines of text on a page. Thessian had a kind heart. He would make a great emperor. If she asked for money, he would probably pay her without batting an eye.

"Your Highness…"

"You may call me by name in private."

"Thessian." That one word meant she had managed to gain his trust. He did not seem to doubt her no matter what she claimed, which made her feel even worse. "I believe you said we should get to know one another with one question a day."

"Ah." He chuckled. "I thought you did not like me prying into your affairs."

"I no longer mind."

His eyes lingered on her face briefly before he picked up his goblet and had a drink. He appeared to be seriously contemplating the question he was about to ask.

"If you don't mind, may I go first?" she asked.

"Go ahead."

"Have you ever been in love?"

He choked on the wine.

After a bunch of coughs, he wiped his mouth with the back of his hand. "I guess your question makes sense after the situation we've faced today."

"Indeed."

"There was a time I had a fiancée. Imperial customs state that we must get engaged at an early age. I was no exception."

"Did you love her?"

He kept his attention on the drink he was holding as the words seemed to be stuck in his throat. "I did."

"What happened?"

"I left for war at the age of seventeen. I thought we would wed once I returned victorious. I was wrong. In the time I was on the battlefield, her family broke off the engagement and had her marry someone else."

Emilia stared at him in disbelief. Breaking an engagement with the Imperial Family was next to impossible. Just how much did her family pay to break the engagement? An even greater question plagued her. Who was the madwoman who did not find him attractive enough to marry? He was a prince of a powerful empire, a war hero with a long list of achievements, the best swordsman on the continent, handsome and with a great body. Had she been in his ex-fiancée's shoes, she'd wed him in a heartbeat.

She blanched at her thoughts.

*No, no, no.* Thessian was not someone she could date. Her job was to help him claim the throne and live quietly in the hinterlands.

"Who would dare decline your hand in marriage?" Emilia

asked.

"I believe it is my turn to ask a question."

*Shoot! I guess he's not going to tell me who the lady is.* "Ask away."

"Why didn't you ask me to compensate for the damages?"

"You have figured it out..."

"It was hard not to when the view, despite being beautiful, includes the section of the city that was affected by the fire my men caused."

She finished her wine in one mouthful. The alcohol warmed her chilled body from within. "I felt guilty."

"Why? The guilt is mine, and I am responsible for my subordinates' mess."

"I won't stop you if you wish to pay for the damages. The sum is quite startling, though."

"Does not matter. Send the bill to my estate in Darkgate."

"Thessian, I—"

He narrowed his eyes and took a step closer to her.

Whether it was the buzz from the alcohol, or because she found him to be attractive, her heart began to race.

"Do not move, Emilia," he said in a deep rumble that sent a shiver through her.

As he leant in, she heard something whooshing past their heads.

Thessian immediately pulled her against him into a protective hold.

Her nose hit his rock-solid chest, and she mumbled, "Ow!"

With two long strides, he retreated with her inside, taking cover behind the nearest wall.

Before she knew it, he was already holding a dagger in his hand and scanning the area for their enemies.

Emilia peeled her head back and studied the object that flew at them. A knife-shaped icicle was lodged in the castle's wall and reflected the moonlight. She rolled her eyes as next to it was an arrow.

"It is not an attack, Your Highness." She moved away from him. Returning to the balcony, she shouted, "Clayton! Ambrose! Come here this instant before I banish you from the kingdom!"

The leaves of the trees rustled, and she heard someone landing on the ground below.

She returned to the room and waited for her subordinates with her arms crossed.

*How could they shoot at Thessian?*

Had he been hurt, her plans would have gone up in smoke. She spared a nervous glance over her shoulder to gauge the prince's mood. He did not seem angry, merely amused.

She blew out a breath as the culprits entered the room. Ambrose's eyes grew wide when she saw the rose petals and the candles. Her expression darkened for a second, telling Emilia that the maids in charge were going to get an earful for the inappropriate decorations.

Clayton stormed across the room with an ice shortsword in hand. "How dare you try to kiss my master!"

"Kiss?" Thessian's brows drew together. "There was a spider in her hair. I was attempting to remove it."

Emilia looked at Clayton's and Ambrose's embarrassed faces and burst out laughing. "Why would Prince Thessian kiss someone like me?"

"Your Majesty, you must not know how attractive you are!" Ambrose said with gusto.

"I may be pretty for someone in Dante, but His Highness can pick any beauty he wants from the Empire." Her expression hardened as she pointed to her two aides. "Apologise to him. If he was harmed in any way, I would have you removed from your posts."

Ambrose did not make a fuss and curtsied low. "I have made a grave mistake. Please forgive me for misreading the situation, Your Imperial Highness. You may punish me as you like."

Clayton grumbled under his breath and lowered his head. "I also apologise."

"Your maid was trying to protect your honour." Thessian sheathed his dagger in his boot. He straightened his posture and moved to stand in front of Clayton.

They were tall men, but Thessian was two inches taller and a lot more muscular. Like the sun and the moon, they were equally attractive in their own way. Once more, she regretted not having a smartphone, so she could take a picture of the hunks and fangirl about them online.

The tension in the room rose as they sized each other up.

"Your dog needs to learn to control its greed," Thessian commented. "One day, it may bite its master."

"I would never harm her." Clayton's fingers gripped the shortsword so tightly, that Emilia could see the veins in his hands bulging.

"Put your weapon away this instant, Clayton," Emilia ordered.

He glanced in her direction and reluctantly complied. Firing one last glare at the prince, Clayton went down on one knee in front of Emilia and bowed his head. "I will receive any punishment you deem appropriate."

Emilia covered her eyes with her hand. She knew they were trying to protect her reputation. Rumours were a scary thing. If it was known beyond the castle's walls that Emilia was alone in a bedchamber with foreign nobility, who knows what the nobles would do? No. Even her closest subjects may think she has become a puppet or a mistress. She had half a mind to let them go unpunished, yet the royal etiquette required for the punishment to be severe.

Thessian must have noticed her struggle and said, "I am not offended. Let us forget this ever happened."

Relief flooded through Emilia, and her legs nearly gave out. She did not wish to lose Clayton's loyalty. His magical abilities and position among the nobility could prove useful in the future. His desperation to remain by her side gave her a strange sense of calm and possessiveness. It did not hurt that he was a visual treat, either.

"Thank you for your generosity," Emilia replied.

Thessian gave her a curt nod and strode out of the room.

Emilia dismissed Ambrose with a wave of her hand. Once the door was tightly shut, she studied Clayton's submissive posture. He was still as a statue and tense. He acted as if he expected her to hit him. She recalled a passing comment Lady Isobelle made, how their father used to beat Clayton into submission when he made a mistake.

A sick feeling settled in the pit of her stomach. She lowered to her knees and lifted his chin with her fingertips. "I am not going to punish you, Clayton."

He avoided her gaze but did not push her hand away.

"Please look at me," she whispered.

Clayton met her gaze. A mixture of emotions battled for dominance, one of which she recognised right away—anger. "I do not regret my actions, Master. That man is undeserving of you."

"If a prince of the largest empire on the continent is undeserving of me, I fear I may never marry," she joked.

He did not smile. Instead, his expression darkened. "He killed your family and is using you."

She retracted her hand and rose to her full height. "We use each other. Thessian and I have a deal. We will support each other's goals and then go our separate ways."

"What if he wishes to keep you by his side?"

"That's ridiculous."

"Ambrose is right. You are too kind and innocent. Men like him are sure to try to take advantage of your heart."

*Kind? Innocent?* She nearly burst out laughing. Ambrose had put Emilia on a pedestal, and Clayton was no different. They saw what they wanted to see through rose-tinted glasses. Their loyalty was a great gift and a burden at the same time.

*Should I prove him wrong?*

"Rise, Clayton."

When he stood up, he towered over her. His handsome face was hard to ignore. "Do you have a fiancée?"

He frowned. "I do not."

"Then perhaps a lover or someone you love?"

"No, Master. My only reason for living is to be your shadow and protect you."

"Are you saying you are mine and mine alone?"

"Yes. I belong to you."

Emilia cupped his cheeks and pulled his face down until they were an inch apart. "I hope you will take responsibility for those words."

She closed the final gap between them and kissed him.

# 8
# A HAREM OF MEN

### EMILIA

**Emilia enjoyed the feel of** Clayton's velvety lips against hers as she pressed their bodies closer. Her fingers climbed his shoulders and wound around his hair. His dark locks felt as soft as mink to the touch.

Breathless, she pulled back enough to gauge his reaction.

Clayton appeared dazed. He touched his lips in wonder, and his eyes widened.

In an instant, he went down on his knee. "Your Majesty, I-I will take this as a form of punishment influenced by alcohol and fix my behaviour towards the prince."

He muttered a flurry of apologies and scrambled out of the room.

Dumbfounded, she stared at the opened door.

*Am I that bad at kissing?*

*Wait.* She palmed her forehead. "If kissing him is a punishment, is moving to the next stage considered a death penalty?"

In her jumbled mind, realisation finally dawned. Technically, she was his superior. Had her boss started kissing her out of the blue, she, too, would freak out. The same could be said if a Pop idol she revered started showing interest in her.

*It's too bad. I guess I'll apologise when I see him next.*

Ambrose stuck her head around the door frame. "Have you finished your business, Your Majesty?"

Deflated, Emilia replied, "I suppose so."

Taking a quick study of Emilia, Ambrose hastened her approach. "Did something happen with Lord Armel? He seemed perturbed on his way out."

"Ambrose, imagine your superior gave you a kiss. How would you react?"

"If you kissed me, Your Majesty, I would die happy on the spot."

Emilia let out a musical laugh. *That's such an Ambrose response.* "Never mind. Nothing happened. Prepare a relaxing bath for me. I shan't be long."

"Yes, Your Majesty."

Emilia grabbed the unfinished bottle of wine and sauntered to the vacant balcony. She gave the view another minute of appreciation before drinking straight from the bottle's neck. Her throat warmed as the sweet alcohol descended to her stomach. Her new world had magic, dragons, and handsome warriors, yet why was it still so hard to get a date?

"I should have run away with all my money and became a rich merchant with a harem of men."

# 9

# A KEPT MAN

## LAURENCE

**For the second day in a row,** Laurence woke up next to Cali's sleeping face. Yesterday, he could have flatly rejected her, and they could have resumed their professional relationship. Yet, after seeing her so mesmerising and dressed up for him, like a night nymph, he could no longer hold back the attraction. His palms were so sweaty, he would not have been able to hold a sword.

Gingerly, he brushed a long lock of her blonde hair away from her face. He was in too deep to back out now. Thessian may even send him back to the Empire should Laurence mutter the wrong word.

She slowly opened her unfocused eyes and smiled. "Good morning, Commander."

He smiled back. "We are well past being formal with each other, Calithea."

"I suppose we are."

Laurence sat up. His action seemed to agitate her, and she immediately did the same.

"I will be leaving with Ian and the other squad leaders in search of the beastmen in less than a week. I think we should decide what to do about us going forward." He took a hold of her hand and raised her knuckles to his lips. He could feel the rough callouses on her palms from years of earnest training.

"What is it you want, Cali?" he muttered against her skin.

Cali looked down. Her long hair covered her face like a veil. "I know I cannot expect a marriage with you. I am of common birth and am unqualified to wed someone from a marquess' household."

He clenched his jaw. Cali already knew what held him back and dared not dream too big. He did not deserve her kind heart. "Should we elope? I do not have any savings as of yet, but I—"

She lifted her head and studied his face as if searching for something. "Are you serious?"

"I know I joke around often, but this is a matter of honour. I should warn you, my mother may send assassins after us."

"You do not need to worry about money, Sir Laurence. I have more than enough."

"What do you mean?"

She blushed. "We are always deployed or travelling. I have not had the time to spend much of my salary." She had a thoughtful expression for a second and added, "I did send a bit of money to my mother who started a small trading business. She and Father can support themselves now."

The fact that Calithea had more money than a noble's son did not sit well with him. "I cannot ask you to use your savings. I will do what I can to provide for us."

Cali hugged him so tight, that he struggled to breathe. Her naked chest pressed against his, and he could not help thinking inappropriate thoughts.

"Even if I have to face hundreds of assassins for the rest of my life, I would choose to be by your side, Sir Laurence. I cannot express how happy I am at this moment."

*Think clean thoughts, Laurence, before she takes note of the growing tent between your legs.*

She peeled away and glanced down. Smirking, Cali said, "Want to go another round?"

"It would be my pleasure." He grinned and pulled the thick blanket over them.

---

The week flew by quicker than Laurence wanted it to.

In the blink of an eye, Ian had completely healed without a single scar.

That morning, the group was meeting in the stables to depart for their new assignment. While Yeland, Sergey, and Eugene were busy checking their personal belongings, Laurence reluctantly patted his horse on the side. Its shiny brown mane and muscular body proved it was healthy and ready for the long journey. He wanted to see Calithea one more time before departure, but she was too busy. Last night, she gave him an oval silver locket on a silver chain. On the back of it were engraved Cali's initials. Apparently, it belonged to her mother who gave it to Cali as a good luck charm on the battlefield. In return, Laurence gave Calithea his family's ring as a promise to stay true to her. He even told her to throw it away if she ever suspected him of cheating.

"Sir Laurence, Sir Ian has arrived. Should we set off?" Yeland asked.

"What about His Highness?" Laurence scanned the stables. "Have you seen him?"

Yeland shook his head.

Ian picked out a black horse at the back of the stables, expertly secured his minimal luggage, and pulled on the reins to guide the steed outside.

"Ian, wait!" Laurence chased after him.

The elf halted outside. He looked over his shoulder and asked,

"What?"

"There is no need for you to come if you're unhappy about it. I promise to return with the beast-girl as soon as possible."

"I am tagging along to supervise you," Ian explained. "I fear you may cause more havoc if left to your own devices."

Laurence let out a loud guffaw. "When did you get a sense of humour?"

"That was not a joke." Ian pushed his boot into the stirrup and pulled himself up into the seat. "I will wait at the castle gate." He rode off without looking back.

Laurence felt a heavy hand on his shoulder.

"It will take a lot more grovelling to get him to like you again," Thessian said behind Laurence.

Laurence let out an exaggerated sigh. "Yes, I have assumed as much."

"Here, take this with you." Thessian handed him a leather satchel.

Taking a peek inside, Laurence let out a low whistle. "There is a castle-worth of healing potions in here."

"Beastmen are dangerous. You may encounter more than one on your journey. Use them in case of an emergency."

"I will. Thank you, Your Highness."

Thessian studied his friend for a long moment. "How are things with Dame Cali? I hope she won't be weeping once you leave."

"We promised to write each other." Laurence scanned the area. With no witnesses around, he draped his arm over Thessian's shoulders, pulling him down to his height. "I must ask for a favour."

"What is it?"

"I need a raise."

Thessian shook Laurence off and folded his arms over his wide chest. "Why?"

Laurence balled his hands at his sides. "I will not be a kept man! It is a matter of pride."

Thessian chuckled. "You get paid enough to buy a mansion every year. Where did it all go?"

"You know I had no reason to save money till now. If I am to leave the Oswald family—"

"I never thought you would abandon your clan for a woman."

"Neither did I!" Laurence raked his fingers through his messy hair. "You know how my parents are, especially Mother. They won't leave Calithea alone if they find out we are together."

"Is it due to Dame Cali's status?"

Laurence nodded.

Thessian rubbed his jaw in thought. "I will think on it."

"Thank you, Your Highness." Laurence beamed at him and climbed into the saddle.

The other knights joined them shortly, and, with a brief goodbye from Prince Thessian, they left Newburn.

# 10
# THE TRUTH BEHIND THE SHADOWS

### EMILIA

**Emilia tapped her index finger** on her desk as she intently stared at her office door. Since she kissed Clayton, he began avoiding her. When she called for him, his sister, Lady Isobelle, would turn up instead to give Emilia a report on the progress of the trial preparations.

*Speak of the Devil...*

A knock sounded on the door, and Lady Isobelle was escorted in by Sir Rowell, who promptly excused himself and left them alone. Today, she was dressed in a frilly black dress that matched her pinned-up black hair. The lady never wore any jewellery or expensive accessories nobles often donned. Not like Isobelle needed them. She would look gorgeous even in a filthy sack.

Emilia could no longer contain her curiosity. "Lady Isobelle, is Lord Armel avoiding me?"

Isobelle produced a beatific smile that could sell sand in a desert. "He said he is busy with the task you have given him, Your Majesty. The trial begins tomorrow, and he wants everything to go swimmingly."

"Is that the truth?"

Gliding closer to the Queen's desk, Lady Isobelle lowered her voice and playfully replied, "For the most part. He has been working non-stop during the day and training at night. As much as I enjoy seeing his perfect façade falling, he may collapse after the trial is over."

"As I thought, I should speak with him…"

"Worry not, Your Majesty. He will snap out of it soon enough. Our family members are trained not to have weaknesses. I will simply remind him of the fact."

Intrigued, Emilia leaned in. "Could you tell me more about House Escariot?"

"It would be my pleasure." Isobelle motioned to the sofas at the other end of the room. "Shall we get more comfortable, Your Majesty? It may take a while."

Emilia ordered the guards outside to not let anyone in until her business with Lady Armel was concluded. She joined Isobelle on the sofa. Taking a quick study of the lady's rod-straight posture and delicate features, Emilia struggled with the idea that Isobelle was an assassin with such a slim body.

Lady Isobelle smiled. "What would Your Majesty like to know?"

"From what I've heard from you and Lord Armel, you have grown up in a tough environment."

She let out a giggle as she covered her mouth with her hand. "Our family has its traditions like any other."

It was no news to Emilia that the nobles often neglected or abused their children. Most simply hired a nanny and forgot the children existed until it was time for succession classes. Even then, abuse was masqueraded as education.

"Initially, our parents had five children. As Your Majesty knows, only one person may become the head of the house and inherit the curse. The rest are lucky if they survive at all."

Emilia did not know how to react. Their childhood sounded worse than hers. "What happened to your siblings?"

"They did not survive the trials." Isobelle did not display a single emotion as she spoke her words matter-of-factly, almost as if she was reading a boring report rather than talking about the death of her siblings. "At the age of ten, each of us was given a dagger and a loaf of bread before we were discarded in a forest with monsters for a week. Those who did not make it out alive were buried in unmarked graves."

Emilia's heart ached at the idea of children being tortured in such a way. *How scared must they have been to fight wild beasts at such a young age?* "Are you and Lord Armel the sole survivors of that test?"

"Yes. Our brothers were weak and failed."

"Did you not get along with them?" Emilia gingerly asked.

"We are taught that caring and loving each other is a grave weakness. Therefore, it is a rule within the household to marry people with whom we have no emotional attachment. Our father even created an additional test for us with those words in mind. Once Clayton and I became the sole survivors, he told us to raise pets and keep them by our side at all times. Once we showed even a slight emotional interest in the animal… Well, you must get the idea. From then on, it was rinse and repeat until we no longer grew attached to anything."

Emilia felt the blood draining from her face. What kind of maniac made his children kill their pets over and over again? No, what was worse was that the parents showed no love for their children throughout the entire process. To the adults, their children were simply tools to inherit the curse. Perfect, emotionless shadows for a monarch. And, after all that torture, they had to choose to serve or die.

Emilia felt her blood boil. *How horrible…*

Isobelle pulled out a handkerchief and offered it to Emilia. "I did not mean to upset Your Majesty."

Emilia touched her damp cheeks. She did not realise she had shed tears. Accepting the handkerchief, she wiped at her eyes. "I had no idea—"

Isobelle gave Emilia a reassuring smile. "I am glad someone as kind as you became our master. To witness our queen shedding tears for our sake is a moment to engrave in my heart." She smirked. "I bet Brother will be furious with me for making you cry."

"May I ask, why did he become the head and not you?"

"I did not want that curse engraved on my flesh, so I did the bare minimum. Clayton, on the other hand, was eager to please Father to get even the smallest of praises and trained until his hands were bloody and his muscles tore. There was a time he came home covered in blood from head to toe, holding an ogre's severed head, because Father spoke in passing of his interest in them."

"I suppose I should be careful with my words from now on," Emilia muttered under her breath. Balling her hands in her lap, Emilia asked, "What happened to your father?"

"Under the curse, if you do not accept your master, you will die a slow and painful death. Every day, you will have seizures and feel like you are being stabbed by a thousand knives. Father lasted until Clayton turned sixteen and was able to take over. He then begged Brother to finish him off with his last shred of sanity."

Emilia was speechless. Her mind struggled to come to terms with what Clayton had lived through. In comparison, her isolated life in her tower was a walk in the park.

Isobelle gently touched Emilia's hand, giving it a light squeeze. "I told you our story so you would pity us, Your Majesty. This way, you won't give us any tough missions."

Despite Isobelle's obvious attempt to lighten the mood, Emilia could not bring herself to smile. Now, more than ever, she had the urge to speak with Clayton and apologise for her insensitive behaviour last week. "Could you arrange a meeting with Lord Armel at the town square this evening? I wish to speak with him directly."

"I will pass on your message, Your Majesty." Isobelle bowed her head. "With your permission, I should return home. There are many reports to look over regarding Duke Malette's territory and his son's movements."

"Travel safely."

The door clicked shut behind Isobelle, and Emilia buried her face in her hands. No matter what, she had to help Clayton break the curse. He had suffered enough.

Emilia received confirmation about the meeting with Clayton via a crow sent by Isobelle. She dressed in a commoner's attire, donned a long brown wig, and snuck out of the castle after informing Ambrose of her outing. No doubt her head maid would secretly follow.

Walking through the emptying cobbled streets, she recalled the day of the king's funeral. The citizens were wary of her because the Church had spread lies about her existence. It had been a while since she sent a letter to His Holiness. If he refused her offer, she would be put in a tight spot. Nobles she could control through money or backdoor deals, but the citizens needed to see her in a positive light. She did not have a strong military or influence to prevent an uprising of the common people.

She rubbed her neck nervously as she recalled the French revolutions from her past life. They often ended with the king's head parting from his neck at the guillotine.

The lanterns were lit as she reached her destination. The fountain in the town square was shaped into a statue of King Gilebert, clad in armour, riding his warhorse. Water poured from the horse's mouth, which made her hide her laughter with a cough. She had no idea what the king was going for, but it looked like the horse was vomiting. Then again, the king did have an atrocious taste in objects. Any merchant who came his way, as long as they grovelled and complimented the king, would make enough gold to last them a year or two.

"Your Ma—I mean, my lady, you have arrived." It was Clayton's smooth voice.

She tore her gaze away from the statue and looked at the man standing next to her. He had a pallid complexion, dark circles under his eyes, and a growing beard that hid half of his face. Although he was dressed down to not attract attention, somehow, he still exuded a noble's aura.

"Shall we get something to eat?" she asked.

Clayton offered her his arm. "As you wish, my lady. I know just the place."

Emilia slid her hand up to his bicep, enjoying the feel of hard muscle under her palm.

*Buff men are the best.*

At her pace, they headed away from the fountain and in the direction of many taverns and inns that were situated in the bowels of the city.

"May I ask what it is you wish to discuss with such urgency?"

Emilia avoided stealing glances at him. "I can see you are pushing yourself too hard for my sake, Clayton. It gives me no joy to see you in such a state."

"What do you mean? I am perfectly fine."

She rolled her eyes. If she looked like him, Ambrose would have strapped her to a bed and not allowed her to go anywhere for a week.

An idea came to mind, and she grinned. "I think we should change our destination."

He paused. "Where would you like to go, my lady?"

"To the nearest inn. I would like to book a room." Peeking at his face, she saw his panicked expression. His reaction made her want to tease him more. "Do not worry, Clayton. I do not plan on eating you alive."

She took a hold of his hand and pulled him in the direction of the inn sign she was familiar with.

Emilia pushed open the wooden door and dragged him to the bar where a chubby man with a receding hairline was busy pouring an ale for a customer. She recognised him as someone working with the guild and was often seen affectionately chatting with Sally.

"Evenin'. We'd like a room," she stated boldly.

The owner, without looking up, muttered in a gravelly voice, "Ten coppers."

She slid a silver coin across, finally getting the man's attention. "Make sure no one disturbs us."

The owner gave a curt nod, handed her a key from under the counter, and pointed to the staircase on his left. "Last room on the right."

"Please bring up a meal for us," she replied.

Emilia pulled Clayton along, who seemed to be so confused, that he could not speak.

Scaling the stairs, she felt like a rebellious child as she propelled her escort into the tiny room that contained a single bed with yellowed sheets and a grey woollen blanket next to a crate that was used as a bedside table. Letting go of Clayton's hand, she moved to light the lantern hanging on a rusty hook.

"Your Majesty, if you wish to rest here, I will wait outside…"

She spoke over her shoulder. "The one resting here is you. Get on the bed."

"I assure you, I am fi—"

Before he could finish, she pulled on his arm and pushed him to sit on the bed. He could have easily shaken her off but didn't. "Please, Clayton. I do not like seeing you suffer on my account."

"I apologise for making Your Majesty worried about this useless shadow."

Emilia scowled. "If you are truly sorry, get some sleep. The Duke's trial is tomorrow. I cannot have you being sleep-deprived."

"I promise to return to my estate and get some sleep." He started to get up, and she placed her hands on his shoulders, keeping him from rising.

"Rest! That is an order." She gave him a pointed look to show him that she meant every word.

Clayton nodded, and Emilia stepped back and leaned her back against the wall.

Reluctantly, he removed his boots and stretched out on the blanket. His frame was so big, he took up most of the bed. "Please wake me in an hour, Your Majesty. I cannot keep you waiting for a long time."

Emilia nodded. It was a white lie. She wanted him to sleep for at least four hours to regain his energy.

Surprisingly, when his head hit the pillow, his breathing became even within minutes, and he was as still as the dead. Once she was certain he was in a deep sleep, she collected the food at the door from the innkeeper with a murmured 'thank you'.

Emilia placed Clayton's portion on the crate and sat on the floor with her back resting against the wall.

She ate her fill of the meaty stew and drank sweet ale to wash down the hard bread. Occasionally, she stole glances at Clayton's sleeping face. Her initial plan was to apologise for the kiss at the right time and part ways. Seeing how haggard he had become drove Isobelle's words further home. Clayton was in desperate need of acknowledgement whether from his father or his master. As she was the said master, she had to teach him to find balance before he drove himself to an early grave. Still, having someone trying so hard for her sake was strangely comforting. She was no longer alone and with no one to rely on. The years she spent in that dreary, cold tower had stayed with her. To that day, she secretly feared that she would wake up to find she never left those stone walls.

Hours passed.

Her limbs grew stiff, so she got up and stretched. Light on her feet, she inched towards the door. If she stayed any longer, Ambrose would probably burst into the inn in search of Emilia.

"Your Majesty?" Clayton asked in his half-asleep state and sat up with a strained creak of the bed frame.

"I was planning on letting you rest some more."

"No need. I have survived on less sleep for a month before."

*Is he even human?* "The trial begins today. I soon hope to see Malette's head on a pike outside the castle walls."

He climbed off the bed and bowed low. "Everything is prepared and will happen as you desire, Your Majesty."

Emilia balled her hands at her sides. She wanted to reach out and give him a bit of comfort or praise but feared he would distance himself again.

"I look forward to it." Biting her lip, she added, "I apologise for kissing you. It was insensitive of me."

He straightened his posture. His cheeks displayed a faint blush under the low, orange light from the lantern. "Your Majesty can do nothing wrong to me. I am bound to you as a servant for life."

Her brows furrowed, and she was ready to storm out. "And what did Clayton as a person think of the kiss?"

"I—" He stopped, and his lips formed a thin line.

*I guess, it was too much to ask for him to enjoy it...* "I only wished to deliver my apology to you, Lord Armel. Have a good night and good luck in court."

She started for the door when he caught the material of her cloak and tugged on it. "I-I liked it, Master. A lot."

# 11
# MATTERS OF THE CHURCH

## EMILIA

**H**earing Clayton's admission made her whole face burn. She quickly pulled the hood of her cloak on to hide her appearance. "I really should be going."

"I understand, Your Majesty." Without turning, she felt him letting go of her cloak. "Thank you for allowing me to rest in your presence."

"It is what anyone with a conscience would do." She reached for the door handle when his fingers brushed hers. He was so close, she could feel the heat from his body against her side and back.

"Allow me," he said, opening the door for her.

She bobbed her head and strode out in a hurry.

No matter how much distance she put between her and the inn, her heart did not settle down nor did her blush wane. She briefly considered a visit to the royal physician to check if she had developed heart problems, but she knew it was just her brain making excuses for the suffocating attraction she felt for her shadow.

*Of all the clichés, I had to get a crush on my bodyguard!*

---

The next day, Emilia chewed her breakfast without tasting any of it. Her mind was too preoccupied with the trial that was about to begin in the city's courthouse. She had entrusted the trial to Clayton and Isobelle. Just to be on the safe side, Dame Cali was to serve as the guard for Duke Malette during the proceedings and until he was convicted of high treason. Even Thessian said he would observe the trial as a spectator.

Ambrose inched closer to Emilia. "Your Majesty, what is bothering you?"

"I cannot shake the feeling that something bad will happen today."

"There is nothing to worry about. Duke Malette has been under strict surveillance by Lionheart and Dame Cali. Lord Armel and his sister have diligently prepared the legal case to strip the Duke of his title and territory. The Duke may have sway with some nobles due to being the former king's cousin, but he is not a direct descendant like you."

"He is also not cursed to bring destruction to Dante."

"Do you believe the Church of the Holy Light will act against your will?"

Emilia set down her cutlery on the plate. She couldn't eat another bite as her stomach grew heavy with worry. "They would not dare act openly, and I doubt His Holiness will allow for any more interference without his express permission."

"Then was the bishop acting on his own?"

"From what Lionhart told me, the new pope has the greatest power of Luminos among the priests and the support of the common people, which is why he rose within the ranks quickly. I doubt everyone was happy to suddenly work under a man who came out of nowhere."

Ambrose commented, "He may be a puppet."

"No one knows for certain. He has not left the City of Light since his appointment. There are even rumours that he has been confined by the cardinals."

Ambrose tilted her head to one side. "Can they confine someone of such importance?"

"I would not know."

The level of power the Pope possessed was a mystery. Most priests emitted a bit of light from their hands and healed the injuries of others through something they called a 'miracle'. The only difference between the priests and the mages that she noticed was the said light. After getting to know Clayton and Lady Riga, Emilia was more inclined to learn about the mages and the types of magic in the world. Some mages could cast light spells, and their secondary ability was healing.

*Could the priests be mages?*

*If so, why would they so actively persecute their own kind?*

And, had they truly been mages, wouldn't the Mage Assembly voice their suspicion also? At that point in time, she could only speculate without concrete evidence.

Sir Rowell entered the dining hall and bowed low. "Your Majesty, two people are asking for an appointment with you. One of them has a royal invitation."

"Who would they be?"

"Mr Jehan Wells of the Lionhart Guild and a young cardinal from the City of Light."

Emilia raised a brow. *A young cardinal?*

That rarely happened. In her past life, they were all old men who had served the church for many years. She was in two minds about making the cardinal wait.

Her mood turned sour. It should have taken her messenger two weeks to reach the Pope. The response was too quick.

*Was he intercepted?*

Dabbing at the corners of her mouth with a cloth serviette, she got up from the dining table. "Have Mr Wells wait in my office and the cardinal in the drawing room. I will meet with the Church's representative first."

"At once, Your Majesty." Sir Rowell backed out of the room.

"Ambrose, you know what to do."

"Of course, Your Majesty." Ambrose smiled and disappeared into the secret passageways.

Emilia patiently waited for twenty minutes before heading to the drawing room. She did not want the cardinal to think that she dropped her work and ran to see him. A part of her felt bad for making Jehan wait. She ran into him a few times at the guild, but they never spoke.

Emilia asked the two knights at the door of the drawing room to follow her in. From their appearance, she knew they belonged to Thessian's army and would report about the meeting to His Highness later.

Having two looming bodyguards was not bad. She could easily protect herself from a priest with the dagger she kept strapped to her thigh, but revealing all of her cards too early could put her at a disadvantage.

Appearing as a typical noblewoman was better, for now.

One of the knights opened the door for her, and she glided inside.

In the drawing room, two people awaited her arrival.

The man on the right appeared to be in his mid-twenties and was easy on the eyes. He was dressed in a black robe that reached his ankles. A two-toned, scarlet-and-gold, stole was draped over his wide shoulders. At a glance, his athletic body suited a knight more than a pious man of God. He even sported a tan on his hands and face which was uncommon for high-ranking clergy members. From under his mussed, sandy hair, he silently observed her with gentle, grass-green eyes.

As she approached the cardinal, she noted that his shoes were made of the finest leather but were covered with dirt as if he had been walking outdoors for many days.

The second man was a holy knight. He was tall—almost Thessian's height—and had short black hair, dark eyes, and an equally docile demeanour. His shiny silver armour with the church's emblem was a huge eyesore. The sweeping navy cape on his back was useless in battle situations and more suited for pompous events.

The cardinal lowered his head in greeting, and the knight followed suit. "It is a pleasure to meet Your Highness. I am Cardinal Valerian Knox and this is Sir Klaus von Erenel. May the blessings of Luminos guide you."

She felt her eye twitch. He was either misinformed or pretending to be. "I am no longer a princess, Your *Eminence*. Since King Gilebert's passing, I am the sole owner of the Dante Throne and would appreciate it if you would adjust your words accordingly."

He did not raise his head. "My deepest apologies, Your Majesty. And please, call me Valerian."

Leaving them standing there, she made her way to an armchair and sat down. The marble table in front of her looked empty, so she glanced at one of the knights. "Please bring tea and refreshments for our guests."

The knight wordlessly bowed and walked out of the room in search of a servant. His partner moved to stand guard against the wall, behind Emilia.

She carefully folded her hands in her lap, taking on the well-practised posture of a monarch. "You may join me, Cardinal. Sir Erenel may do so as well."

The holy knight pulled out a chair for the cardinal before taking the other seat at the small round table. All the while, Emilia felt the cardinal's eyes on her. She did not feel any malice from his gaze, merely curiosity.

"May I ask what brought a cardinal to the Dante Kingdom?" she asked, keeping an eye on his expression.

He reached into his pocket and pulled out her letter. "I came because of this, Your Majesty."

"I believe the letter was addressed to the Pope and not a cardinal," she retorted.

Valerian shot her a boyish smile that showed off his dimples. "His Holiness is quite busy with the matters within the City of Light and is, therefore, unable to respond to every letter."

That was a backhanded way of telling her that she was not important enough. She returned his smile. "He must be awfully preoccupied dealing with a single city-state while I am only looking after a small kingdom."

For a split-second, she thought his smile reached his penetrating eyes. "In your letter, Your Majesty mentioned Bishop Lagarde conspiring to commit high treason with the kingdom's duke. Do you have any evidence?"

"I have plenty of witnesses and reports from an information guild."

He lowered his head and let out a heavy sigh. "It is a pity he turned away from Luminos. Lagarde will be dismissed from his post, effective immediately."

"You do not wish to see the evidence I mentioned?"

"I trust your words, Your Majesty," he replied nonchalantly.

For a lackey of the Church, he was more easy-going than she thought possible. "What about the other matter I mentioned in the letter?"

"Ah," Valerian tucked the letter back into his pocket, "I will give you an answer after we see Lagarde."

She raised her hand, getting the attention of the knight behind her. "We are going to the dungeon."

"Yes, Your Majesty," the knight replied and moved to open the door for her.

Emilia got up first. The cardinal and his holy knight followed a safe distance behind her and her escort to not crowd her.

Something did not sit right with Emilia. The longer she thought about Cardinal Valerian's appearance and personality, the less she believed his identity was real.

Halting at the entrance to the dungeon, she smiled pleasantly. "I forgot to ask, but could I see your identification, Your Eminence? I have never met someone in such a high position among the clergy, you see."

"Your Majesty is being cautious, I understand."

Valerian reached into the inner pocket of his robe and retrieved a palm-sized golden plate with his credentials and the holy symbol of Luminos embossed on it. It was unmistakable. He was, indeed, a high-ranking official. The common priests who worked at the temples had wooden identification. Bishops and archbishops possessed a silver plate. Only the cardinals and the Pope had the golden identification.

"My apologies for doubting you, Cardinal."

He dismissed her apology with another kind smile.

With an escort of a dungeon guard, they descended the staircase and followed the lengthy corridor to another set of stairs, leading them farther into the depths of the dungeon. Soon after, they came to a stop in front of Lagarde's cell.

The bishop's facial hair had grown out, and he seemed to have lost some weight. Lifting his tired eyes from the stone ground he sat on, he gasped and scrambled backwards on all fours. His back pressed against the wall and panic filled his eyes.

There was no way he was acting that way because of her. She turned her head and noticed a change in the cardinal's expression.

Long gone were pleasantness and warm smiles. They were replaced with a stone-cold glare focused on the criminal.

"Lagarde," Cardinal Valerian began with a voice full of authority. "For crimes committed against Her Majesty, the Queen of Dante, you are sentenced to immediate execution. Sir Klaus, proceed."

The holy knight took the key from the guard with Emilia's permission and entered the cell, his sword drawn.

"Sir Erenel! Please, I did nothing wrong! I am being framed!" Lagarde bowed so low, he was almost flat on the floor. With a terror-filled expression, he turned to Valerian. "I beg you to forgive me. Just this once? Please? Your Holi—"

His head flew off with a single powerful swing of the knight's sword.

Emilia was stunned as Lagarde's bloodied head rolled towards the metal bars.

The ex-bishop's eyes glazed over as his mouth remained open.

"A pity, indeed," Valerian muttered, wiping the small splatter of blood from his hands with a handkerchief.

The shock from the brutal scene finally subsided, and Emilia stared at Valerian in disbelief. "You're the Pope?"

# 12
# THE DUKE'S DEFENCE

## THESSIAN

**On the morning of the Duke's** trial, Thessian wrote a letter to his father and dressed to attend the trial. Laurence had become such a handful during their stay in Dante, that Thessian contemplated sending him back to Darkgate once his friend returned from his mission. There was a glimmer of hope in Thessian's heart that Dame Cali could tame that wild horse before more disasters could occur.

He ran a hand through his hair. *One can hope...*

Thinking about Laurence's romantic endeavours made him pause. It had been a few days since the prince's conversation with Emilia in that overly romantic bedroom her servants had prepared.

He couldn't help but smile every time he remembered the look of shock on her face. The Queen could act older than she was when it came to court affairs and strategies, but she was a timid young lady with no experience in matters of the heart.

Not just that. She had the absurd belief that she was not beautiful enough for him. Perhaps, her maids covered up the mirror in her bedchambers out of spite. No doubt, in the near future, she would have a line of suitors stretching all the way to the Reyniel Kingdom. Some would want her for her power, some for her beauty, but, hopefully, there would be one or two who wished to share their hearts and cherish her for her intelligence and bravery.

Thessian pulled a charcoal-coloured cloak over his shoulders and secured it with a silver clip. The trial was due to begin in an hour, giving him more than enough time to get to the courthouse on foot.

Making certain he had everything for the last time, he left the palace.

The leisurely walk to the courthouse was uneventful. Newburn had suffered greatly due to the fire, displacing an entire street worth of people. He heard that Count Baudelaire had paid for the temporary accommodation of over a hundred people at the local inns. Such generosity from a noble towards the commoners was suspicious. Emilia trusted the Count, yet what if Lord Baudelaire was trying to steal the throne from under her? He managed the nobles on Emilia's side and was liked by the people. Taking one more step could lead Lord Baudelaire to become a monarch.

Not like Thessian would let that happen.

Stopping at the foot of the steps that led to the courthouse's entrance, he studied the gloomy stone structure with a pointed wooden roof. Unlike the high court in the Empire, this little courthouse could not fit more than fifty spectators.

The crowd gathered outside seemed eager to be involved with the trial's gossip. After all, the only duke of the kingdom could be executed for high treason less than two weeks after the previous king's funeral. The nobles must be getting worried about a purge.

He pulled his hood on farther over his face and strode to the entrance where he presented a letter with Her Majesty's seal.

The guards on duty permitted him entry.

He was greeted and promptly guided by a clerk to a separate

balcony on the second floor that overlooked the entire courtroom. After a mumbled 'thank you kindly' from Thessian, the clerk returned to his duties.

Staying hidden in the shadows, Thessian assessed the mood below.

From the balcony, Thessian could see the nobles who managed to get in. They were seated according to their rank. Among them, he spotted Count Baudelaire.

In the same row, a familiar hulking figure of Count Edgar Fournier was hard to miss. He must have finally arrived to track the dragon and could not turn down the spectacle that was about to unfold. In front of them sat Marquess Lenard Carrell among a few other marquesses.

At the top of the courtroom was the judges' bench with three empty seats.

One of the guards walked over to the rope barrier that separated the room in two and announced to the spectators, "Now entering the honourable judges."

The door to the judges' chambers opened, and three men filed out. The two old gentlemen in burgundy robes ambled to their seats at the judge's bench. The last to take his seat was none other than the Queen's shadow, Lord Clayton Armel.

Thessian smirked. No matter whether Lord Armel was a judge or a viscount, all of the attention would be on the opinions of his seniors.

Once the judges were seated, the guard announced the entry of Duke Malette and his legal counsel. Under Dame Cali's stern watch, they headed to the defendant's table on the left side of the courtroom. Seeing Malette's hands bound with chains made some of the noble ladies in attendance gasp or fan themselves.

The guard cleared his throat loud enough to get the attention of the distracted nobility.

The Queen's shadow stood and announced, "The trial of Duke Anatole Ferdinand Malette will now begin. The charges against him are high treason against the Crown, murder of His Majesty, King Gilebert Verne Roderick Dante, His Highness the Crown

Prince, and His Highness the second prince, conspiring to murder Her Majesty Emilia Valeria Dante, and attempting a coup by sneaking soldiers into the city. How does the defendant plead?"

Malette's scrawny lawyer rose and pushed his round spectacles up his hooked nose that reminded Thessian of a parrot's beak. "My client pleads not guilty on all accounts, Your Honour."

Lord Armel kept his expression neutral the entire time. "The evidence has already been submitted and reviewed. Does the Duke's legal counsel have anything else to add?"

A light knock behind Thessian drew his attention. He opened the door to find the spymaster standing there.

"May I join you, Your Highness?" Lionhart inquired.

Thessian stepped aside, allowing the man to saunter onto the balcony.

They remained standing closer to the door to avoid drawing unnecessary attention.

In a low voice, Lionhart asked, "How is Your Highness finding your stay in Dante?"

"What is it you want, Lionhart?"

"I thought some casual conversation would lighten the mood. If you are not inclined to talk, I will simply observe the trial from here."

Thessian eyed him from under his brows. Lionhart was a man who was hard to read. His dark, cold gaze reminded Thessian of the butchers he met on the battlefield who had killed one too many people. His ethnicity was also hard to ignore. The man obviously came from the desert kingdom of Asmor or was the offspring of someone who hailed from there. To arrive on the continent, he would have had to cross the Misty Ocean.

"The defendant may rise to speak in his defence," Lord Armel announced.

Thessian returned his attention to the ongoings below.

The Duke proudly rose and adjusted the cuffs of his coat to hide the chains ever-so-slightly. "Your Honours, I am being falsely accused by the fake queen who has no relation to the royal family."

A flurry of gasps and chatter erupted from the audience.

Thessian glanced at Lionhart.

No reaction came from the spymaster, which solidified in his mind that the Duke's words were make-believe.

Duke Malette continued, "When I heard that something happened to my dear cousin, King Gilebert, I dropped everything in my estate near Newburn and rushed over to find a strange girl sitting on the throne. As we all know, the real princess spent her life in the Tower due to her terrible curse. King Gilebert was too kind-hearted and could not kill his child. The truth that no one knows to this day is that the princess died there. This fact is only known to those within the royal family..."

The nobility in the room began to question everything. Their voices grew so loud that one of the older judges slammed his hammer down three times to get them to stop.

Clayton cleared his throat. "Your story is intriguing, Your Grace, but Princess Emilia's name has not been crossed out from the royal genealogy tree. Had she truly died, her name would have been removed, especially if it had been years since her passing."

Malette's face grew red. "That is merely because the former king held the princess close to his heart and did not allow for the name to be removed."

"Your Grace, are you telling us that the royal protocol is so loose that it would leave an opening for an impostor to claim a royal's identity?"

"I-I guess, I must have misheard the late king's words," Malette muttered.

Thessian chuckled.

"The fact that the princess is cursed remains," Malette added. "An archbishop personally came from the City of Light and looked into that child's future. It was prophesied that she would bring destruction to this kingdom." He spread his arms out as much as the chains would allow. "And look! The prophecy came true! The king was murdered along with the two princes. A child is sitting on the throne with no one to guide her. And worst of all, she is being manipulated by a foreign power. They even have an encampment north of Newburn where thousands of soldiers are waiting for an order to attack us all."

Thessian raised a brow. A few thousand men could take over a city as defenceless as Newburn in a matter of days, but to take over an entire kingdom? Even the best of strategists would be unable to secure such a victory. And thousands of soldiers? He had a few hundred men at camp awaiting orders. Malette certainly knew how to spin a tall tale and scare the nobles.

Lord Armel retained an indifferent expression. "Your Grace, how religious are you?"

The Duke seemed taken aback by the question. "I follow the will of Luminos and his teachings, Your Honour."

"According to your own words, you follow a *foreign* religion that has sprouted less than a century ago. Since the beginning of time, it has been known that the king and queen are chosen by God. And, if Luminos is the true god, then he is flawless. It is us, mortals, who are full of faults and sin. Would you not agree that this could also mean that the archbishop may have misinterpreted the words of God?"

"I-I think…"

Clayton cut the Duke off. "By this logic, we may also conclude that it is God's will for the princess to survive and become the Queen of Dante."

Thessian was tempted to applaud Emilia's shadow for his speech. The Duke could not deny that he followed a religion created in a fallen kingdom nor could he fault God as that would mean that God was imperfect.

Thessian never gave the time of day to the priests' ramblings. After all, they hid safely away in their temples while the people died on the battlefield. Had they truly been selfless, they would have endeavoured to heal the injured, regardless of what side they were on. Although the Church of the Holy Light claimed they were neutral, they only healed the royals and the nobility of nations that pushed for more temples to be built. Dante was no exception. King Gilebert must have given the priests quite a lot of leeway for them to have built a massive temple the size of a small castle near the capital.

The lawyer whispered something in Malette's ear, and the Duke's face darkened.

"If that is all you have to say on the matter…" Clayton said in a loud voice.

The Duke's shoulders trembled as he balled his hands. "I am not finished, Your Honour. I have proof that the soldiers outside of Newburn belong to the Empire! I have witnesses who have seen soldiers visiting the towns and villages while speaking in the Empire's common tongue."

Clayton rubbed his tired eyes with his thumb and index finger. "Your Grace, your witnesses have already been interviewed and their testimony recorded. I must say, it is not uncommon for a band of mercenaries to travel from one kingdom to another. We have even sent out a messenger to the encampment you mentioned. According to the man in charge, they are waiting for supplies before heading south to assist with border control. They even provided a contract signed by Marquess Rigal and Marquess Azema who are present here today."

"That's impossible! They must have colluded—"

"Your Grace," Clayton growled in a tone so cold, it could freeze a person to the bone. "Unless you have *evidence* of said collusion, please refrain from dragging through the mud the honourable names of noble families who have protected our borders for many generations."

Malette cursed under his breath and slammed his fist against the table. "I demand a fair trial! This trial is rigged by that scheming wench!"

From above, Thessian could see Clayton's fists shaking with silent fury. If the Duke was not killed by the executioner, Lord Armel would no doubt finish the job for insulting his master.

"I did not kill the king! She did it! It was her!" Malette yelled despite his lawyer's attempts to silence him.

"Malette got the Queen's dog angry," Lionhart commented.

"Do you think it will affect the trial's outcome?" Thessian asked.

"No. He will do his job and complete the task perfectly."

"What makes you so certain?"

Lionhart smirked. "Beasts like him, once they've found a master, will happily pretend to be a good, harmless dog and stay on a leash."

"I doubt it will last. He has too much greed in his eyes. What if he bites his master's hand?"

"Then I will cut him down."

# 13
# GUT FEELING

## THESSIAN

The trial dragged on despite Lord Armel's efforts to stop the Duke from rambling on, but he kept producing one outlandish theory after another about the new queen. He even claimed that, due to her young age, she was unfit for the throne and needed a mentor, glossing over the fact that there were plenty of kings in the past who took the throne at thirteen and fourteen.

To Thessian's surprise, Emilia had given his army a perfect excuse to travel south to the Duke's territory and deal with the uprising before it grew too big. She had not mentioned anything or asked for help, which confused him. She had no military of her own and could not deal with the Duke's forces unless she hired mercenaries.

At one o'clock in the afternoon, the judges announced a break for two hours and left the courtroom.

"Shall we get some lunch, Your Highness?" Lionhart asked, drawing Thessian's attention. "You seem to have a lot on your mind."

"Shall we?"

They left the courthouse and walked a while until they found a tavern with a free table. Due to the commotion caused by the trial, Newburn was overflowing with travellers from other parts of the kingdom.

On their way, he spotted dozens of carriages of nobility parked in the square.

Taking a seat at a table in the back and away from prying eyes, Thessian lowered his hood.

A barmaid came over and took their order so quickly, he barely had the chance to see her face. The poor woman seemed rushed off her feet as she went from one table to the next.

"The Duke has nothing to prove his innocence," Lionhart said, reclining in the creaky wooden chair.

"It is amusing that Lord Armel is trying to blame him for the death of the former king."

"Why not? The Duke has killed a lot of people to remain in his position. What's adding a few more?" Lionhart stopped talking as the barmaid brought their stew and drinks over. She stole a glance at Thessian from under her long lashes and blushed.

The sound of dishes breaking had her jumping out of her skin. She groaned and excused herself, sparing one last flirty look at the prince.

"You are quite popular with the tavern maids, milord," Lionhart joked.

Thessian swallowed a mouthful of his ale. "Getting looks from women like her is better than the fierce stares from the Empire's noblewomen who wish to wed a war hero."

"No need to sell yourself short. They must be staring because they find you attractive. You being a war hero and a duke of the Empire is a bonus."

"What about you?" Thessian asked. "Surely, you also find yourself often surrounded by women."

## QUEEN OF HOPE

Lionhart burst out laughing. "I am not interested in having a romantic relationship."

"Did your last one end badly?"

The spymaster's face darkened. Although he retained a crooked smile on his face, his eyes lost their spark and seemed almost dead. "The past doesn't matter. It is not as if we can return to it."

Thessian sensed Lionhart's apprehension and did not pry further. It was none of his business what kind of love life Emilia's spymaster led.

To change the subject, Thessian asked, "Did you come from Asmor?"

"Milord is quite curious about my past…"

"I am interested in the kind of people the Queen keeps by her side."

"I did not seek Emilia out. She found me and sold me information that made us a lot of money. Our relationship was mostly transactional until she saw me beating up some drunks at the guild. She then demanded I teach her to fight in exchange for a location of an untapped mineral mine."

"How old was she?"

Lionhart's expression softened as if he was talking about a daughter and not a business partner. "She claimed to be thirteen at the time, but her malnourished body looked no older than that of a seven or eight-year-old. When I learned of her identity, it was not hard to calculate her true age. Despite her appearance, her eyes had no innocence in them. She was, and still is, an enigma."

Thessian contemplated the new information. With her ability to see the future, she even uncovered mines. She could have escaped from the castle at any moment and lived off her money. Yet, she stayed behind and waited for *him*. She wagered her life on the line to meet Thessian and help him become emperor.

*Why? What did she see that requires me to take the throne? Why not side with my brother, Cain?*

An urge to see her came over him. He stopped his train of thought. He could ask her about the future in the evening. After all, they had been getting to know each other by keeping the promise of asking one personal question a day, or whenever their schedules allowed.

They ate their meal in silence until Lionhart asked, "Do you fancy Emilia?"

Thessian choked on his stew. He covered his mouth and coughed until his throat burned and his eyes stung.

Glaring at the spymaster, he demanded, "Where did that come from?"

"It is but a simple question."

Done with his meal, Thessian abruptly pushed himself up from the table. "I hold no romantic feelings for her. We simply share common goals."

"I hope it stays that way, milord." Lionhart smiled and muttered something under his breath that sounded similar to, "Having to deal with more suitors would be troublesome…"

Upon their return to the courthouse's second floor, they met Lord Fournier, who was waiting for Thessian.

Lionhart inclined his head in greeting to Lord Fournier and went on ahead to the balcony.

"Your Grace!" Lord Fournier cheered with a big grin. He spread his arms out and gave Thessian a warm hug. "It has been a while. How is my youngest doing?"

Thessian laughed. "Lady Riga is doing quite well. Last I heard, the Queen found a magic tutor to help the lady hone her skills and control mana better."

Lord Fournier bobbed his head in approval. "As long as Riga is not a burden to you, Your Grace. It has certainly gotten quiet in my castle since she left. No more fires to put out in the middle of the night or explosions to deal with." He chuckled. "Worry not, my wife gave Riga a stern talking to before she left with you. She promised to only practice her magic with her future teacher."

Thessian recalled Riga hurling fireballs at the dragon they'd encountered. To not shatter her father's high expectations, Thessian decided not to tell him that the promise was long since broken. All for a good reason, as Lady Riga made a promising addition to his forces.

Leaning in, Lord Fournier lowered his voice. "Is it true that you have found a dragon in Newburn? Is that the reason why an entire district went up in flames?"

"Yes, the dragon is real, and no, those are unrelated."

"Is it big? Young or old?"

"It is young and the height of a fully grown ogre."

Lord Fournier stroked his long brown beard that had some grey hairs in it. "Never hunted a dragon before. A wyvern, sure, but they are not intelligent." He nodded as if confirming something. "Very well, after the court closes for the day, I will greet the new queen and get to work. I even brought Lenard with me. He and I always enjoy a good hunt."

"After the trial, ask for Dame Cali. She will provide the reports and witness statements about the dragon's appearance and abilities."

"Thank you, Your Grace." Lord Fournier inclined his head. "I shall take my leave. It seems the trial is about to resume."

Thessian joined Lionhart on the balcony. By the time he arrived, the judges were walking to their seats.

Taking a quick study of the Duke's relaxed demeanour, Thessian asked Lionhart, "Do you think he has something up his sleeve?"

"What could have changed in two hours? He was under guard the whole time."

Dame Cali undoubtedly would only permit the lawyer to interact with Malette. That did not stop the lawyer from talking to people outside.

A bad feeling came over Thessian. On the battlefield, he learned to trust his gut. No man on the brink of death behaved so calmly.

*Not unless he knows there is a way out for him.*

"I think it best I observe the rest of today's events from the ground floor," Thessian said.

"Do you believe he will make a run for it? There are more guards here than at the castle. One of your strongest knights is right next to him, and the Queen's dog is not going to let Malette out of his sight until the Duke's head is separated from his shoulders."

"This is merely a precaution on my part."

Lionhart frowned. "Well, you are not wrong, Your Highness. He is definitely up to something. I think I should return to the castle, in case he tries to harm the Queen in our absence."

They parted ways.

Thessian descended to the ground floor and exited the courthouse through the back door and gave a cursory sweep of the area. The surroundings were as busy as that morning. The chroniclers were camping outside the front entrance, sitting on the stone steps and chatting with one another. The commoners who were interested in gossip, too, were waiting against the courthouse's grey walls.

His eyes were drawn to the group of five men who were working in the side alley. Two of them were rolling large wooden barrels into the manor next door while another gave them directions. The remaining two were busy unloading more barrels from the wagon parked on the street.

The bad feeling Thessian had earlier grew.

He slipped on his hood and approached the workers. There were no inns or taverns down that alley. The courthouse's guards only guarded the entrances, so no one paid too much attention to the sides.

He approached the men unloading the wagon. Despite their simple worker attire, they wore leather gloves, and their shoes were more expensive than what a commoner could afford.

"Oi, you! Move! We're busy here!" The man with a thin scar across his round face snapped at Thessian.

Standing so close to the barrels, Thessian caught a waft of coal.

"You seemed to be struggling, so I was planning to help," Thessian said. "For a small fee, of course."

"He looks sturdy," the second man in a woolly hat muttered, stretching his back. "We could finish the job faster if we had more hands."

"Ugh, fine! We'll give you five silvers for your trouble," the scarred man offered.

"Ten," Thessian bartered with a charming smile.

"Seven or get out of here!"

Thessian grabbed the nearest barrel to him and picked it up. The muscles in his well-trained arms ached from the sheer weight of what was inside. He could not hear any liquid sloshing around, so they were not transporting wine for a party.

As Thessian trudged into the alley, he pretended to trip and dropped the barrel. The lid popped off and a mix of fine charcoal and sulphur fell out.

*Is that...serpentine powder?*

# 14
# WANDERING HANDS

## THESSIAN

"**Oi! You're meant to help**, not hinder!" one of the men from the wagon shouted.

The serpentine powder was highly volatile and unstable. A single barrel could cause a house to explode. Ten of them could destroy an entire street. It had been used by the former King of Darkgate during Thessian's last battle. He nearly lost half of his men to that cursed powder. To that day, he had his secretary, Viscount Ludwig Esker Cressben, investigating who developed such a dangerous thing and who supplied it. Since it reached Dante, too, the prince had to capture those men alive for questioning.

"Are you deaf?" the scarred man yelled, grabbing Thessian's shoulder.

Thessian raised his hands in defence. "Sorry. It slipped out of my hands."

"Do you know how much this stuff costs? Are you gonna compensate us for it?"

His partner nudged him. "Rich, we are drawing too much attention. Let's finish the job."

Muttering foul curses under his breath, Rich wiped his sweaty brow with his coat's sleeve. "You are lucky we won't charge you for the damages! Now hurry and bring it inside."

Thessian knew exactly why the men were nervous. One wrong move, and they could all be blown asunder into bloody fragments. The distraction the Duke planned for his escape was as clear as day. Regardless of the lives of the innocents Malette sacrificed, the man was eager to survive.

"I'm sorry for the trouble. I'll finish the job for five silvers instead. How's that?"

Rich waved in dismissal before returning to the wagon with his partner.

Thessian gingerly picked up the barrel, set it upright, and carefully secured the lid on top. Knowing what was contained within made his palms sweaty. He held his breath as he lifted the barrel and carried it in the direction of where the other workers went.

He walked around the corner to find three men chatting away on their break.

A short, lean man in his late thirties, who was giving the others instructions earlier, raised a brow at Thessian's approach. "Who're you?"

"I got hired to carry some barrels," Thessian informed him.

He frowned. "You look like a noble."

Thessian laughed. "I get that a lot. Perhaps my father was one."

"You from the Empire?"

"I was born there." Thessian grunted and pretended to nearly drop the barrel. "Sir, this is quite heavy."

The man pointed to the opened back door of the manor. "Alright, bring it in there. Sara will tell you where to put it."

Thessian adjusted his hold on the barrel. The muscles in his arms were beginning to burn from the weight of the load. Once he stepped through the threshold, he set the barrel down and rubbed his aching biceps better.

A tall, muscular brunette approached him. Her mature, sun-kissed skin set her apart from the rest of the men outside, as did the flashy sapphire earrings that dangled from her ears. What caught Thessian's attention the most was the sword strapped to her side. The hilt was encrusted with jewels, and the scabbard had a crest with a roaring jaguar on it.

"Looks like they've finally hired someone strong."

Thessian picked up on her foreign accent. He had spoken with traders from all over the continent and knew she hailed from the Reyniel Kingdom.

"You're a quiet one." She studied him from almost eye level with her dark, inquisitive eyes. "And better lookin' than the rest of 'em." She pointed to the barrel. "Get a move on and leave it in the master's chamber with the others. Be careful not to drop it, or you might lose your life."

Thessian lifted the barrel one more time with a grunt and carried it up an aged staircase that seemed too small for him. He spotted the only unlocked room with an opened door from which he could smell a strong stench of sulphur.

Two more men were inside. They wore thin gloves, goggles, and a white sheet over their noses as they cautiously divided and mixed the charcoal with the sulphur.

Thessian tried not to show his surprise when he counted fifteen barrels stacked against the wall. They must have been at it since before the trial began. With that much serpentine, they could destroy half of Newburn.

He had to inform the Queen and his men.

Wordlessly, he left the barrel in the corner and made his way back down the stairs.

At the bottom of the staircase, the same woman approached him. He assumed she was 'Sara' the other smuggler mentioned. "Hey, when we're done 'ere, how 'bout grabbing a drink?"

Thessian smiled pleasantly at her. "That would be great." As he moved past her, he felt her hand landing on his buttock, and she gave it an appreciative squeeze.

"Fine down 'ere too," she purred.

Thessian held in the urge to cut her hand off and strode out of the manor. While the two men in the wagon were distracted, and the others were busy rolling the barrels down the alley, he slipped past them and merged with the crowd on the street. Since the city guard could be taking bribes and permitted them to smuggle the barrels, Thessian decided to only inform those he could trust.

He spotted a street urchin sitting cross-legged across the road from the courthouse while chomping on a bread roll. Thessian had seen the kid lurking around Lionhart a handful of times. It was safe to assume the boy worked for the guild.

Approaching the dark-haired child, Thessian asked, "What is your name, boy?"

"Depends on who's askin', milord." He gave Thessian's frame a once over with his doe-like eyes. "I know ye. Ye work for Lady Em."

Thessian did not correct the boy and tossed him a silver coin. "I need you to deliver an urgent message to her."

The boy rubbed the coin with his grimy fingers and tested it with his teeth. "Wha kinda message?"

"Ask her to send two dozen knights to the manor near the courthouse as soon as possible. The Duke may attempt an escape."

"Is it coz of dem barrels?"

"Yes. There is a dangerous powder inside that could harm many people."

"And who's tha message from?"

"Thessian."

The boy pulled out his hat from his pocket, dusted it off, and slipped it on his head with the silver coin inside. Climbing to his feet, he said, "It's Rime, milord."

"What is?"

"Me name." The boy waved his half-eaten roll and ran off towards the castle.

# 15

# NOT A PUPPET

## EMILIA

**E**milia was faced with a man who held equal power to a king. She could not afford to make a mistake or mistreat the Pope.

"Your Majesty, this is an unofficial visit," Pope Valerian said with a smile so kind, she could have fallen for it had his servant not beheaded the bishop a minute prior. "I came to punish the sinner personally for betraying Luminos, and, of course, for attempting to harm royalty."

"Why would His Holiness waste time by tracking down the bad apples of the Church?"

"To keep the rest from rotting."

Demanding any more answers would be considered rude, so she added, "Shall we return to the drawing room? The refreshments should have arrived."

Valerian offered her his arm. "Would you allow me the honour of escorting you, Your Majesty?"

Emilia couldn't refuse even if she wanted to. She needed him to force the temple and its priests in Newburn to proceed with her coronation as soon as possible.

Gently placing her hand on his arm, she allowed him to guide her out of the dungeon and towards the main castle. The material of his robe was soft to the touch and easily let her know that he was all muscle underneath.

By the sound of their footsteps, she gauged that Sir Erenel and her guard walked three paces behind them.

"I would prefer it if we could forego formalities in private and speak comfortably, Your Majesty," Valerian said in a silky yet mesmerising voice. He could give day-long sermons and not a single churchgoer would fall asleep. "I liked it better when you were less on guard with me."

She had nothing to lose by pretending to be close with the Pope. If she could use him and his influence, many of the nobles and citizens who follow the Church's doctrine and beliefs would accept her. "I will try."

"You are not what the rumours said you were."

"And what did Your Holiness hear?"

He tsked when she used his title. "I heard you were a grotesque, hunched-over woman who has lived in the dark all her life and has never seen the sun. That you are uneducated, cruel, cursed, and ambitious." He listed off the nasty rumours while keeping his eye on her reaction.

Emilia shrugged one shoulder. "People will always be afraid of the unknown."

"You believe they are afraid of you?"

"Of what I can become."

He accepted her words with a nod. "I think I like you very much."

"Does that mean you will fulfil my request?"

"I will personally assist with your coronation if you do me one favour."

What could he possibly ask of her? Money? The royal treasury probably had more rats than gold. She could use her personal funds, but that would be using up her retirement fund. If he asked for land for the temples, she needed to consult with Thessian. The prince did not seem like a religious man and would probably refuse more of the Church's influence in his territory.

"I would like to go on a date with you."

She was so preoccupied with her thoughts that she must have misheard him. "I apologise. My mind was elsewhere for a second. Could you repeat your request?"

"I wish to go on a date with you, Emilia."

Her legs turned to stone, making him stop as well.

She raised her eyes to study his unnecessarily attractive face. Seeing that he was serious, she felt her ears burning. "Is the Pope even allowed to date?"

"Why not? The Pope can marry and have children if he so wishes. Luminos does not prevent one from pursuing love and happiness."

"And you wish to go on a *date* with *me*?"

His bright smile reached his amused eyes. "That would be correct."

She was stumped for the second time that day, all because of a man who confused her to no end. *Is he a womaniser? With a face like his, he could easily score a date or ten. Maybe he likes a challenge?* "How about an outing instead of a date?"

Valerian lowered his head, and his shoulders sagged. For a second, he looked like a sad puppy.

She would not be fooled by his flawless acting that made her heart pang with guilt. Valerian was a ruler of the City of Light and the owner of the Church of the Holy Light. He could become a powerful ally or a formidable enemy. Once again, the choice was out of her hands.

Swallowing her nerves, she replied, "One date."

He perked up and beamed at her, making his dimples re-appear. Without realising it, she was becoming weak to his smiles that were as addictive as chocolate.

"I will make arrangements," he whispered in his velvety voice.

Emilia blinked several times before daring to ask, "What about the matter of my coronation?" She sucked in a breath. "It is not as if I am eager for the throne, but I need the Church's support to take the necessary steps to improve the lives of my people."

His eyes narrowed slightly as his lips curled up.

Still surprised by his beauty, she now pondered that maybe having a charming and handsome pope was another way to convert people to their religion. After all, in her old world, celebrities were often worshipped like deities and whatever they sponsored was eagerly bought by their followers.

Patting her hand on his bicep, he replied, "I will speak with the priests and have them begin preparations. How about holding it a month from now?"

In a month, she would be turning eighteen. She had to hold a birthday banquet for the nobles and forge connections with those who were on the fence about supporting her.

"I would like for the ceremony to happen within the next two weeks."

"A new queen's coronation requires attention to detail and time. Rushing it could make it less memorable for you and your citizens."

He had a point. Every new monarch showed off their wealth and power during the coronation. A subpar ceremony would displease the nobles and make them doubt her. The citizens may see her as frugal at first but would soon begin to question her wealth.

"Very well, as long as the ceremony happens before my birthday."

From the corner of her eye, she saw Ambrose quickly approaching them.

On instinct, Emilia took a step away from Valerian. The Pope might not be as kind as Thessian if her servant made an attempt on his life, just because he was too close to her.

Ambrose gave a fleeting glare at Valerian before she whispered in Emilia's ear, "Rime from the guild is here on urgent business, Your Majesty."

The bad feeling from that morning resurfaced. The guild members were keeping watch over the trial, so something must have happened.

Keeping her expression in check, Emilia smiled politely at Valerian. "Your Holiness, I must attend to some urgent matters. I apologise for not being able to entertain you for longer."

"Not to worry. We will see each other again soon enough. May the blessings of Luminos guide you." He turned to face his holy knight. "Sir Erenel, we are done here for today. Let us return to our lodgings."

"Where are you staying, Your Holiness?" Emilia asked, in case she needed to send him a message.

"In a small tavern outside the city. Everywhere else was booked due to the Duke's trial."

*Ah, I shouldn't have asked...*

"If it would please Your Holiness, you and Sir Erenel can stay in one of our guest rooms." Not like she could allow the Pope to reside in some decrepit tavern. It would send a terrible message about her hospitality to any other monarch or noble who wished to visit.

"It would be our pleasure." He gently lifted her hand by the fingers and left a feather-soft kiss on the back of her hand. Letting go, he announced, "We will return with our luggage."

Sir Erenel and Pope Valerian left with the knight who was ordered to escort them to the castle gate.

Ambrose pouted. "Was that the Pope, Your Majesty?"

"It sure was."

"Puppet?"

"I doubt it."

"I wish he was uglier."

Emilia stifled a laugh. "Shall we go see what young Rime has to say?"

"Of course, Your Majesty. I had him brought to your office to stay with Jehan Wells."

"And did you learn anything after observing Jehan?"

"He did not move from his seat the entire time nor seem displeased about the wait. He even spoke politely to the servants. I think he will make a good Guard Captain."

"I hope he accepts the offer."

# 16

# A WEEPING BEAR

## EMILIA

**Emilia confidently walked into** her office with Ambrose trailing behind her. Upon entering, she saw Rime jumping on the cushy sofa seat. Jehan was waving his hands in the air in an attempt to stop him.

The boy's eyes grew wide when he spotted Emilia. He slipped and fell flat on the floor.

Lifting his head, Rime produced a cheeky grin. "Lady Em, it's been a while!"

"It's not 'Lady Em', it's 'Your Majesty', Rime," Ambrose chided.

Rime rolled his eyes.

Jehan pulled Rime up by the collar and forced the boy to bow properly alongside him. "Greetings ta Her Majesty, the Queen of Dante. This humble servant apologises fer any slights this young one has committed."

"I take no offence," Emilia replied. "Rime is a spirited boy who does good work for the guild. I appreciate his efforts a great deal. You may raise your heads." Manoeuvring to the nearest available sofa, she sat down and motioned for them to sit across from her. "Now, Rime, care to tell me what urgent message you have?"

Rime scrambled into a seat while Jehan bowed one more time and sat down next to the boy.

"Tha huge blond with tha name somethin'-sian said tha Duke might try his luck at escaping. Said tha barrels in a manor near tha courthouse are dangerous."

*The huge blond?* She could only think of one who fit that description. "Anything else?"

"Oh, 'n' he wants twenty knights."

Emilia's expression grew grim. The castle would be defenceless if that many left their posts, yet Thessian would not ask for no reason. The situation had to be dire. They had to be up against, at least, a dozen enemies. In the grand scheme of things, that was nothing.

A series of knocks drew her attention. She turned her head to find Lionhart closing the door behind him.

"Are we having a guild meeting without the guild master?" Lionhart joked.

Rime hopped off the sofa and ran to Lionhart with his arms wide. Once enveloped in a tight hug, the kid grinned from ear to ear. "Mister Lionhart, when're ya coming back? Sally's been super strict with bedtime!"

Lionhart patted the boy on the head, shifting his hat until it slipped over Rime's eyes. "I have some work to do at the castle for Her Majesty, so not for a while."

Rime pulled back and readjusted his hat. A silver coin fell on the floor and rolled around.

Lionhart gave the boy a stern look.

"I didn't steal it! I earned it!" Rime picked up his coin and wiped it with his brown shirt as if it were a precious gem.

"His Highness contacted me through Rime," Emilia interjected. "There is a situation at the courthouse. He needs twenty men."

Lionhart's brows jumped up. "I was with him not too long ago. Seems he found the cause for his worry."

"We cannot leave the castle defenceless," Emilia added.

Lionhart sauntered over and collapsed into a seat next to Jehan.

Rime pointed at the seat and yelled, "Mister Lionhart, that's mine!"

Ignoring the comment, Lionhart crossed his legs. "Send fifteen knights. I will tag along."

"I, too, will join," Ambrose offered.

Emilia eyed Jehan. "Mister Jehan Wells, I was told that you lost your position in the military due to my brother's foolishness. I wanted to extend an apology to you and an offer to work for the Crown once more. If you are willing to, that is."

Jehan lowered his bald head and sat there in silence for a long minute, staring at the carpet. When he lifted his face, he had tears in his eyes. His formal speech slipped as he said, "Yer Majesty has nothin' ta apologise fer. Ye never did me any wrong."

Seeing a grown man cry made her eyes sting with unshed tears. Had this been her past life, she would have freely given him a comforting hug. In her new shoes, she couldn't go around being too affectionate. For a second, she recalled the kiss with Clayton and shook her head to clear the image away.

"Jehan, will you accept the position of Guard Captain? I promise to pay you well."

Jehan wiped at his eyes with his beefy palms. The sight was similar to witnessing a battle-scarred bear weeping. He corrected his speech the best he could. "Of course, Yer Majesty! I would be happy to be of service. I will even swear a knight's oath to you!" With a hope-filled expression, he turned to Lionhart. "D'ya think my wife will come back to me?"

"We will have to wait and see, old friend."

Emilia said, "Ambrose, have Sir Rowell order a new badge for *Sir* Jehan Wells. Also, inform Dame Cali that she will have to fill him in on the details of the job once she returns."

Lionhart elbowed Jehan in the side. "Hear that? You're a knight again, *Sir* Wells."

Jehan burst into another round of tears. This time, they were tears of joy as he sported an unmistakable grin on his aged face.

Emilia glanced at Ambrose who produced a handkerchief from her hidden pocket.

The head maid wordlessly offered it to the crying man.

"Thank you!" Jehan eagerly wiped his face with it.

"Back to the important issue at hand." Emilia folded her hands in her lap. "Sir Jehan, will you come with us to investigate the manor?"

"Us?" Lionhart scowled. "Emilia, are you planning on going?"

"Of course. Rime said whatever is in those barrels is dangerous." She peered over her shoulder at the boy. "Did Thessian mention anything else?"

Rime shook his head.

Ambrose knelt in front of Emilia. "Your Majesty, should anything happen to you, this kingdom will fall into chaos. There would be no end to the fight over the throne among the nobility, as you have no heir."

"I agree with her," Lionhart added. "If those barrels contain what I think they do, it is too dangerous to take you."

"And what do you suppose is in them?" Emilia inquired with a cold stare.

"There have been reports of a new weapon appearing on the Black Market. No one knows where it's from or who produces it. The merchants who sell it are different every time it surfaces. Nevertheless, it is said to look like a fine black powder and is highly unstable. If used correctly, it can create a sea of fire."

*Is he talking about gunpowder?* She couldn't be certain as the technology in her new world was a combination of Medieval Europe and magic. Things like recording crystals also existed and operated on the mana stored within the magical crystal. They were similar to video cameras in functionality. Yet, she still had to relieve herself using a chamber pot. She missed toilets a great deal.

"Lionhart, Ambrose, I appreciate your concern, but I cannot sit back and watch you get hurt on my behalf. To ease your minds, I will keep a safe distance." She sucked in a breath as she looked from one person to the next. "No matter what, you must not let Prince Thessian die."

Ambrose gasped. "Your Majesty, have you fallen for the Empire's second prince?"

"What? No! Thessian is vital for our survival. I cannot explain the details, but I hope you can trust me."

Lionhart crossed his arms. "Is it another piece of information you can't tell even your closest allies?"

"I—" Emilia looked at her fists in her lap. She knew she was asking for unconditional faith while she shared nothing in return.

Ambrose slapped her hand to her chest. "I will protect the prince with my life, Your Majesty!"

Sir Jehan nodded. "I'm 'ere ta take orders, Yer Majesty. Questioning 'em is not ma job."

"You lot..." Lionhart let out a long sigh and pinched the bridge of his nose. "Very well. The prince's survival will be our priority."

Emilia's heart swelled, and she said with a growing smile, "Thank you, everyone. I promise I will explain my reasoning in due time."

They agreed to take fifteen knights and sent the knight on duty to gather the men outside. Before they had the chance to leave the office, Sir Rowell arrived with a messenger.

"Your Majesty, this is the clerk from the courthouse, Mister Jeremy Piltz," Sir Rowell introduced, motioning to a lean man in his late twenties who wore all black and a well-worn pair of leather boots. "He is here to deliver a message."

Emilia permitted the clerk's approach.

Jeremy kept his head down and pulled his hat off in respect. "Y-your Majesty, I was asked by Lord Armel to inform you that Duke Malette has requested a trial by combat."

"Malette must know he is losing the case," Lionhart grumbled.

"Or he is stalling," Emilia added. "Mister Piltz, whom did the Duke ask to fight on his behalf?"

"A knight named Sir Galleon Vigrass, Your Majesty."

Emilia turned to her spymaster. "Do you know him?"

"Sir Vigrass is well known for being exceptionally strong. Before he was hired to serve the Duke, Vigrass won multiple sword-fighting tournaments hosted here in Newburn. He is talented, no doubt."

Sir Jehan bobbed his head in agreement. "I've seen his fights. He has no qualms about crippling his opponent as long as he wins."

"What a fitting pair…" Emilia said with distaste. "Mister Piltz, and who is the knight assigned to fight by the court?"

The clerk wiped his sweaty forehead with his hat. "That would be Sir Adrian Mallory."

From the little knowledge Emilia had about names, 'Mallory' meant 'unfortunate'. Truly, should Sir Mallory face Sir Vigrass, he may, indeed, become an unlucky person. "What is his combat experience?"

"I-I would not know. He recently began working at the courthouse after he transferred from his position at the city guard."

Emilia did not like uncertainties when she was getting close to beheading the Duke.

"You could overrule Malette's request and deny him the trial by combat," Lionhart suggested.

Sir Rowell took a step forward. "Your Majesty, may I suggest assigning Dame Calithea Louberte as the opponent for Sir Vigrass. She possesses real combat experience and is already at the courthouse."

Emilia contemplated her options.

Interfering with the trial directly could turn the nobles against her and lose their trust in the process. The original goal was to eliminate Duke Malette through the court's ruling and have him beheaded. Yet, Vigrass did not seem to be a simple opponent a weak city guard could win against. That was the only time she regretted not having Sir Laurence around. He might be a troublemaker, but he was a skilled fighter. She couldn't ask Thessian for fear of him getting recognised by the nobles. As much as Emilia would have liked Cali to take over the fight, she was a foreigner who fought alongside Thessian in many battles. And Emilia was beginning to like the dame too much to let some brute hurt her. Also, to keep a short leash on the nobles, Emilia couldn't let them think she was a puppet queen who was influenced by the Empire's royalty. She had to set the stage for a fluid merge of her kingdom and the Empire to cause the least problems for Thessian.

She still had time to decide. The fight could take days to arrange, if not weeks.

"Mister Piltz, return to the courthouse and tell Lord Armel to accept the Duke's request and to encourage the other judges to end proceedings for the day." Emilia glanced at the head butler. "Sir Rowell, inform the stables to have our horses ready as quickly as possible. Lionhart, Ambrose, go ahead and gather as much information as you can. Sir Jehan, meet me in the courtyard with the knights."

Rime raised a hand. "What about me?"

Emilia pulled the kid to one side when the others swiftly filed out of her office. "You have the most important job, Rime. Gather as many children as you can and have them cause a distraction near the manor on my signal. I promise you all will be well compensated for your trouble."

"I'll get right on it!"

Emilia watched the boy running out of her office and sighed. She did not like putting kids in danger, but they would be least suspected by the enemy. And, as long as they did not get too close to the manor, they should be out of immediate danger.

All she needed now was more information on the situation.

In the courtyard, she folded her arms behind her back as she eyed the three rows of knights who stood to attention.

"Who is the Vice Captain?" Emilia demanded.

A man in his late twenties, with short chestnut hair and rugged good looks, stepped forward. Although he was clad in heavy royal armour, she could tell he had a strong physique because of how effortless his movements were. The fact he looked her in the eye without keeping his gaze downcast gave her a good idea of how little respect he had for her position.

"Name?"

"Sir Regis Lacroix, Your Majesty." His voice was gruff and sounded bored.

"Are you from Lord Baudelaire's territory?"

"That would be correct, Your Majesty," he retorted.

Emilia gritted her teeth. She could behead him on the spot for his rudeness. Lucky for him, she had no time to lose by bloodying her hands.

"Sir Jehan Wells will be taking over as Guard Captain from Dame Calithea Louberte in the coming weeks. During this mission, he will act as your superior. Understood?"

Sir Regis assessed Jehan with a single glance. "With all due respect, Your Majesty, there is enough tension within the knighthood between the two factions. Bringing in an old man with unknown skill as a commanding officer will only make the rift grow further."

*Old man?*

Last Emilia checked, on paper, Jehan was barely forty-three. He served in the king's army since he was fifteen and as a vice general for over five years. Had it not been for her stupid older brother's mistake, he would have long been promoted.

The post of Royal Guard Captain for Jehan was merely a stepping stone. If he proved useful, she would eventually reinstate him and grant him a general's position. She needed to keep an eye on the former king's dwindling military force from within. There was no end to the number of mistakes King Gilebert made during his long reign. He lost countless talented people because he refused to pay them their worth.

Emilia smirked. "Sir Jehan Wells, what say you?"

Jehan bowed his head to Emilia and pronounced each word with care and loud enough for the knights at the back to hear. "I respect the Vice Captain's concern and ask to give him the lead in this mission. I will act as yer personal guard instead. With yer permission, when we return, I would like to formally duel Sir

Lacroix to prove my skills."

She gave a curt nod. They had no time to dilly-dally. Lionhart and Ambrose were waiting, and Thessian could be in danger. "Sir Lacroix, I hope your leadership won't disappoint after the display you have put on. I will fill you in on the situation on our way. Move out!"

# 17
# IN THE COMPANY OF SMUGGLERS

### THESSIAN

**A**fter giving the message to Rime, Thessian headed back to the wagon.

"Where have you been?" Rich demanded and narrowed his eyes.

"I went to take a piss." Thessian wiped his hands on his cloak for effect.

Rich grimaced. "Hurry up! We ain't paying you for slacking."

Thessian picked up the next barrel with a grunt. Putting his legs and back to work, he slowly made his way to the manor. With each barrel he brought, the suspicion around his presence lessened, especially since Sara continuously kept flirting with him. The only person who remained on edge around him was Ulrich—the man in charge of organising the workers and general management within the group.

He dropped off his sixth and final barrel in the master's bedchamber which was now so full that the two men—Dalton and Cyan—could barely move away from their table.

Being the recipient of Sara's incessant affection, and overhearing their conversations, allowed Thessian to observe the smugglers. From what he learnt, the organisation was made up of nine people. Sara Sayeed was the leader, and Ulrich was the second-in-command. Rich and Hyde were in charge of transportation. Cliff, Sean, and Spade did the grunt work. The remaining two were Dalton and Cyan, who knew how to mix the serpentine powder correctly as it was often separated into its components during transportation. They were the first group of people who were closely associated with the creator of the powder. With any luck, Thessian could learn the location of the production site and either take it over or shut it down. As much as he hated to admit it, serpentine powder was a useful product during wartime.

In the hallway, Sara planted her hand on Thessian's shoulder. "We're done here for today. Got the message that the trial will resume tomorrow at noon." She winked at him. "How 'bout that drink?"

Thessian put on his best smile and wiped the sweat off his brow. He was still wearing his cloak despite his shirt being drenched with sweat. "Sure thing. I'm parched."

"Oi, Sara! You gon' be long? We are gon' leave ya behind," one of the workers Thessian came to know as Cliff shouted from the staircase.

"I am! Give me a minute." She slid her arm to Thessian's waist and frowned. "What kind of worker carries a sword around?"

"I never said I was a worker," Thessian replied matter-of-factly. "Until recently, I worked as a mercenary in the Empire."

Her eyes started twinkling with curiosity. "Did you fight in the Battle of Darkgate?"

"Yes…"

"Then you must have seen what a handful of those barrels can do!" She leaned in so close that he could smell her spicy perfume and a hint of wine on her breath. "I hope the Duke loses tomorrow. That way, we can showcase the merchandise." Unexpectedly, she roughly slapped his butt. "If you're currently unemployed, come work for me. I pay well, and you'll get *extra benefits*."

Thessian stepped out of her reach and lifted her hand to his lips. Giving her a suggestive look, he said, "We can discuss the details—"

"Sara!" Cliff yelled. "Ya comin' or what?"

She rolled her eyes. "I'm going to kill him."

Thessian motioned for her to take the lead. "Ladies first."

"Oh, at last, a gentleman in my organisation!"

After everyone had gathered outside the manor. Sara pointed to Ulrich and Sean. "Stay behind and make sure those two don't blow themselves up in there. We are going out drinkin' to welcome a new member."

Ulrich scowled. "You know nothing about the guy! How can we trust him?"

"What's there to trust? Money talks best," she retorted. "Everyone's got a price, even Mister Mercenary here."

"I guess we do need more fighters in our group." Ulrich ran a hand over his sour face. "Be quick. We can't leave the place unguarded for too long."

"Yeah, yeah. Not like anyone knows we're here." Sara draped her arms over Cliff's and Hyde's shoulders. "Shall we get drunk, boys?"

"As long as you don't start singing," Cliff joked.

"There's noooothing wro-o-o-ong with maaah VOOOOice," she sang in a tone so grating and off-key, the men covered their ears and complained.

"Whatever. Last one there pays the tab!" Without warning, Sara sprinted off.

"There she goes again..." Ulrich muttered as he slapped his forehead.

Thessian stared at the men in disbelief as a bunch of them cursed and started chasing after their leader.

Ulrich shook his head and then tossed a coin purse at Thessian who caught it mid-air. "Your wages for the work." He rummaged in his pocket and produced a much larger purse. "And this is for Sara's drinks." He handed it to Thessian with a glare. "Better not make a run for it with the coin, friend, or they'll be fishing you out of the river tomorrow."

A part of Thessian wanted to see how Ulrich, who was barely above half of Thessian's height and weight would achieve such a feat.

Pretending to be intimidated, the prince took the second purse. "Where should I go?"

"The Impolite Duck. It's a tavern on Meritare Road, not far from the slums."

As Thessian walked away, he felt Ulrich's burning stare on his back. Not long after, Thessian noticed he was being followed. Sara may let anyone she fancies into the gang, but Ulrich was on the cautious side.

Thessian did his best not to deviate from the path to the tavern.

Along the way, he felt a light weight colliding with his legs and stumbled backwards. Looking down, Thessian found a willowy girl sitting on the road and dusting off her patchwork dress.

She glared at him. Her face was covered with grime and dirt. Even her large, round eyes were the colour of murky water.

Thessian offered her a hand. "Are you hurt, young lady?"

She slapped Thessian's hand away, shot up, and then jingled Thessian's coin purse in front of him. Although she looked frail, she ran off before he could process the situation fully.

*Was I just pickpocketed?*

Launching after the kid, Thessian's leg muscles screamed in protest. He had done more than enough hard labour that day, adding sprinting was pushing it.

The girl was quick but always remained in his sights as if taunting him. When he neared her, she sped up, and when the distance grew too large, she slowed her pace.

The sun had set over the city, and the shadows grew in places where the light could not reach.

Eventually, they came to a dead end surrounded by tall walls of wooden houses. At that point, Thessian was certain he managed to shake off his tail some time ago.

The girl smirked and threw the coin purse back at Thessian's wide chest while the prince caught his breath.

Rime stepped out from behind a pile of crates and beamed at him. "You run fast, milord."

Thessian grabbed his purse and shoved it in his pocket. "For a second there, I thought I was truly robbed."

Rime gave the girl three coppers and whispered something in her ear.

She nodded and scurried off past Thessian.

"A friend of yours?" Thessian asked.

"Ya talkin' 'bout Mouse? Nah, she's mah assistant." Rime came over and craned his neck to look up. "Follow me, milord. Lady Em wishes ta speak with ya."

"Has she deployed the knights?"

"She told 'em ta keep outta sight. Their armour's too fancy, ya see, so Ernesto is helping 'em change. Once they're ready, my friends and I will cause a dis-action."

"A distraction?"

"Yes, milord."

They backtracked to the corner and followed the tight street to a decrepit shack that used to be someone's home. The roof had many tiles missing, and the windows were barricaded with wooden planks from the inside.

Rime opened a door that hung on one hinge for Thessian. "In ya go, milord."

Thessian had to duck his head to pass the threshold. The floorboards under his feet seemed unstable as they produced strained creaks under his weight.

In the middle of the mostly empty room was a round table and two chairs. A single lantern rested on the table's surface, creating shadows of the two cups and a teapot. It was also the sole source of light.

One of the seats was occupied by Emilia who had two burly men standing behind her. The man on the right of her was Thessian's age and seemed unhappy to be there while the much older man, with a scarred face, kept his eyes on Thessian's approach.

"Sir Jehan Wells, Sir Regis Lacroix, wait outside," Emilia ordered.

The men wordlessly shuffled towards the door. The younger of the two appeared relieved to be away from the cramped space.

As the door closed behind them, Emilia rose. "Your Highness…"

Tired and parched, Thessian waved for her to sit down and took the remaining seat at the table. Grabbing the teapot, he poured tea into the second cup. For once, Emilia's hobby of tea-drinking helped him stay hydrated.

He took a sip. The tea was lukewarm, which meant Emilia had been waiting for him for a while.

Allowing for the stress to seep out of him, he relaxed his posture a little and studied her concerned expression.

"Are you unharmed, Thessian?"

He smiled at the use of his first name. "As always, you never fail to surprise me, Emilia."

A tint of red surfaced on her cheeks which made his smile grow wider. For a moment, he forgot why they were there.

She took a sip from her cup. "You did a dangerous thing."

"I can't let anything else happen to this city. After all, I would have to pay for the damage," he said in jest.

She hid her smile behind the rim of the cup. Straightening up and placing her teacup on the saucer, she replied, "I have no higher moral ground to stand on as I would have done the same thing. Care to share your findings?"

He tapped his finger on the table while he rearranged his thoughts. "Duke Malette hired a band of smugglers to fill the manor next to the courthouse with serpentine powder. They mentioned that if the trial fails, they will set off an explosion." He poured another drink. "How did the trial progress?"

"The duke requested a trial by combat. He even has his knight chosen."

"Of course, he does. Malette is not short on imagination on how to save himself." He sat back in his seat and finished his drink in one go. "What about the serpentine powder? Have you devised a plan?"

"I was waiting for your return to see if my plan is viable. After all, you must have something in mind when you requested more manpower."

He nodded. "They don't trust me yet, but their boss, Sara, likes to flirt around. It seems she is my best option to know more about their plans."

"Oh!" Emilia cracked a smile. "You are planning to seduce her?"

He frowned. "Do you believe I cannot pretend to be Laurence for a day?"

Emilia laughed, which surprised Thessian, and then waved her hands in denial. "I apologise, Your Highness, I am not laughing at you. I am laughing at the idea of you pretending to be Laurence to seduce a woman."

"I am not proud of this." He balled his hand on the table. "Still, the serpentine powder is a powerful weapon and has killed many of my men in the past. I will not let them use it here to kill innocent people."

"Of course, that is why I chose you."

Emilia's words had a calming effect on him, allowing his tense shoulders to relax. "Nothing improper will happen. I will not soil myself with the likes of her."

Emilia leaned forward. "Does that mean you are going back?"

He nodded and smiled at the evident concern in her crystalline, blue eyes. "I need something to write with and paper to draw you the layout of the property."

She pulled out a folded piece of parchment from her pocket and a piece of charcoal. "Do you know how many they are?"

"So far, I counted nine, but not all know how to fight. At this time, five of them are at a tavern, celebrating, and another four are guarding the manor." The prince grabbed the parchment and the charcoal. "Our main objective will be to prevent the serpentine powder from igniting. The barrels are many and heavy."

Thessian quickly sketched a blueprint of the areas he had access to within the manor. He highlighted the entrances and the windows while he explained about the group of smugglers.

Moments later, he put the charcoal on the table and wiped his hand on the handkerchief Emilia offered him. "I should leave before they suspect something."

"Where are you meeting them?"

"The Impolite Duck."

Emilia covered her small laugh with her gloved hand. Her smile and presence soothed him. She had never made him feel uncomfortable and rarely looked at him like a prime cut of meat. As for the immoral Sara, who had brazenly touched him every chance she got, he could not wait to put that wench in prison alongside her band of criminals.

Getting up, he tried to look presentable. "Do not fret, Emilia. I have been to worse places."

"I am worried about your honour, Your Highness." She produced a teasing smile.

He did his best not to scowl, even if he was happy that she was feeling more relaxed around him. "All jokes aside, please take care of yourself."

"Don't worry, I will deal with the serpentine powder," she informed him as she rolled up the sketch. "Once we have the men in the manor in custody, and the powder secured, I will send knights to the tavern to capture the rest. Please be safe until then."

"You will be dealing with a much more dangerous situation." Thessian hesitated about getting too close as he smelled of sweat.

"I know what to do, Thessian. Trust me."

He inclined his head. "I will take my leave. Good luck."

"Once this is over, let us meet for a late supper."

The prince genuinely smiled for the first time that day. "Indeed."

# 18
# THE IMPOLITE DUCK

### EMILIA

**E**milia waited until **Thessian** was gone to sit down and study the blueprint he drew. For a man who spent almost a decade on the battlefield, he was quite skilled with his hands. No matter how hard she tried to improve in Art, all she managed was stickmen doodles and messy cross-stitch. Even Ambrose, who was born a commoner, was better at embroidery than Emilia, which bruised the Queen's ego.

"Your Majesty, may we come in?" Sir Jehan called from behind the door.

She was beginning to grow fond of Jehan. He was quiet, obeyed her orders, and did not act out of turn. On the other hand, Sir Regis Lacroix seemed too full of himself. She was eager to see the duel between him and Jehan. Should he win against Jehan, she may be stuck with him as Guard Captain—a scenario she dreaded.

"Come in," she called back.

Sir Jehan lumbered into the single-room shack that was used as one of the temporary hideouts by the Lionhart Guild. Before it was taken over by Lionhart, it was a place where opium addicts gathered. According to her spymaster, the problem was not solved, it simply moved to the growing slums in the city.

*Just another headache waiting to happen.*

Sir Lacroix waltzed in after Jehan.

Compared to Emilia, they were like two massive boulders. She somewhat hoped Sir Lacroix would hit his head on the low ceiling and cut the attitude.

*No. You're a queen. You need to show a good example.*

"I have the layout of the manor." She spread out the blueprint on the table and moved the lantern to illuminate the charcoal lines better. "There are three entrances. The side door, the back door, and the front door." She pointed at each one as she spoke. "The windows are blocked by furniture on the ground floor. The serpentine powder is located in the master's bedchamber on the second floor. The windows to that room face towards the road."

"What's serpentine powder, Your Majesty?" Sir Lacroix asked.

"It is a highly unstable powder and can erupt into a storm of fire when ignited. The quantities of it in this manor could destroy two or three streets, possibly more."

The men tensed at her explanation.

It was a dangerous mission. She knew that. It was also why Lionhart and Ambrose did not want her anywhere near the site. However, she was the only one equipped with the knowledge of documentaries and articles from another world and knew how they could safely neutralise the powder.

"According to the information I have received, half of the smugglers are getting drunk right now. The other four are still at the manor. We won't have a better opportunity to capture them and the powder."

"What if they ignite the barrels when they see the knights?" Sir Lacroix asked.

"That is one of the possibilities. That is why I am waiting for one more person to arrive."

As if on cue, the door opened, and Clayton walked in. He bowed low to Emilia and came close when she ordered. She was glad to see that he had shaved off his unkempt beard, and the circles under his eyes were almost gone.

"Lord Armel, these are Sir Jehan Wells and the Vice Captain of the Royal Guards, Sir Regis Lacroix," she explained.

Clayton greeted them with a curt nod.

The knights replied in kind.

"What is your command, Your Majesty?" Clayton asked in his smooth voice.

"I need you to sneak into a manor and freeze the barrels that hold serpentine powder. There are two dozen of them. Can you do it?"

"It would be my pleasu—"

Clayton didn't finish his sentence, because Sir Lacroix cut in with, "Your Majesty, maybe we should ask for the opinion of an expert on how to deal with this dangerous substance. After all, what could a young queen know about strategy and explosives?"

Emilia glared at him. "Sir Lacroix, do you know how serpentine is made?"

He shook his head.

"Seventy-five per cent saltpetre, fifteen per cent charcoal, and ten per cent sulphur," she said matter-of-factly. In a patronizing voice, she continued, "A low-ranked soldier such as yourself must not know what these ingredients are. But, let's say that once the serpentine powder is created and exposed to high temperatures or a flame, it goes *boom!*" She waved her arms to add drama to her words. "Adding water to it is the safest way to render it harmless, but it would be unwise to lose such an asset as it could be useful in the future." She folded her arms over her chest and faked a smile. "Now, if you are too afraid to join us on this quest or cannot take orders from a woman who outranks you, maybe you should go back to Lord Baudelaire's territory and leave this to the *experts*."

Sir Lacroix's face became red as he lowered his eyes to the floor.

Emilia glanced to Jehan who was trying to conceal his wide grin.

Clayton had taken a step closer to her and was pursing his lips to contain his laughter.

Emilia inhaled deeply, squared her shoulders, and used her commanding voice. "Vice Captain Regis Lacroix, do you want to be relieved of your duty?"

He raised his head. "N-no, Your Majesty."

"Do you still have doubts about my orders?"

"I...I will do as Your Majesty commands."

She removed her glove and held out her hand with the ring bearing the monarch's seal. "Then kneel, kiss the ring, and swear the knight's oath of fealty right here. I cannot afford to have a Vice Captain who does not trust and obey his monarch."

Regis was silent and completely still. She could see sweat beading on his forehead. For a prideful man like him, obeying a young lady who seemingly knew nothing of the world had to be difficult.

As an abandoned and hated princess, Emilia learned that she was not above killing. Her survival came first. Keeping an untamed beast like Sir Lacroix by her side could cause her to lose her life one day. But if she could prove herself worthy of his trust, then his loyalty was worth the risk she was taking by allowing him to live.

"Make your choice," she warned for the last time.

The knight knelt and gingerly took her offered hand in his much larger one. Bringing the ring close to his lips, he gave the seal a peck.

Unexpectedly, he lowered his head until it nearly touched his knee. "I swear to protect my queen and her kingdom and do no harm to both. I shall serve faithfully and with honour until I can no longer hold my sword or breathe my last breath."

"The crime for disrespecting their ruler is to have the culprit flogged or killed, Your Majesty," Clayton reminded her.

Sir Jehan added, "A worse punishment would be to strip him of his position and have him put on dungeon guard duty."

"A true knight does not break their vow," she claimed, sliding her glove back on.

Sir Lacroix raised his head to look at her with what she assumed to be surprise.

"A wise ruler can offer a second chance to their subjects to redeem themselves. After all, Sir Lacroix and Sir Jehan promised to have a duel once this mission is over. I am looking forward to the outcome."

"Ah, yes." Sir Jehan rubbed the back of his neck. "I'll give him a good beating fer disrespecting Yer Majesty."

"I shall remember your words when I'm sweeping the floor with your face," Sir Lacroix countered.

"That's tha spirit!" Still laughing, Jehan nodded to Emilia. "We can keep him fer now. I'll discipline him if he goes back ta his old ways."

Emilia smiled softly. She really liked Jehan.

Clayton grumbled, "He won't live to be disciplined if he ever questions my master again."

Emilia felt her cheeks warm and noticed an ice dagger forming in Clayton's hand.

She moved closer to her shadow and whispered in his ear, "Play nice. You cannot go around killing every man who looks at me sideways or gets too close."

"Why not?" he asked as if he truly did not know the answer.

"We need them to fight for the kingdom. Once I prove to them that I am a worthy queen, they will fall into line."

Clayton grunted, and the ice blade melted away.

Emilia clapped her hands to draw everyone's attention. "Great. Now that we are all on the same page, shall we save our capital from another fire?" Directing her next words at Sir Lacroix, she ordered, "You can rise and prove your loyalty with your actions. I will do the same, so I can gain the trust of the nobles and the soldiers of this kingdom."

Regis got up and nodded, seemingly a bit flustered. Not scared, though, even at the sight of an ice blade.

*Maybe he will make a good Guard Captain once Jehan gets promoted...*

"What are your orders, Your Majesty?" Clayton asked.

Emilia's skin prickled with the chill emanating from her shadow's body.

Regaining her composure, she walked to the table and tapped her finger on the wood, bringing their attention back to the layout of the building. "Sir Lacroix, divide the knights into three groups. Each group will guard one entrance. My associate will keep an eye on things from the rooftops and inform you of any changes by firing an arrow. Sir Jehan, I need you to contact the guild and investigate the city guard. Those responsible for allowing this dangerous substance into my city must be punished."

Sir Jehan asked, "Who will guard you, Your Majesty?"

"Do not fret, I do not plan to put myself in danger." She smiled at them. "I'm thinking of getting a drink at The Impolite Duck."

A single oil lantern glimmered on Meritare Road, illuminating the rotting wooden sign for The Impolite Duck as it swayed in the wind. The inscription seemed to be carved with a dull hunting knife, and the drawing of a duck was similar to a slug. The tavern was wedged between intimidating houses that seemed ready to collapse. Emilia was well aware of the poor state of certain areas in Newburn. Apart from the well-guarded streets where the nobles and the rich merchants resided, the local guards rarely visited anything beyond the invisible line that split the city.

Emilia pulled her hood low over her face and approached the tavern. A bard's pitchy song assaulted her ears as she opened the door.

In the busy tavern, most patrons were too drunk to notice her entrance.

Stepping inside, she got a brief nod of greeting from the barmaid.

On the left side of the busy tavern, she spotted Thessian's broad back. He had his hood up, but he was impossible to miss.

Emilia slid onto the sole available barstool from which she could listen in on the conversations around her. Beyond the booming laughter of the drunkards behind her, she picked up on the smugglers' discussion.

"... know why we call him Cyan?" one of the men asked.

Thessian replied, "Does he turn blue when you throttle him."

The smugglers laughed hard until the same man shushed them. "No. It's 'cause he poisoned a bunch of people he didn't like with cyanide!"

The barmaid rapped her knuckles on the counter in front of Emilia to get her attention. "What'll it be?"

Emilia smiled at the redhead and slid a silver coin across the counter. "A meal with your finest ale."

The older woman raised a brow at Emilia. "I ain't got change for ye."

"None needed."

"Suit yerself." The barmaid shuffled towards the kitchen in the back and picked up a couple of empty pitchers along the way.

"...hear about Spade?" the same overly-cheerful man asked Thessian. "We call him that 'cause he stepped on one, and it broke his nose. That's why he's got a crooked nose! Ah-ha-ha-ha."

Thessian let out a sound that seemed close to a forced laugh and asked, "Since your name is Rich, does that mean you were once rich?"

"Oi, Sara! The new guy is trying to be funny," Rich grumbled.

The only woman in the group replied, "Gotta say, his jokes are better than yours."

When Emilia glimpsed at the smugglers over her shoulder, Sara's gaze focused on the door of the tavern.

The Queen followed the woman's gaze and noticed a small figure in a green cloak near the entrance. The person pulled down their hood to reveal a young girl no older than Emilia with deep creases of concern etched onto her round face.

Sara draped her arm around Thessian's shoulders and whispered something in his ear. She climbed off the bench and made a beeline for the new arrival.

Thessian's attention was split between the lively chatter of the smugglers, who wanted his input on the best place for a night of pleasure, and Sara's retreating form.

The food and ale arrived as Emilia slid off her stool.

"Where're ye going?" the barmaid asked.

"I need to use the outhouse."

"Be quick then or yer food 'll get cold."

Emilia snuck out of the tavern and pretended to be drunk, steadying herself against the barrels out front.

Sara marched ahead, looked around, and pulled the girl in close. They spoke in hushed tones to each other until Sara's voice could no longer be contained.

"What do you mean the knights found out!?"

The girl shushed Sara. "They must've been tipped off. Did something happen while I was away?"

Although it was dark, Emilia felt ants crawling up her spine when Sara looked at the tavern. That woman was bad news. Even from such a distance, Emilia sensed enormous bloodlust.

Sara whipped out her scimitar from its sheath. "Wait here, Rose."

"Mother, you can't go in there with a weapon. It'll draw too much attention!"

"Then I'll bring that swine out here!" Sara shook off Rose's hands and stormed back to the tavern.

Emilia saw Rose pulling out a shortbow and readying an arrow.

Cussing under her breath, Emilia scrambled back inside just in time to see Sara slamming her fist on the table in front of Thessian.

"Come out! Now!" Sara yelled.

"What's happened?" Rich piped in.

"You drunk again, Sara?" another asked.

Sara glared at them, silencing the bunch of men in an instant.

Thessian left the table and followed Sara towards the door where Emilia stood. He must have finally noticed her because his eyes grew wide.

There was no time to think. Emilia took two steps to the table on her right, ripped the half-empty tankard out of the hand of the meanest-looking man there and threw it in his face.

For effect, Emilia shouted, "How dare you cheat on me!"

The men at that table were completely stumped.

She muttered an apology under her breath and, with all her might, punched the same man in the face. Everything from her fingers to her wrist pulsated on impact as if she hit a brick wall.

While the stranger cradled his bleeding nose, two men from the same table got up and stalked towards Emilia.

The first man took a swing at her.

She ducked to the left, making him land a punch on another patron.

"Mah drink!" an older man, who had enough weapons and scars on him to be a seasoned mercenary, yelled.

With a flurry of spit-fuelled cuss words and shrieks of a terrified bard, a massive brawl erupted.

# 19
# AROUND THE CAMPFIRE

## LAURENCE

"**I bet His Highness misses me** dearly right about now," Laurence mused while sitting on a log next to a crackling campfire.

Across from him, Yeland, Eugene, and Sergey were digging into the stew they worked hard to prepare.

Laurence breathed a sigh of relief. After a long day of riding their horses, taking a break to fill their stomachs and allowing their muscles to relax felt heavenly. The scene would have been perfect had it not been for Ian's vehement refusal to sit down with them for a chat. That elf had a stick up his posterior the size of a unicorn's horn.

Eugene finished chewing. "I find that hard to believe, Commander."

"Quit it with the titles!" Laurence replied cheerfully. "We are on a journey where rank does not matter. What better way to form friendship bonds than to eat, sleep, and enjoy the outdoors together?"

"No offence, but I'd rather sleep with a lady," Sergey said with a laugh.

"Me too," Eugene commented.

Yeland simply nodded in agreement.

Laurence pouted. "I do not see why you'd reject me, Sergey. I've been told that I am quite sightly."

"You are no longer on the market, Sir Laurence," Sergey replied. "You should consider yourself lucky. Dame Cali has quite a lot of admirers in His Highness' army."

The warm bowl and spoon in Laurence's hands nearly fell from his grasp. "She does?"

"Of course. Even Eugene here had the hopes of asking her out on a date one day."

Eugene's face turned bright red. He got up and shuffled to the stew pot that was bubbling over the fire.

"Eugene, is that true?" Laurence asked.

"Sir—" Eugene kept his gaze low as he refilled his wooden bowl. "I admire Dame Cali for her swordsmanship."

"That's not what you said two months ago while we were playing cards," Sergey countered.

Laurence managed to put on a hurt expression. "Eugene, I am sorry to say this, but I taught Dame Cali her sword-fighting skills. I believe the one you truly admire is me."

Sergey and Yeland burst out laughing and nearly fell off the fallen tree they sat on.

"I think it is time for me to turn in…" Eugene left his bowl near the dwindling fire. He turned and marched to the tent they had set up earlier.

"It was a jest!" Laurence called after him. He looked at the other two who were busy gasping for air. "So how many men are interested in my woman?"

"Worry not, sir." Yeland wiped tears from the corners of his eyes. "None would dare approach her now that you two are courting each other. As a matter of fact, she has beaten so many knights during sparring that most are afraid to admit their feelings for her."

The explanation Yeland had given Laurence did not ease his worry. They may be together now, but what if she found a more suitable man while he was away? From what Laurence could tell, the Queen's shadow had an unnecessarily attractive face and great fighting abilities.

Sergey elbowed Yeland in the side. "I believe we should follow Eugene's example and rest early."

They hurried off, leaving Laurence to stare at the waning flames.

He picked up on light footsteps behind him and knew exactly who it was without looking.

"Are you not going to sleep, Ian?"

Ian sat on the available log and began sharpening his arrowheads with a fine stone.

"Not going to talk?"

"I will keep watch tonight." Ian spoke in a low drone.

"We are half a day's ride from the nearest village. Who would bother us in the middle of nowhere?"

Ian ignored him.

Laurence grumbled, "It would not hurt you to get off your high horse now and again. We are travelling as a group, after all."

Having gotten no response from the elf, Laurence threw his arms up in the air. "Do not complain to me when you feel tired tomorrow."

Ian lifted his eyes with a silent question, "Have I ever complained?"

Laurence cussed and began tidying. He put aside the remaining stew and put a lid on the pot. Then, he gathered the used bowls which he rinsed in the nearby stream. All that was left was checking the area one last time for wild animals, and he could turn in for the night.

He muttered under his breath, "Why did His Highness hire someone like him in the first place?"

Laurence could never figure out the relationship between Thessian and Ian. They weren't friends nor were they limited to a commander and subordinate relationship. Although Thessian was careful not to show it, Laurence had picked up on a change in his friend's behaviour every time he was with Ian. Thessian sometimes spoke to the elf as if they were on the same level.

Scratching his head, Laurence blew out a frustrated sigh. It is not as if they had spent a lot of time around other elves. They were a secretive bunch and did not get along with humans. Any time the delegation arrived in the Empire from Shaeban, Ian would disappear for days. Thessian would ignore such strange behaviour as if it were a given.

Judging by the fighting skills Ian displayed, Laurence suspected the elf used to be a high-ranking warrior.

*Does not matter, I guess. Thessian would not allow another troublemaker into the ranks. I am more than enough.*

His heavy boots made the melting snow under his feet crunch with each step. Spring was almost upon them, and, in the coming weeks, the emperor would send summons for them to return. The season of royal balls would soon be in full swing. His Highness would no doubt be forced to attend to find a suitable wife.

Laurence, too, had to face his family sooner or later. He had agreed with His Highness in private that if their party did not find any traces of the beastmen tribe, they would return to Newburn after a month.

After all, scouring the entirety of the Hollow Mountains could take years. The biggest problem was the large quantities of monsters that roamed the mountain. If beastmen could blend in with the monsters or had the ability to control them, then it made sense why they chose that place as their hideout.

The sound of light footsteps behind him caused him to stop. He rolled his eyes and started to turn. "Ian, I know—"

Before he could finish, he was floored by a cloaked figure.

Laurence grasped the slender wrists of the stranger and used his legs to push himself off the ground and roll them over. Once he was on top, he ripped the hood off the person in question to reveal the beast-girl from the brothel. Only now, she appeared to be a decade older, and her scantily-clad body had become fuller.

Had it not been for her face, he would have thought it was someone else.

Her fiery hair fell around the snow like a river of blood under the moonlit sky, and the silver in her eyes was almost aglow.

Lifting her head off the ground, she sniffed him. "*Mir.*"

Laurence frowned. "Did you follow my scent?" His frown deepened. "We rode horses all day. How did you catch up?"

She nuzzled her face against his neck.

Laurence jumped off her faster than a deer escaping a hunter and wagged his finger. "I will not be bitten a second time, young lady!"

Her expression hardened as she sat up. "*Vosie ntes mir, arikesh. Jya otarkert vosie.*"

"I. Cannot. Understand. You," he explained in a louder voice, hoping to get the meaning across.

She got on all fours and crawled towards him. Then, she grabbed his hand and pulled him down again.

Laurence managed to land on his knees, making them eye-level. All of his senses screamed for him to run. He tried to yank his wrist out of her grip, but she wouldn't let go.

With inhuman strength, she pushed him down and climbed on top of his chest. "*Mir.*"

"Yes. Mir. Now let me go please."

She grinned at him. Her eyes lost their focus, and her head fell onto his chest.

Dumbfounded, Laurence stared at the starry sky above while the beastwoman softly snored on top of him.

"Are you cheating on Dame Calithea already?" Ian's harsh words arrived before the elf's boots stopped next to Laurence's head.

Laurence glowered at him. "I am certain you have witnessed the whole scene."

"Have you been bitten, Sir Laurence?"

"Not this time."

"So, you were..." Ian looked at him with pity. "You may not know this, but it is a tradition among beastmen to bite their future mate. They believe it to be a sign of possession."

"What are you saying?"

"I am telling you that you are doomed."

The wheels finally turned full circle in Laurence's head. "No! I promised Cali—"

Ian shushed him. "Be quiet, or she will wake. Take her to the tent and do not leave her side."

"What do you mean? I cannot stay near her if she thinks of me as her mate."

Ian shrugged. "That is your problem. We need her to find the rest of her tribe."

"Can we return instead?"

"That would not complete the mission."

"I promised His Highness to bring the girl," Laurence countered.

"Yet you are not getting on your horse with her and riding to the castle."

Grumbling under his breath, Laurence pushed himself up and gathered the sleeping woman in his arms. With Ian's help, he managed to stand upright.

"Is it normal for beastmen to age rapidly in the span of a few weeks?"

Ian thought for a moment. "I once read that when their kind selects a bride or groom, they will mature to be able to breed."

Blood drained from Laurence's face. "Cali will neuter me."

"And I will support her decision fully," Ian replied dismissively and sauntered towards the campsite.

# 20
# ONE DREADFUL NIGHT

### THESSIAN

The tavern erupted into a fistfight before Thessian's eyes. With his height that towered over most patrons, he managed to avoid punches aimed at his face with ease. As he moved to separate from Sara, she grabbed him by the arm.

"Where do you think you're going?" Sara's hostility was impossible to miss.

Emilia must have sent the knights to the manor, which meant that one of the smugglers had escaped or there was one he was not aware of.

Thessian captured Sara's wrist and squeezed hard.

She winced and unsheathed a small knife from around her waist. In an attempt to swing her arm, she cut someone's shoulder who, in their panic, screamed and pushed her away.

Suddenly, unsteady on her feet, Sara fell backwards with her eyes widening. Her grip on his arm loosened, and he quickly shook her off.

Thessian felt another, smaller hand wrapping around his other hand. He looked down to find Emilia.

She pulled him to her height and shouted over the commotion, "Let us get out of here. Keep your head down."

Pushing their way between the people appeared easy for the Queen. She picked up the pace and dodged the shuffling legs while Thessian felt a knee connecting with his side on more than one occasion. As far as he could tell, he avoided getting anything broken.

Eventually, Emilia pulled him behind the counter. At the far end of it, Thessian spotted a cowering bard who clung to his mandolin and muttered something about his mother being right.

Emilia whispered in the barmaid's ear and handed over a gold coin.

The exasperated redhead pointed to the door that led to the kitchen. "Ye can leave through tha window in tha attic. Take tha ladder on the back wall."

"Thank you," Emilia replied. "I will send someone to compensate you for the damages tomorrow."

Sighing, the barmaid opened the door to the kitchen for them. "Just leave."

Once more, Emilia took a hold of Thessian's hand, as if it was natural, and led the way to a cramped kitchen. The chef was gone, most likely too busy attempting to calm the rowdy patrons.

The door shut behind them, and Emilia ran to the ladder next to the preparation counter. With little effort, she scaled the steps. Unlike other noble ladies who were constantly worried about their outward appearance, she did what had to be done and in the most efficient way. He liked that about her.

Making certain she reached the attic safely, he followed after her. The crooked steps had him tightening his grip on the sides of the ladder as he ascended.

Finally off the unstable contraption, he closed the trapdoor behind them and pushed a nearby sack of vegetables over it. It may hinder the owners from getting up there, but their problem right now was avoiding Sara's pursuit.

Emilia inched to the grimy window, which was the only source of moonlight in the dark and dusty attic. She checked the opening mechanism and then pushed the window open. A strained groan from the wooden frame made him grimace.

Taking a step back, Emilia stumbled over another sack.

Without thinking, Thessian rushed forward and caught her before she met with the floor. His hands steadied her around her thin waist, emphasising to him how delicate she was compared to him. From up close, he could smell the scent of rose oil in her hair. She smelled nice.

*How long has it been since I've spent a night with a woman?*

"Your Highness, you can let go now…"

Thessian jerked back. "I do apologise."

"No need. You saved me from a fall. Help me climb out."

The prince walked past her and knelt on one knee under the window. "Please use my leg for support."

The Queen nodded, seemingly unaffected by the fact she would be using an Imperial Prince as a stepping stool. She placed her booted foot on his thigh and used the window frame to pull herself up.

Taking a moment, she climbed through the opening.

"I can see the entire Meritare Road from here," her breathless voice reached his ears.

Thessian forced his body through the tight window. Compared to how easily she slipped out, he nearly got stuck. He only hoped that the tiles and roof beams would be strong enough to support their combined weight.

"I will go first," he suggested, shuffling past her.

Together, they traversed the connected rooftops until the end of the street.

Peering over the edge to check on the situation below, Thessian slipped on a mossy tile. He felt Emilia's arms quickly wrapping around his middle, but his weight proved too much for her.

With a yelp and a shriek, they fell off.

Thessian groaned as his face and body met with the wet dirt. Luckily, Emilia landed on his back.

She rolled off him and muttered, "Good thing that was only the first floor."

"Indeed." He pushed his aching body upright and wiped at the fresh dirt in his eyes.

"Allow me."

A moment later, he felt her soft handkerchief brushing against his face. Once he could see again, he noticed that she was standing on her tiptoes and trying her best not to laugh.

"I must look ridiculous."

"Not at all, Your Highness. Merely a little muddy." She smiled as she withdrew the handkerchief. "This will have to do until we get to the castle."

"There he is!" Sara pointed her scimitar at them from the roadside.

The leader of the smugglers pushed past the drunks, and her comrades, who also managed to get out, and sprinted at them full speed.

Thessian drew his sword from the scabbard. "Emilia, I suggest you step back."

Panic filled her eyes. "I would prefer it if we make a run for it."

"I am more than capable of fighting her off."

"That's not the—" Emilia did not finish her sentence as Sara's curved blade clashed against his sword.

Thessian was taken aback by Sara's strength. Had his grip been even slightly loose, his sword would have flown away. Although Sara put her entire weight into every swing, he managed to parry her incessant attacks that were as aggressive as her flirting style. Her quick footwork spoke volumes. Undoubtedly, she was an experienced warrior.

"How dare you sell us out!" Sara used her scimitar to guard against his attack from above and kicked out, barely missing his privates. "I even offered you a job."

Thessian leaned back and avoided her incoming swing at his neck. He caught her wrist mid-air, yanked her towards him, and punched her in the gut. "I suggest you and your company turn yourself over to the guards. There is no need for more bloodshed."

Sara gasped for air on her buckling knees. Her scimitar fell from her hand. With eyes that burned with hatred, she glowered at the prince.

Behind her, he saw the other smugglers running over. None of them were combatants, so he dismissed them as a threat.

"Sara!" Cliff yelled.

Spade and Hyde held the young man back.

Thessian did not care for their animosity. His goal was to capture the smugglers. "Emilia, we need them—"

"Alive, I know," she replied, holding her shortsword and advancing towards the others.

"Oi, who's this little lady?" Rich snapped, pointing at Emilia.

Emilia ignored him and swung her blade in warning anytime one of them attempted to get too close to Thessian and Sara.

Thessian returned his attention to Sara once she stopped wheezing.

"Eat this, imperial swine!" She threw a handful of dirt at his eyes.

*Not again...*

He was too slow. His eyes stung, and his sight became impaired. Staggering backwards, he rubbed at his face with the back of his hand.

"Thessian!" Emilia shouted.

He could not see what was going on but heard blades clashing not far from where he stood. Although Emilia knew how to defend herself, she would not be able to fight off Sara who was on par with Laurence in strength.

His heart raced as sluggish seconds felt like hours. He did not wish to see Emilia hurt, or worse. She may not admit it, but he felt like they had grown closer since the night of the coup. At that moment, he realised that he saw her as more than a mere vassal or a means to control Dante's territory. She was a friend with whom he did not wish to part.

A pained cry came from one of the women as he finally managed to clear most of his vision.

Emilia's shortsword was back in its sheath while she held one dagger in her left hand. A dagger with the same design was lodged in Sara's right shoulder. He also spotted an arrow sticking out of Sara's back.

Behind the smugglers stood Lionhart, with two daggers drawn, and Emilia's head maid, with a bow and arrow at the ready.

Sara struggled to lift her scimitar. Each movement brought out a pained groan from her tightening lips. "I won't go down like this!" Raising her voice, she shouted, "Kill him, Rose!"

Emilia dropped her dagger and collided, at full speed, with the prince like a battering ram just as an arrow came flying from one of the rooftops. She managed to push him off his feet until they fell backwards.

Thessian's head hit the ground. His vision swam, and he moved his hands to lift Emilia off when his fingers touched something solid sticking out of her back.

Dread filled his stomach.

Through hazy sight, he spotted the arrow's shaft, and his fingers came away with blood.

Emilia lifted her head and produced a sheepish smile. "I told you we should run."

Then, she passed out on top of him.

## 21
# CHILD OF LUMINOS

### THESSIAN

**Thessian carefully moved** Emilia's unconscious body off him. He noted that in the time he spent on the ground, the royal knights appeared and surrounded Sara and her friends. Sparing a glance at the rooftops, he realised that the last member of the smugglers had escaped without a trace.

Thessian ordered the nearest knight, "Help me lift Her Majesty onto my back. Hurry!"

The knight stammered and was pushed aside by Lionhart.

"She really cannot live a quiet life," Lionhart commented. The indifferent pretence he attempted failed as the spymaster's hands shook when he lifted Emilia's limp body and draped it over Thessian's offered back.

The head maid was next to arrive. "How is Her Majesty? What can I do to help?"

"Find a horse and bring it here," Thessian replied.

The panicked head maid bobbed her head and scurried off. Her personality did a complete turnaround when, up the road, she yanked a royal knight off his horse and nearly bit his head off for attempting to refuse.

Thessian held on to Emilia's thighs, keeping her in place. He could feel her body heat warming his back.

"Where is the Queen's shadow?" Thessian asked Lionhart.

"He got delayed wrapping things up at the manor."

"We need his healing ability. Send a messenger to retrieve him while I bring Emilia to the castle. Hopefully, the royal physician will be able to keep her alive until then."

The head maid arrived, pulling the animal by the reins. "I brought the horse, Your Highness." Tears wet the young woman's eyes as she patted the horse's neck. "Please make sure Her Majesty gets to the castle quickly."

With Lionhart's help, Thessian used one arm to support Emilia's backside and, with the other, he pulled himself into the saddle. They cut the head maid's cloak with a dagger and used the material to strap Emilia to Thessian's waist.

Even after all that, the Queen did not wake.

Thessian gripped the reins and nudged the horse into a trot with his heels.

Once he was past the knights, who parted ways for him, he pushed the animal to its limit.

As they galloped through the empty streets of Newburn, his mind and heart raced along with the horse. He ran the scenario of what would happen if Emilia passed away. His friend would be gone, and the kingdom would be consumed by a civil war over the throne. The greedy nobles would tear the land apart to get their share.

Thessian could place her double on the throne. After all, she had not had the opportunity to present herself before all the noble houses. The first event where she participated in an official capacity was the king's funeral, and those present only got to see her briefly or from a distance. The nobles who had met her could be persuaded to remain quiet or be silenced.

*What am I even considering?*

In the worst-case scenario, he would need to join forces with his supporters and take the throne by force. Emilia truly had handed him her kingdom on a platter when they met. Without her, too many lives would be lost to count as a victory.

"Hang in there, Emilia," he said over his shoulder. "Don't you dare die on me. A lot of people hope for you to live, including me."

After what seemed like forever, he arrived at the castle's gates. "Open the gates and call for the head butler. The Queen is injured!"

A knight on watch duty scampered to the mechanism and began to lift the portcullis with a grunt. The second guard ran ahead to inform the others.

Once the opening was big enough, Thessian urged the horse to move.

The horse bobbed its head and trotted inside.

They went up the cobbled road that led to the main castle. By the time Thessian got there, Sir Rowell was waiting for them at the entrance. One look at the head butler's stern expression told Thessian that the man cared a great deal for his monarch.

Sir Rowell barked orders to the servants who helped lower Emilia off the horse.

"I will carry her," Thessian growled at the men. "Find the physician and bring him to her bedchambers."

The prince took Emilia from the quivering manservants. No doubt they remembered the night when he slaughtered their king in front of them. Before they could protest, he carefully lifted her into his arms. He rested her lolling head against his shoulder and did his best to avoid shifting the arrow in her upper back.

"Fetch the physician!" Sir Rowell barked at the stupefied men.

The servants scattered immediately.

Thessian strode into the palace with his hands tightening on Emilia's body. From above, he could see how pasty her complexion had become. Judging by the growing wet stain on her back, he knew she was losing a lot of blood.

Sir Rowell opened the doors for him until they reached her

bedchambers and motioned for Thessian to enter.

To fit in the door frame with her, the prince had to walk in sideways. He marched to her bed where he gently laid her on her stomach, making sure her nose and mouth were unrestricted.

"May I ask what happened?" Sir Rowell inquired.

Thessian wiped a blood-stained hand on his muddy cloak. He must have looked quite a state yet the butler did not bat an eye. "She caught an arrow in my stead."

"I see. Then I hope Your Highness will do everything in his power to keep Her Majesty alive. It may be worth mentioning that His Holiness is currently a guest at the palace…"

"The Pope is here?"

"He is resting in the guest room."

A miracle from the Pope could heal Emilia's wound without a scar, but at what price? Thessian knew next to nothing about the man who became the new pope in recent years. Rather, he was too busy fighting in a campaign to care.

"Shall I send a servant for him?" Sir Rowell pressed.

The butler certainly wanted to save Emilia even if that meant Thessian would be indebted to the City of Light.

*Nothing ventured, nothing gained.* "Go ahead."

Sir Rowell excused himself and hurried out of the room in search of a servant.

In the meantime, the royal physician burst into the room with his hands full of bandages, small jars, and vials.

Benjamin, despite his age, scurried to the bed, pushed past Thessian, and quickly checked Emilia's vitals. His face grew grim when he checked her pulse.

"How is she?" Thessian asked.

"Her Majesty is in a terrible state. Her pulse is very weak." He picked up a pair of scissors and began cutting away her clothes.

Once her back was completely naked, Thessian saw that the arrow was lodged a few inches above her heart.

*She could have easily died on the spot.*

His stomach sank. "Are you not going to take the arrow out?"

"Removing the arrow would cause her to bleed out faster if we are not prepared in advance. There is also no telling how severe the internal damage is."

Thessian glared at him. "Surely, you are not planning on leaving the arrow inside her."

Benjamin cast his gaze downward when speaking to Thessian. "My lord, most soldiers with similar wounds pass away from internal bleeding within days. Her Majesty's body, although kept in good shape, is still that of a woman."

Thessian balled his hands at his side. His body trembled with the need to punch something. How could she be so foolish as to take an arrow for him? And where was her shadow? Lord Armel was wasting precious seconds dilly-dallying somewhere.

*Is begging the Pope for help the only option? What if he declines?*
*I could throttle him...*

Sir Rowel returned with two men behind him.

The man in holy knight's armour was obviously the escort. Thessian ignored him and moved to stand in front of the younger, blond man who gazed at Thessian with unnerving calmness. There was no point in using an alias. Pope Valerian Knox visited the Imperial capital—Erehvin—and greeted the emperor shortly after he received his title. No doubt, he had seen the portraits of the Imperial Family hanging all over the palace.

"I am the Duke of Darkgate, Thessian Alexey Hellios. May the blessings of Luminos guide you."

The Pope smiled and spoke in a velvety voice that made Thessian's eye twitch. "May the blessings of Luminos guide you also, Your Grace. As you may have guessed, I am the tenth leader of the City of Light, Pope Valerian Knox. What has brought the second prince of the *Hellion Empire* at this hour to the bedchambers of a wounded *Queen of Dante*?" His following words came out much colder. "Or were you the cause of her misfortune?"

"Your Grace, Your Holiness, my deepest apologies but this is not the time for long discussions," Benjamin interjected from the Queen's bedside. He ambled over, keeping his head down. Next to Thessian, he bowed low to the Pope. "Please, Your Holiness, use a healing miracle and save Her Majesty. I fear my skills are not enough."

Sir Rowell bowed as well. "I also ask for your generosity, Your Holiness."

Valerian looked at Thessian expectantly.

The Imperial Family did not bow to anyone. Thessian was not about to plead with some jester unless he knew the man's true ability. Rumours spread by the Church of the Holy Light highlighted that the Pope had the strongest healing powers on the continent. A single meeting with such a powerful man cost any noble of high rank at least a diamond mine and at most their entire fortune.

Valerian planted a hand on Benjamin's shoulder. "I will heal her, doctor. Please, remove the arrow."

Benjamin bowed over and over again. "Thank you, Your Holiness! Thank you!"

Thessian grasped Valerian's wrist. "What are you playing at?"

"Let go of him, Your Grace!" came a warning from the holy knight who reached for his sword.

Valerian lifted his other hand, halting his guard. "Does His Grace not believe in the goodness of one's heart?"

"Not when it comes to the City of Light and the extortionists who reside there," Thessian replied.

"Allow me to prove you wrong, Your Grace." The Pope eyed Thessian's hand with distaste until he removed it.

Valerian brushed past him and sauntered to the Queen's side.

Thessian observed from the corner of the room as the physician skilfully removed the arrow from Emilia's back. Even in her unconscious state, she moaned in pain a couple of times. Every time a sound left her lips, Thessian half-hoped she would wake up and tell him she would be fine.

To his dismay, that did not happen.

Instead, once the arrow came out, blood rapidly pooled in the open wound and began to flow out freely.

With swift movements, Benjamin wiped the blood around the wound with a linen cloth. "It is your turn, Your Holiness."

Valerian sat on the bed next to Emilia. He tucked her dark locks behind her ear in an almost loving manner. Then, he placed his palm over her wound and started to whisper something in a melodic ancient language.

A soft glow formed under his hand. With each sentence the Pope finished, the glow grew brighter until Thessian struggled to keep his eyes on the procedure.

Turning his head, Thessian found Sir Rowell with his eyes closed and his palms clasped together in silent prayer. Whoever he was asking for help, Thessian hoped would answer the butler's call.

The healing light dimmed and soon vanished.

Valerian removed his hand and planted a soft kiss on top of Emilia's head. "Be well, Child of Luminos."

The physician wiped off the remaining blood and gasped. "The wound is gone!" With tears streaming down his wrinkled face, he kept continuously thanking Valerian for the miracle.

"The wound may be gone, but why is she not waking up?" Thessian asked, his mood growing sourer by the second.

"That would be a question better suited for the doctor," Valerian replied as he sluggishly stood.

Thessian blocked the Pope from taking another step. "Why? Did your magic trick only visually heal her?"

"I assure you, Your Grace, Her Majesty has been healed and blessed by Luminos' power. If Luminos did not wish for me to heal her, the miracle would not happen."

"What an uncertain power you have…"

Valerian smiled weakly. "You are not wrong. Should I ever betray God, my power may truly become a useless magic trick." He swayed, and the holy knight pushed Thessian away to catch Valerian.

"His Holiness must rest," the knight announced and draped Valerian's arm over his shoulders. "We will retire to our quarters."

Their exit was interrupted by Lord Armel who burst into the room panting. His face was beaded with sweat. All of his attention was on the Queen as he pushed past the people in the way without as much as a greeting.

Lord Armel scanned Emilia's body for imperfections and

frowned. "I was told Her Majesty is gravely hurt…"

Thessian nodded in the direction of Valerian. "The Pope healed her."

The Queen's shadow did not seem pleased with the new development but said nothing. Thessian, too, sensed that the Pope was up to something. No doubt he would ask Emilia to repay him for a second chance at life in the future.

*The question is, what is he going to ask for?*

# 22
# ENDANGERED CHASTITY

## LAURENCE

**Something tickled Laurence's nose** as he woke from his slumber.

He tried pushing the object away. His fingers brushed soft fur, and his eyes snapped open.

On his chest, he found the beastwoman resting her head. Her large wolf-like ears were the cause of his discomfort as they wiggled under his nose. She breathed in a steady rhythm, informing him she was asleep.

Laurence attempted to gently push her off.

With a low growl, she coiled her arm around his waist and trapped him in place with an unrelenting grip.

After five minutes of struggling to get free, he gave up and stared at the tent's ceiling. The others were nowhere in sight. Their belongings and bedrolls were neatly packed, which meant they had witnessed his embarrassing situation and left him to it.

Ian peeled back the tent door and stuck his head in. In a low murmur, he said, "Breakfast is ready."

Laurence waved his free hand helplessly. "A little help here?"

"I think not. We do not know how she will behave if we anger her."

"What about me? I cannot move a muscle!"

"We leave for the Dragon Village in an hour." The elf left Laurence to his dilemma.

With a groan, Laurence nudged the beastwoman's shoulder until she raised her head.

Half-asleep, she nuzzled her face against his neck and breathed in his scent.

Goosebumps broke out on his arms and legs. He yanked her away from him. Finally unrestricted, he scrambled away.

The beastwoman's long red hair fell around her face and shoulders as she sat up. Rubbing her face with her hand, she let out a yawn.

Finally opening her eyes, she smiled at him. "*Mir.*"

"Listen here, young lady, I am not 'mir'. My name is Laurence. La-oo-ren-ss."

She didn't react.

Exasperated, he jabbed his thumb into his chest. "La-oo-ren-sss."

"*Loo-re-z.*" She tested the word on her tongue.

Laurence repeated his name a couple of times until she managed to somewhat pronounce it. He pointed to her next. "Name?"

She tilted her head to one side in confusion.

Once again, he indicated to his chest. "I am Laurence." He pointed at her. "You?"

"*Khaja.*"

He repeated the word uncertainly.

She smiled back and started to crawl on all fours towards him. His hands shot up to stop her. "Khaja, what are you doing?"

"*Vosie ntes mir, La-ooo-ren-z.*"

Whatever she was saying, he suspected it was something strange again. Laurence had no more time to waste. He launched out of the tent. Khaja had tracked him to the middle of nowhere. No doubt, she would not run off on her own.

Seeing his companions enjoying their breakfast without a care in the world made him storm over. Each of his steps heavier than the last.

"Look who it is!" Eugene, who sat on a log next to Sergey, announced with a wide grin. "Did you enjoy your nap, Commander?"

Laurence ripped a roll of bread from Eugene's hand and bit into it as his stomach whined from emptiness. "How dare you all leave me in there alone?"

"You looked comfortable," Sergey added.

Laurence was about to reply when he felt someone's arms wrapping around his torso. Dread filled him as he knew exactly who it was. Holding the bread with his teeth, he attempted to pry the beastwoman off him.

The men laughed. Even Yeland, who was often as quiet as Ian, joined in.

"Dis ish noh fummy," Laurence complained through the food blocking his mouth.

Ian came over, spared a look of disgust at Laurence's situation, and said to everyone. "Pack the tent and clean up if you have finished eating."

"Hey, Ian!" Laurence snapped. "Do something about her! She is too strong for me to move on my own."

The elf sighed. "I told you last night. You have been chosen as her mate. Deal with it until we find her clan. They may know of a way to dissolve the union."

Laurence tried again to peel her off.

This time, she let go.

Blowing out a breath of relief, he indicated to Ian. "Why not take him for a mate? If you ignore his bad personality, he is rather pretty without his headscarf." He tried his luck at getting near Ian's headwear and was met with a dagger to the throat.

Khaja let out a loud growl that sent a shudder through Laurence.

Ian eyed the beastwoman past Laurence's shoulder. "I was

correct. She is protective of you." He sheathed his dagger and stepped back. "I will ready the horses." He spared one last look at the beastwoman. "Put a hood or a hat on her. Her ears are easy to identify."

"Err, Commander..." Sergey said nervously.

Glancing over his shoulder, Laurence saw why the others grew silent so quickly. Khaja's claws had come out, and her narrowed eyes followed Ian's retreating figure as he headed towards the line of tied horses by the stream.

Laurence ran a hand over his face. It was barely morning, and he already felt like all energy had drained from him.

Taking a step towards Khaja, he carefully took a hold of her paw. "I am fine. Relax."

Although she probably did not understand his words, she must have picked up on his calm demeanour. Her claws morphed back into hands, and she stared at their linked hands.

"Does that mean the wedding with Dame Cali is off?" Sergey asked.

Laurence glowered at his comrade. "Calithea cannot find out about this!"

Sergey nodded. "She would be furious."

Yeland scratched the back of his head. "Sir Laurence probably had never seen Dame Cali angry. He was always away with His Highness when we went drinking."

"Why? Is she an angry drunk?" Laurence half-joked.

The men shared a look in awkward silence.

"She cannot be that bad..." Laurence felt his stomach sinking with fret.

Sergey spoke first. "One time, we were in a tavern and a group of mercenaries started arguing with the owner. Dame Cali beat them all black and blue before we had the chance to leave our seats."

"What about that time she punched a knight in the face and broke his front teeth for talking badly about Sir Laurence?" Eugene offered.

"Or the time—" Sergey began.

Laurence raised his hands and cut them off. "I get the point." He looked at Khaja who had not let go of his hand and said to them, "Let us keep this a secret no matter what."

They all solemnly agreed.

Packed and ready to leave, they saddled their horses.

Laurence glanced down at Khaja who was waiting for him to pull her up. He looked to the others. "Anyone wants to ride with her?"

"No," Sergey and Eugene muttered in unison.

"I wish to return from this mission alive," Yeland commented.

Ian ignored him completely and nudged his horse in the direction of the Dragon Village.

Laurence rolled his eyes. He bent down and offered Khaja his hand.

The beastwoman accepted it with a smile, and he pulled her up to sit behind him. He did not want to give her the chance to distract him from the front with her constant sniffing and nuzzling.

The horse neighed in protest under their combined weight.

Laurence pulled her arms around his waist. "Keep them here, Khaja! No sniffing or touching me anywhere else." As he said that, she leaned against him and nibbled on his neck.

He shuddered. "This is going to be one long journey…"

It took the group half a day to reach the outskirts of the Dragon Village which rested three leagues away from the foot of the Hollow Mountains. From a distance, Laurence saw plumes of smoke rising from the chimneys. The village consisted of two dozen wooden houses, an inn, a smithy, a carpenter's shop, and a general store.

The Village Chief's manor was located a small distance away, according to information he received from the Lionhart Guild prior to departure. Laurence also learned that most of the residents worked at the mine, extracting the Dragon's Heart gems.

Ian slowed his horse to a trot and got closer to Laurence. "We should gather information on beastmen while we are here."

"Do you think these people know anything?" Laurence asked.

"We will know soon enough." Ian spared a glance at the beastwoman. "Keep an eye on her, so she does not cause a commotion."

Laurence felt Khaja's arms squeezing his waist in Ian's presence. She must not have forgiven the elf for attempting to attack her groom. Had this situation happened to Sergey or Eugene, he would have found the whole event quite humorous. Yet, as the one receiving Khaja's affection, Laurence felt the weight of his burden growing by the minute.

"Ian, you act as if your rank is higher than mine," Laurence grumbled. "I may be undergoing His Highness' punishment, but that does not mean you are in charge."

"I have acquaintances in the village but feel free to take the lead, Sir Laurence."

Laurence gaped at him. When did the stony-faced elf find the time to make friends in such a remote place? More importantly, why did Laurence feel like he lost the argument?

Biting back a curse, Laurence retorted, "Let's split up and meet at the tavern for dinner."

Ian rode off ahead. Whether he agreed or not was anyone's guess.

At the Dragon Village's entrance, Laurence and the rest hopped off their horses. Snow sunk under their boots and reached to their ankles. The closer they got to the Hollow Mountains, the harsher and colder the whipping wind became. Laurence felt the chill down to his bones despite his warm coat with a fur underlayer.

Taking the animal by the reins, Laurence announced to his men, "I will take Khaja and head for the Chief's home. Subtly query the villagers regarding beastmen sightings."

"Where is Sir Ian?" Sergey asked, scanning the area.

"Off on his own again," Laurence replied. "See you at the tavern at dinnertime. Do not forget to book three rooms for us."

The men waved and shuffled with their horses in the direction of the stalls that were set up by the locals.

Meanwhile, Laurence took the beastwoman by the hand and pulled her aside and out of sight.

She did not protest.

Once he was satisfied that no one was around to hear him, he said, "I need you to be very quiet and obedient from now on." For effect, he put his index finger against his lips in a universal sign of silence.

She tilted her head to one side.

"Qua-ee-et," he repeated.

Khaja's brows scrunched together. She captured his gloved hand and put his index finger against her lips.

Jerking his hand out of her grasp, Laurence stepped out of her reach. He rubbed the back of his neck. *Too bad I cannot leave her in the tavern.*

"*Vosie ntes ukiy kur deche heslich, La-ooo-ren-z.*"

Her ears perked up, and she looked around. Then, she took off.

Laurence had no time to think. He sprinted after her, shouting, "Wait! Khaja, wait! Ugh—"

Following her was nearly impossible. Her full speed was close to a wild galloping horse, which made sense as she had no trouble catching up with his group the day prior.

Before he knew it, he lost sight of her.

Laurence spun around, searching for a trace of her red hair. Despite not wearing much under her cloak, she did not seem cold in the slightest. Had he been half-naked in winter, he would have frozen to death.

"Where did she go?" he muttered and walked over to the nearest villager.

With a single unimpressed look, the elderly woman must have written his life's story in her head. She asked with a toothless mouth, "Whad'ya wunt?"

"Excuse me, have you—" He paused, noting something amiss with the cat the woman was lovingly stroking. It did not move. Upon closer inspection, he realised it had no eyes in its sockets. A handful of bones protruded from under the animal's ginger fur, and he grimaced. "Never…mind."

He picked up the pace in search of Khaja. Hopefully, she did not get into any trouble.

By the time he finished scouring every hole and crate that could fit a beastwoman, the sun was setting.

Someone cleared their throat to draw Laurence's attention. In a voice laced with irritation, the man said, "I have received word of suspicious people arriving in our village today. Who might you be, sir, and what is your purpose?"

# 23
# SUSPENDED SEARCH

## LAURENCE

Laurence smiled at the short gentleman whose round belly could hardly be contained in his tailored fur coat. His greying beard reached his chest, and his dark beady eyes were amplified in size by the round, metal spectacles he wore. No doubt he was the wealthiest man in the village. Not many commoners could afford quality clothes and luxuries.

Behind the nobleman stood a lanky soldier in leather armour that had seen better days.

*Seems this noble spends most of his wealth on himself.*

Laurence inclined his head in greeting. "Good evening, sir. Am I to assume I am speaking with the Village Chief, Baron Bald Lucy?" He did his best to keep a straight face.

"If you know who I am, I believe it is time you introduced yourself," the Baron pressed.

"My name is Sir Laurel."

Laurence reached into the inner pocket of his coat and pulled out an envelope with a royal seal. Emilia said the letter would give them an excuse to loiter in the Dragon Village. He handed it to the soldier who, in turn, gave it to his master.

Lord Lucy's eyes widened. He made quick work of opening the envelope and reading the contents of the letter. His expression changed to a polite smile as he folded the letter and returned it to Laurence. "I did not realise Her Majesty's worry for the miners was so great that she would send her royal guards to investigate the recent collapse in the mine."

Queen Emilia had gone out of her way once again and created a perfect alibi for them. Hopefully, the rest of his comrades were able to gather some information while he wasted his time searching for Khaja. "I am at fault for not going directly to greet you once we arrived, Lord Lucy. You see, my companion got lost, and I was searching for her."

"Aside from you and your men, there has been none other," Lord Lucy assured him with great confidence.

*Khaja must be hiding out of sight.*

Laurence decided to suspend his search and approached Bald Lucy. "It is getting late, my lord. Could you spare some time tomorrow morning to discuss the issues with the mine?"

The Baron stroked his beard. "Tomorrow... Yes, I should have some time to spare. Where are you staying? I will send Paul here to fetch you."

"We will be at the Spotted Dogs Inn." *Why bother asking when that is the only place in the village with spare beds?*

"Good. You must be tired, Sir Laurel. Get some rest."

Laurence bowed to the noble despite being one too. He could not reveal he was Marquess Oswald's son from the Empire. It would cause too much trouble. Yet, Lord Lucy's act of self-importance was rubbing Laurence the wrong way. He would not be surprised to find Lord Lucy dabbling in illegal activities. Since Laurence was already in the Dragon Village, he may as well help the Queen and learn whether Baron Lucy could be trusted with managing the place or not.

With long strides, Laurence headed for the inn. He felt the Baron's eyes burning a hole in his back the entire time, which only confirmed that Baron Bald Lucy was up to no good.

The inn had seen better days, much like the rest of the dilapidated village. The steps groaned under his weight as he scaled them and opened the door. The smell of hot meat stew awakened his stomach, and it produced an audible protest.

Rubbing his stomach, he looked around.

"Over here, sir!" Sergey called from one of the tables near the bar.

Laurence made his way over. The place was empty aside from the grumpy man manning the bar.

Ian lifted his gaze from his untouched meal. "Where is she?"

With a shrug, Laurence replied, "She ran off on me the second we got here."

"How could you lose our only lead?" Ian did not seem happy which meant things did not go well with his acquaintances.

Taking the last available seat at the table, Laurence stole a plate of roasted potatoes and boiled vegetables from Yeland and asked, "What about you, gentlemen? Any news?"

Resigned, Yeland got up. "I will order more food…"

Sergey leaned in. "We asked nearly everyone in the village about any sightings of large animals or animal attacks that looked suspicious. No one was willing to talk."

"What about you, Ian?"

The elf pushed his untouched bowl. It came as no surprise that he abstained from dipping his spoon into the dubious liquid. Compared to the generous amounts of meat in Newburn meals, the stew at the inn looked like mud with floating chunks of carrots. Even the meat must have escaped before it got dunked into that brown sludge.

"The carpenters said the ones keeping track of monsters are the soldiers at the Northern Watchtower," Ian finally said.

"Are you planning on visiting it tomorrow?" Laurence asked.

"No. The watchtower is in Marquess Carrell's territory. I may be suspected of spying if I go alone."

Laurence had to agree. A lone elf claiming to be a royal knight of Dante was a suitable setup for a far-fetched jest. Although Marquess Carrell was Prince Thessian's supporter for the coup, that did not mean his subordinates were made aware that he betrayed the king. Once again, they could not announce that they were Hellion's knights.

"We will leave for the Northern Watchtower once we investigate Baron Lucy."

Sergey, who until now was busy chewing his slice of bread, asked, "The Village Chief?"

"Yes," Laurence replied with distaste.

"Why would you need to investigate him?" Sergey pressed.

Laurence pulled out the royal letter and slid it to the middle of the table. "Seems Her Majesty wishes for us to look into the recent collapse in the Dragon's Heart Mine."

"We serve His Highness," Ian reminded him. "There is no need to waste time here."

"I disagree." Laurence folded his arms over his chest. "Khaja is gone, and we need to find her anyway. So, why not kill two birds with one stone?"

Ian glared at Laurence as he abandoned his seat at the table. "I think I will retire for the night."

The elf stomped up the stairs.

"Sir Ian must hate us for deceiving him with the brothel fiasco," Eugene commented.

Laurence relaxed his posture and dug into the meal that once belonged to Yeland. "I doubt it. He probably hates the world."

Laurence had a difficult time falling asleep that night. As he did not trust the inn's owner to clean the sheets properly between the guests, he threw his cloak over the mattress and lay on top of it.

Tossing and turning on the uncomfortable bed did not help. So, he pulled out the silver locket Calithea had given him and held it in his hand. Staying true to one woman for the rest of his life was a strange feeling. He did not wish to see her cry because of him.

Closing his eyes, he recalled their first meeting...

*Laurence stood in front of two rows of promising recruits. The sun beat down on them, and his skin prickled under the intense heat. The youths before him burned with anticipation and excitement he did not share. The air was thick with the smell of ripe wheat and dry enough to make the back of his throat itch.*

*He let out a heaving sigh. As always, Thessian left the undesirable work to Laurence, which included putting the newbies through the initial training.*

*Planting his hands firmly on his sides, Laurence announced, "My name is Sir Laurence Oswald. I am His Highness' second-in-command. If you think joining Prince Thessian's knights is a walk in the park, you are sorely mistaken. I will not go easy on you. If you are here for glory or because you believe being a knight will make you popular with the ladies, I suggest you leave now."*

*No one moved from their spot.*

*Laurence felt his lips tugging into an evil smile. "The task for today is to run around the wheat field ten times. Any stragglers will be disqualified."*

*"Yes, sir!"*

*"Begin!" he shouted.*

*Among the prospects were two young women in their late teens. A brunette with short, light-brown hair and tanned skin, as if she worked on a farm her entire life, and a pretty, slender blonde who was taller than some of the men. From his experience, women did not last long nor survive the initial training. They often quit at the first obstacle or halfway. Judging by their rough clothes, he could tell they were of common birth. He dismissed his thoughts with a shrug and sat in the shade of an oak tree with a leather bouget of water.*

*His eyes followed the progress of the recruits.*

*On the third lap, three out of twenty were crawling along.*

By the time they were on the seventh lap, fifteen were either lying on the dirt, begging for water, or giving up and heading home.

To his surprise, the two women continued to jog along at a steady pace. Their clothes were drenched in sweat and their faces were damp and red from the strenuous exercise.

The last lap began as the sun started to set.

Laurence rubbed his rumbling gut and slowly made his way to the finish line. He swallowed the remaining water as he looked at the clock tower nearby. It was a little past seven o'clock. The remaining recruits had been running for three hours under the blazing sun while the others were dismissed for lacking perseverance. As a reward, he planned to feed them a hearty meal and congratulate them with a barrel of ale.

Too bad they were so few. As years went on, fewer people could complete the ten-mile run.

Twenty minutes later, the group finally dragged their wobbly limbs over the finish line and collapsed in unison. He picked up a sack he left on the ground earlier that day and approached them.

"Have a drink, everyone," Laurence said with a wide grin and pulled out a bouget for each of them. "I think introductions are in order."

The first person to take the drink was a lean man in his early twenties. He sported a deep tan and short, chestnut-coloured hair. "I'm Leo Ritter. I worked as a mercenary for two years for the Bad Blood Company."

The next was the brunette Laurence took note of earlier in the day. "I'm Verena Vogel, a sailor."

Laurence raised a brow. A female sailor was uncommon, especially in the middle of the continent. Her profession certainly explained the dark tan on her skin. To not make her feel awkward, he moved on to the next lad who did not look a day older than fourteen. He had barely come off his mother's teat, yet the boy was rushing to join the military.

The boy accepted the drink and downed the entire contents of the bouget before he replied, "Sergey Larvios is my name. Third son of Baron Larvios, and possibly the only handsome one."

"Is that the baron who recently came into money?" Laurence asked.

"The very same!" Sergey beamed at Laurence. "I am surprised you heard of my father, Sir Laurence."

Laurence smiled back. It was impossible not to hear the rumours in the *noble circles of how a mere baron made his fortune by getting lucky at cards. Since then, the Baron invested in trading ships and tried to get close to the emperor with lavish gifts.*

A fortune so frail would not last long.

*Laurence moved on to the second woman in the group.*

*When their eyes met, she quickly looked away. Although her cheeks were quite red from the run, somehow her face got redder.*

Oh my, this one fancies me...

"Your name, recruit?"

*She ducked her head.* "Cali... Cali-thea Louberte, S-sir Laurence."

"Cali, welcome to the military." *He offered her a hand in the form of a handshake.*

*Cali took a hold of it, climbed onto one knee, and kissed the back of his hand.*

*Dumbfounded, Laurence stared at his tingling skin where her soft lips were a second ago. He was not the only one who was stumped. The others were openly staring and waiting for his reaction.*

*Laurence let out a chuckle.* "That is the first time anyone has kissed my hand..."

*Calithea lifted her head in apparent confusion.* "Was I not supposed to? I heard nobles do this all the time in greeting..."

*Verena could not contain her guffaw. She doubled over and between gasps, she said,* "Yeah. When greeting...women."

*Cali's mouth fell open.* "Oh..."

"I thought. The Run. Would kill me. Turns out. It *was* this!" *Verena continued between bursts of laughter.*

*The others joined in, including Calithea.*

# 24

# BALD LUCY

## LAURENCE

**At dawn, Laurence got together** with his comrades in one of the inn's rooms. He sat on the bed next to Eugene.

Yeland and Sergey stood by the door, and Ian had his arms crossed by the window.

With everyone present, Laurence began with, "I plan to meet the Village Chief at his residence when his guard arrives to escort me. While I distract Lord Lucy, I need someone to sneak in and take a look at the accounting books."

"I will do it," Ian said with little enthusiasm.

"Great." Laurence could leave the important task to Ian. "I will take Yeland to the meeting. Sergey and Eugene, I would like you to question the miners about the collapse at the mine."

Sergey asked, "What if they refuse to talk like yesterday?"

"Tell them Lord Lucy is eager to get to the bottom of it. I doubt they have a good relationship, so they will likely say something. We will meet back here at sunset." As an afterthought, Laurence added, "Should anything happen, or you feel the situation has become dangerous, get out immediately. We cannot expose ourselves here."

The others gave a nod of agreement and dispersed.

Laurence dressed in his best clothes and polished his boots. He combed his hair and tied it with a navy ribbon to show his false loyalty to the Dante Crown. Then, he shaved his unkempt stubble that had been growing over the past week.

He admired his handiwork in the handheld mirror and winked at his reflection. "Still as handsome as ever!"

An hour later, there was a knock on Laurence's door. He opened it to find Yeland and Bald Lucy's guard, Paul, standing there.

Yeland announced, "Sir Laurel, this man here is claiming he has arrived to escort you."

Laurence smiled at Paul. "Good morning."

The guard managed a weak smile. "Yes. Good morning, Sir Laurel. Please follow me."

"Of course. Lead the way." Laurence stepped out of his room. "Do you think the Baron will mind if my subordinate tags along?"

Paul studied Yeland with his dead eyes. "It shouldn't matter."

"Fantastic!" Laurence cheered and motioned for the guard to take the lead.

Baron Bald Lucy's home was the property situated ten minutes' walk away from the village's market. The front garden had manicured snow-capped shrubs and a fountain that had frozen from the cold.

In one of the upstairs windows, Laurence spied Lord Lucy peeking out from behind thick curtains.

Even the recently-cleaned cobbled path they walked on seemed ostentatious when the rest of the villagers suffered with muddy roads and potholes the size of a horse.

Laurence clenched his jaw so tight it hurt. He hated when nobles abused their power. Their duty was to look after the commoners, yet they drained the lifeblood and coin from the hard-working men and women of the land. No doubt, Bald Lucy was no different.

At the front door, Paul faced them. "Maria will escort you from here. I must return to guard duty."

Laurence waved goodbye with mock enthusiasm as a middle-aged woman with a deep-set scowl, clad in a black cotton dress that covered her from her neck to her ankles, opened the door. She did not seem happy about welcoming guests. The Baron probably had her rushed off her feet all night and morning to prepare a feast for them.

The maid put on the worst fake smile Laurence had ever seen.

In a raspy voice, Maria said, "You must be the lord's guests."

Laurence inclined his head in greeting. He flashed her a charming smile which worked on all women, regardless of age. Maria was no exception. "Greetings, madam. Apologies for coming here on such short notice... You and the other servants must have suffered a great deal."

He nudged Yeland with his elbow.

Yeland produced a boyish smile of his own, which was a rare sight. "Good morning, ma'am."

Her expression brightened from the acknowledgement of her hardships. "Follow me, gentlemen. My lord is waiting for you in the dining room."

Matching her small stride, Laurence got close to Maria and gave a superficial study of the interior. "There must be a lot of servants as this place is impeccable. It is almost on par with the royal palace in cleanliness."

A shade of rouge tinted her cheeks. "Oh, you jest, sir! Paul, I, and the chef are the only ones serving Baron Lucy."

"I never joke about such matters. Do I, Yan?"

Yeland raised a brow at the improvised name. With a deadpan expression, he replied, "No, you do not, Sir Laurel. You are as serious as a thunderstorm."

Maria let out a giggle. "Then I thank you for the compliment, Sir Laurel."

In the same playful manner, Laurence asked, "Has Baron Lucy been treating you well? It must be hard looking after such a mansion all on your own."

"Like any noble, the lord has his mood swings. He has been in a foul mood since the accidents at the mine have increased. There are even rumours going around that a monster has made the mine its lair."

"Do you happen to know what kind of monster it is?" Laurence asked.

"Some kind of lizard, I think."

Laurence shared a look with Yeland. Sergey and Eugene went to the mine. Hopefully, they would avoid any danger.

She came to a halt in front of a door.

In a hushed tone, she added, "My lord is waiting in here."

The men nodded and were escorted to their seats at a table that was suitable for a family of twelve. From Laurence's observation, he saw portraits of a young woman standing next to the younger baron hanging around the manor. Yet, the place lacked a feminine touch, and Maria did not mention a baroness, which led Laurence to assume she was no longer among the living.

Baron Lucy sat at the head of the table dressed in expensive clothes one could only acquire in the capital and with more rings than his podgy fingers could handle. Without a hat to hide it, Laurence spied a grey toupee covering the top of the lord's head.

No doubt, Bald Lucy was balding.

"Welcome to my humble abode." The Baron spread his arms to show off a table full of delicacies that the villagers probably had never seen in their entire lives. "Please, join me for a meal." He spotted Yeland and asked, "Is this another royal knight, Sir Laurel?"

"This is Sir Yan." Laurence nudged his friend, who bowed and muttered a greeting. "As you can see, he is not much for conversation."

A look of disappointment settled on Baron Lucy's aged face. He was most likely expecting praise for his lavish living when none came. "And what of the other knights? I heard there were five of you."

"You are well-informed, milord." Laurence smiled and offered nothing else.

The Baron let out an awkward laugh. "I should not be holding you back from your breakfast. Please, join me."

He asked Maria to place a bit of everything on his plate—from a variety of meats and cheeses to grapes and olives—and motioned for Laurence and Yeland to do the same.

Laurence kept the banter with Bald Lucy light during the meal to get on the man's good side. He may be a royal knight in name only, but he had to keep up appearances and represent Queen Emilia.

As a final boon, the chef wheeled in the dessert on a metal tray with a custard base and caramelised sugar crust Laurence was quite familiar with. The pricey ingredients were hard to come by in the middle of nowhere, especially sugar and cream. There was no obvious trade route attached to the village, meaning that Lord Lucy had gone out of his way to hire a merchant who brought goods directly to his abode.

Unable to contain himself any longer, Laurence asked, "My, what an extravagant dessert, milord! Isn't that Dragon's Breath Cream from the Hellion Empire?"

The Baron beamed with pride. "I spent some time there last spring. While recuperating from lung disease in the warm climate, I discovered this dessert by chance."

*What a load of hogwash!*

That dessert was quite popular among the upper nobility of the Empire. The chefs who could make it properly were quickly hired by the Imperial Palace, a handful of marquesses, and Prince Kyros. It was one of the gossips that occupied the nobles during the balls of last spring.

Yeland gave the dessert a try. "It is delicious, Lord Lucy."

"Of course, I have the best chef in the kingdom!" the Baron

boasted.

Laurence raised a brow. "Better than the royal chef?"

Baron Lucy cleared his throat. "Tolik is skilled, but I fear he cannot compare to His Majesty's chef."

"Don't you mean, *Her* Majesty's chef?" Laurence corrected him.

The Baron wiped the forming sweat off his forehead with a napkin. "Me and my memory! I apologise. King Gilebert was a good friend of mine, and I miss him a great deal. So, forgive me for the slip of the tongue and…please do not tell Her Majesty."

Laurence wiped the corners of his mouth with a napkin and pushed the untouched dessert away. "Could you tell us about the collapse at the mine?"

Baron Lucy downed a goblet of ale to wash down his dessert and glared at his servants.

Maria and Tolik bowed their heads and scurried out of the dining room.

The Baron reclined in his seat and patted his round belly. "What is there to say? There was a small earthquake and a part of the mine got blocked off. Some of the miners came up with a silly tale of seeing a monster, so they could avoid returning to work."

"Are you certain the monster they saw is imaginary?" Laurence asked.

"I sent Paul to check the tunnels. He reported that there was no trace of any large beasts and only human footprints to be found."

Although Paul's report did not give Laurence any assurances, the guard did seem to take his job seriously. Yet, why would the miners avoid going to work if they had to provide for their families and put food on their tables?

"How many miners claimed the creature exists?"

"Oh, not many. Four or five," Baron Lucy replied.

"When was this?" Yeland inquired.

"Hmm." Bald Lucy stroked his beard. "I would say, a week ago. I wrote a report to the palace as soon as I learned the collapse reduced the quantity of the gems that could be mined. We may miss the next mining quota because of this."

Emilia did not seem to be the type to concern herself over loose change. No doubt, she wanted Laurence to get to the bottom of Lord Lucy's affiliations and whether he could be trusted to operate the mine going forward. From what he had seen, the outlook for the Village Chief was grim. All that remained was to get Ian's report and hear what Sergey and Eugene uncovered.

Laurence engaged in his best acting. "Yes, the Queen is quite upset by what has occurred. She was so worried for your health, Baron Lucy, she could not sleep properly since she read the report."

"I did not realise Her Majesty knew of my health problems... I should visit the castle as soon as this issue is resolved."

"That you should, milord," Laurence added, getting up from his seat. "I apologise, but we must get going. There is much to do and a report to write."

Lord Lucy's eyes bulged at the mention of the report. "I hope you will only write good things about my territory."

From what Laurence heard from Emilia, the mine was rented out to Baron Bald Lucy on the promise that he would split the income with the Crown and look after the village. "I believe you are mistaken once again. This territory belongs to the Crown."

The Baron's face turned a shade of an over-ripe tomato.

At that moment, Laurence thought of an opportunity to catch the foul man red-handed. He put out the bait with a charming smile. "My hands ache a lot these days, milord. I think I will put off writing the report to Her Majesty for a day or two as a thank you for treating us to such a delicious and *expensive* meal."

"You would?" Bald Lucy seemed taken aback. He grinned from ear to ear and stood, offering Laurence a handshake. "That's right! Great knights such as yourselves should spend more time relaxing while away from the palace."

Laurence shook hands with him, feeling the sweat on the Baron's skin. He nearly wiped his hands on his cloak right there from disgust.

"Come by once more before you leave, Sir Laurel. I will be sure to have a parting gift ready for you and your men." Bald Lucy winked.

"I look forward to it."

Once they were back on the dirt road, returning to the village, Yeland finally asked, "Were we just bribed?"

Laurence chuckled. "That we were."

# 25
# A TOKEN OF LOVE

## LAURENCE

**The day at the village** was quiet, to say the least. Laurence saw an open-roofed carriage collecting the men that morning shortly after dawn to slave away at the mine. The women were either at home or shopping at the handful of market stalls for groceries.

Passing by the market, Laurence could tell the choices were limited to dirt-covered potatoes, carrots, and root-like vegetables the colour of a ripe bruise. The butcher's cart had slabs of salted, unknown meat hanging from metal hooks. Fruit and greenery were nowhere in sight. Animal products also appeared to be a luxury.

Laurence wondered what kind of reaction the villagers would have if they got to see Baron Lucy's breakfast spread. Would they fetch their pitchforks and torches? Or stab him outright with rusted carving knives?

The crisp air prickled his skin, and Laurence pulled his hood over his head in a poor attempt to keep his stinging ears warm.

Walking along the road and away from the market stalls, he felt the dirty looks fired their way. The entire settlement had to be aware of why his party was there. Gossip hardly ever sat still. Their visit to the Baron's home had to have excited the wagging tongues.

Back at the inn, and out of sight, he felt his stiff shoulders diving.

"What do we do from here?" Yeland asked.

"Check on our horses and head to the mine. If the monster Maria mentioned is real, then Sergey and Eugene could be in danger."

"I will check on the horses." Yeland went back outside.

Laurence headed for his room. He gave it a quick study, making sure nothing was out of place. Satisfied, he strode to the storage chest and flung it open. He pulled out two daggers, three throwing knives, and the leather satchel with two healing potions Thessian had given him in case of an emergency. Making quick work of sheathing the knives in his boots and securing the daggers behind his back, he was ready for a fight.

He draped the satchel over his shoulder and protectively covered it with his cloak. As a final check, he pulled out his sword and tested its sharpness against his thumb. It made a light cut on his skin at the slightest pressure.

*Perfect.*

Before he had the chance to sheathe his sword, he heard a scuffling sound coming from the room next door.

*Are Sergey and Eugene back?*

He gripped the hilt of his sword and made his way to the hallway. His ears strained past the bickering of the innkeeper and his wife on the ground floor.

He tested the handle to the room next door.

It was opened.

Raising his weapon, he pushed the door open in one swift move and tore inside.

Laurence froze at the stomach-churning sight before him. The stench of blood invaded his senses. Everything from the floorboards to the windowpane was an unnerving shade of crimson.

On one of the beds, Khaja sat with a wide grin. Aside from her face that was splattered with dried blood or dirt—he could not be certain which—her arms and feet were painted red. Next to her was a huge head of an ogre. By the looks of it, the head was ripped off the monster's shoulders with inhuman strength.

"La-ooo-ren-z." She proudly pointed at the head.

He blanched. "Do you wish to behead me also?"

Her sudden decision to stand had Laurence stumbling backwards. In less than a second, she was in front of him, staring right at his face. Her hands steadied him around the waist and kept him from moving.

He pushed her away with his free hand, but she refused to budge. Despite her feminine appearance, she was sturdier than a fortress. Raising his sword against her could cause her to panic, so he lowered the weapon and rested it against the opened door.

This time, he placed his hands on her shoulders and gently nudged her away. "Young lady, you need a wash."

Half-turning on the spot, she pointed to the head with her sharp nail. *"Khaja zaregh golnad oin."*

Laurence did not sense any malice coming from the beastwoman. Instead, she appeared to be asking for praise like a child who learned to ride their first pony.

He patted her on the head and ruffled her hair with a smile on his face. "Good job, although I have no idea how I will explain the bloody mess to the innkeeper."

Thinking back, he did not see any gore in the hallway, which meant she came in through the window.

*Eugene and Sergey must have forgotten to lock the door again.*

Prying himself out of her hold, he avoided the puddles of blood on the floor and made his way to the widow. He pushed it open and stuck his head out.

He was right. There was blood smeared on the windowsill and the roof above.

*It must look quite picturesque from the outside...*

Her eyes had not left him. He felt her hot gaze as he moved around the cramped room and between the two beds that were slapped together with cheap oak. He avoided looking at the ogre's head as it reminded him of how dangerous she truly was.

He heard booted feet scaling the stairs. Fearing that it may be the host of the establishment, he lunged across the room, pulled her against him, and slammed the door shut.

The sword clattered on the floor until it settled.

His heart pounded in his chest and echoed in his head as the booted feet stopped outside the door. A series of four intermittent knocks let him know it was someone from Thessian's knights.

Laurence blew out a breath and opened the door.

Yeland eyed the situation Laurence was in. "I did not realise I was interrupting—"

"No!" Laurence released her and stepped away as far as the space permitted. "You are not in the way, Yeland. Your appearance is rather timely."

Yeland stepped into the room, and his jaw nearly hit the floor. He was five years Laurence's junior. Being barely twenty, the young man had probably never encountered an ogre in Darkgate. "This is…"

"Her doing, yes," Laurence replied quickly. "We must clean this up before the innkeeper finds out."

Yeland's dark brow quirked. "How? We have no rags or buckets or— Well there is no way we will get the smell out."

Yeland was not wrong. They not only needed to get the place into tip-top shape, but Khaja also needed a bath or two.

Running his hand through his hair, he realised his ribbon had come undone some time ago. "Ask the owner to fill the bath in the room next door. Once Khaja is cleaned up, we will use the remaining water to tidy the place up. We will use the bedding as rags and pay for the damages later."

"Would it not be easier to pay the madam of the inn for the cleaning?" Yeland asked.

"And have the entire village cowering in fear?"

Yeland pulled a face which showed much reluctance to the task at hand.

He lowered his head and droned, "I will speak with the

innkeeper and his wife." Giving Laurence's attire one final look, he added, "It may be best you find a change of clothes. You are covered in blood, Commander."

Three hours passed by quickly.

They managed to clean up most of the mess and hid the ogre's head in the storage chest in Laurence's room.

Laurence wiped the sweat off his forehead with the back of his shirt's sleeve. Out of the corner of his eye, he found Khaja sitting cross-legged on his bed. She washed without his help, for which he thanked the gods, and was dressed in his clean clothes.

Resting his hands on his hips, he told her in a stern voice. "Listen, Khaja. I hope you will not be bringing more monster heads here. This is not a place for a monster exhibition."

Khaja tilted her head to one side in evident confusion.

He huffed and pointed to the storage chest. "NO. MORE. HEADS."

She shrank away from his outburst, and he regretted shouting.

"I do apologise," he said in a softer voice and sat beside her.

Whatever was going through her head was a mystery suitable for the knowledge-seeking lunatics of the Mage Assembly.

Before he knew what was happening, his world spun when she pushed him down onto the bed and climbed on top of his chest.

He averted his eyes at the sight of her round breasts that peeked out from her half-buttoned shirt.

"This is quite inappropriate." He tried to get up and failed.

She kept his wrists and chest pinned down with ease. Her nails dug into his skin every time he struggled.

For once, Laurence felt like a dainty lady instead of a knight who had trained for over a decade. "Khaja, this is—"

Her soft lips collided with his, and his eyes bulged.

Laurence did not return her attempt at affection. Instead, his body stiffened while his mind raced. He was betraying the one woman whom he pledged to spend the rest of his life with. Yes, Calithea and he were recently made a couple. Their feelings of love were new, and he was still learning to navigate romantic relationships as a whole.

*She may be pregnant with my child.*

The thought sobered him. He bit Khaja's lower lip until she hissed and jumped off the bed.

Laurence did not wait a second more. He pulled out his dagger and pointed it at her.

With a warning growl, he snarled, "Never again, Khaja!"

Blood trickled down her chin, and her tongue jutted out to lick it. She seemed to hesitate between standing in place and approaching him. She chose the former.

After getting off the bed, Laurence stormed out of his room. He had had enough of beastmen and their strange customs.

*Why couldn't she pick the pesky elf as her groom?*

Laurence's foul mood tasted as bitter as the ale in the inn's bar. He nursed his drink with a permanent scowl as he did not dare return to his room. Yeland was of no help, either. The young lad ran off to check on Eugene and Sergey after disposing of the ruined bedsheets.

The door to the inn opened with an ear-straining creak.

Laurence peered over his shoulder at Ian who took one look at Laurence's miserable posture and rolled his eyes.

Laurence's fingers gripped the wooden pitcher. *I must not waste this piss-poor drink on the elf. I must not!*

"What is the matter this time?" Ian slipped onto the stool next to him.

"I do not know what you mean. Everything is marvellous and brimming with daisies."

Ian made a show of peeking over the rim of Laurence's pitcher.

"I am sober!" Laurence yelled and yanked the pitcher towards him, causing the ale to spill down his shirt and trousers. "Oh, this is just—"

Ian clasped a hand over Laurence's mouth. "Mind your manners. Remember whom you serve and act accordingly."

Laurence straightened his back at the harsh reminder that he was not a poor sod whose only troubles were related to his busy love life. He was a knight and Prince Thessian's second-in-command.

"I-I was not myself. I am sorry for my terrible conduct, Ian."

Ian reduced his voice to a whisper. "I assume the beastwoman returned to your side."

"How did you know?"

"I can smell her on you."

Laurence sniffed his sleeves. His nose picked up on the light scent of his citrus perfume and the overpowering smell of the bitter ale. "What does she smell like?"

Ian thought about it for a moment. "She carries a scent of wilderness and freshly fallen leaves on a dewy morn."

"What?"

The elf sighed in resignation. "Never mind. Let us go to your room and discuss today's events."

"Oh, great idea."

Laurence left a silver coin on the counter, next to the pitcher, to pay for the spillage. On second thought, he left another to clear his conscience.

They went upstairs to Laurence's room. He was half-expecting Khaja to pounce on him a second time. Yet, to his surprise, she was sprawled out on his bed and dead to the world. In her hands, he recognised an article of his clothing that should not be held by a lady.

Rushing over, he yanked his undergarments from her loose hold. Thankfully, she did not wake from her deep sleep.

Grumbling a curse, he snuck away from the bed. *I did not realise beastmen could be perverts, too.*

Ian covered his nose and mouth with his hand. "Why does your room stink of foul blood?"

"The answer is in that chest. Feel free to take a gander," Laurence commented in a low voice.

"Did you kill someone?"

"I am quite good at restraining my murderous desires outside of the battlefield, Ian." Laurence nodded in the direction of the sleeping beastwoman. "She brought an ogre's head back with her."

Ian chuckled. "I once heard there is a ritual among beastmen to gift hunted prey during the courting period. It displays affection and strength of the prospective mate."

Laurence raised a hand. Realising he was still clutching his underwear, he bundled it into a ball and threw it into a corner. "No more of these jests. I am not planning on dating or courting or having anything to do with her. Once this is over, she can return to her people or find another groom."

"Does that mean you are set on marrying Dame Calithea?"

Laurence glared at the elf and walked over to the window. "Report, Ian."

In a few strides, Ian closed the gap between them.

The elf kept his voice barely above a whisper. "I spent as much time as I could in Baron Lucy's office, yet I could not find the accounting books. There were some old letters from King Gilebert, demanding for greater quantities of the Dragon's Heart to be mined, and a dull exchange with an infatuated noblewoman from the Empire."

Laurence clenched his fists. Bald Lucy was sneakier than he thought. The Baron must have hidden the accounts somewhere. But where?

*No matter.* Laurence had set a different trap for the cunning hog. If Bald Lucy took the bait and bribed them before they headed to the Northern Watchtower, Laurence could take Bald Lucy into custody.

"Do you have another plan?"

Laurence smirked. "Of course."

## 26
# THE DUKE'S END

### THESSIAN

**T****hessian did not dare rest** all night for guilt wracked his mind. Sitting on a chair provided by Sir Rowell, he watched Emilia's sleeping face.

She did not stir nor wake. Her breaths were even and so faint, that he often panicked she had stopped breathing altogether.

The royal physician swore on his life Emilia was physically well after the Pope's healing miracle. Yet, no one knew why she did not open her eyes to the many calls of her friends or tears of her head maid.

Emilia's close maid approached him wearing an expression fit for a funeral. If he recalled it correctly, Ambrose was her name. "Your Highness, I suggest you have breakfast in the dining hall. I will notify you should there be any changes in Her Majesty's condition."

Only when Thessian was upright did his stomach voice its emptiness. To salvage his dignity, he asked, "Where is Lord Armel?"

"He left at the crack of dawn to speak with the judges."

*I cannot mope around while the Queen's dog is keeping busy.*

Thessian cautiously gave Ambrose's shoulder a light squeeze. With much assurance, he told her. "Emilia is strong. She will be up on her feet in no time."

Ambrose's harsh features softened. "I thank you for your kind words, Your Highness."

Sparing one final look at Emilia's peaceful face, Thessian left her bedchambers.

Soon after, he found himself standing in front of her office.

Sir Rowell appeared like a soundless shadow. "May I be of some help, my lord?"

"While Her Majesty is indisposed, I was planning on helping her with the paperwork."

"I do apologise, but I cannot allow anyone to enter Her Majesty's office in her absence."

Thessian studied the stubborn head butler with interest. Undoubtedly, Sir Rowell knew exactly who the real owner of the kingdom was, yet the old man displayed his loyalty to Emilia openly and without fear.

*Commendable yet foolish.*

Thessian could easily part the man's head from his body or carve a hole in his chest with his sword.

*But that would not make Emilia happy when she wakes.*

"Very well. Then have breakfast served in my room."

Sir Rowell bowed low. "I shall have the servants prepare a filling meal for you within the hour."

Thessian decided to stop by Lionhart's office before returning to his room.

He spotted Emilia's spymaster sitting with his feet up on his messy desk and staring blankly at a bottle of expensive wine.

"Planning to start drinking early?" Thessian asked from the doorway.

Lionhart's grave mood was no better than that of Emilia's head maid. "I am considering it. The only thing stopping me is the possibility that Emilia may awaken. If she finds out I drank during working hours, I will hear no end of it."

Crossing his arms and resting his shoulder against the door frame, Thessian commented, "Everyone here is quite devoted to her."

"I would not set foot in this pit of snakes if she was not the queen." Lionhart spat on the floor. "The nobles and royals are all the same. They use others and then throw them away at the earliest opportunity. They are no better than the filth at the bottom of an unwashed chamber pot."

Thessian ignored the open insult. "Why serve her? How is she different from the royals you hate?"

Lionhart went silent. He lowered his legs and sat properly in his chair. There was a lot of emotional pain in the spymaster's gaze to fill an ocean with misery.

Unlike Laurence, Thessian did not see the need to pry into the business of others. Yet, he was unable to keep from doing so when it came to Emilia and those around her. She was young and decisive, smart and caring, strong and beautiful. A woman like her could win the hearts of the people wherever she went. If the prince had not orchestrated the coup, she would undoubtedly find another way to claim the throne.

"I heard Lord Armel left to deal with the Duke's trial," Thessian said to break the awkward silence. "Should you be sitting here, lamenting over the past?"

"There is nothing to worry about. Clayton will have the trial by combat dismissed by presenting the evidence of the Duke's terrorist act to the other judges. They will have no choice but to convict and execute him."

"You have much faith in the Queen's dog."

Lionhart sighed. "He will not betray her. Emilia is...a monarch worth serving."

"Do you resent me for what's transpired?"

"To be perfectly honest, Your Highness, I do not blame you. I blame myself for focusing solely on the capture of the smugglers." He slammed his fist against his desk, making an ink pot dance on its surface. "I should have considered Emilia's safety first and sent Ambrose. I will not make the same mistake again!"

"I agree. She needs to be well protected to survive in her position."

Lionhart grinned and rubbed his hands together. A fire reignited in the spymaster's eyes. "I think I know what to do."

"What about the smugglers? Have you learned anything?"

The spymaster's excitement from earlier fizzled out at the mention of the troublemakers. "I have not dared to go near the dungeon for fear that I may kill them."

"Their leader—Sara Sayeed—I think she hails from the Reyniel Kingdom."

"That would not surprise me," Lionhart replied, stroking his chin. "I know that Duke Malette and the King of Reyniel are tied in business. Hmm, now that I think about it…" He clenched his jaw and slammed his fist down again. "Yes, it makes sense! I should investigate…"

Thessian figured the man was off in his own world of mussing as his muttering continued even as Thessian was leaving the office.

Rain battered the capital on the morning of Duke Malette's execution, swallowing Newburn into its grey gloom.

Thessian had to make certain the duke's head rolled off his shoulders once and for all. No mistakes could be made when Emilia remained indisposed. The thought that she could not witness the sight cheered him up and brought his mood plummeting down at the same time. She deserved to know that this was her achievement. The former king's cousin who coveted the throne deserved the fate he got. Had Malette stayed quietly in his duchy, perhaps things would have turned out differently.

Despite the miserable weather, a crowd began to form at the foot of the makeshift execution scaffold. Nobles and commoners alike buzzed with excitement, eager to see the duke's demise once word of his villainous acts spread. He could have destroyed half of the capital with the serpentine powder he purchased from the smugglers. Whether the people realised the depths of danger they were originally unaware of was anyone's guess.

Thessian spotted the Queen's dog, Viscount Clayton Armel, arriving in his carriage.

Lord Armel got out without an escort, his face gaunt and eyes sharp. He pulled a hood over his head and went over to the scaffold to speak with the guards.

The executioner joined them, and soon after, he began to sharpen his sword for theatrical effect in front of the crowd. Malette was, after all, a nobleman and could not be beheaded with an axe.

In a way, Thessian wished for him to be drawn and quartered or publicly tortured instead of a swift noble death of a beheading. Too bad the old judges chose the humblest of punishments.

A chill crawled up Thessian's spine when his eyes met with Lord Armel's. There was nothing but murder in that man's fierce glare.

On a certain level, Thessian could not blame him. He felt equally as guilty for the state Emilia wound up in. That guilt gnawed at him with each passing day she remained unconscious.

Lord Armel finished his discussion and came up to Thessian. Side by side, and under the roof of a tailor's store to keep out of the rain, they exchanged no greetings.

Another unmarked carriage arrived, followed by a troop of city guards that cleared the bystanders out of the way.

The door opened to reveal Duke Malette's hunched-over figure and two knights sitting across from him.

Dame Calithea climbed out of the carriage and yanked on the rope tied to Malette's bruised wrists.

The duke cussed and nearly fell flat on his face as he descended the steps. Muttering things under his breath, he was marched to the foot of the execution stage.

Calithea handed over Duke Malette's restraints to a guard, who chained the prisoner to a tree stump at the centre of the stage.

"Emilia will pay for this!" Malette yelled. "How dare she do this to me?"

The executioner readied the sword and waited for Lord Armel's command while Calithea quickly read out the charges to the public. No doubt she did not wish to prolong the event for much longer.

Malette turned his head to one side, and he spotted Thessian beyond the crowd. His eyes widened with recognition.

"YOU!" That one word was filled with enough venom to kill a man. "So that's why she was able to escape her tower! You planned this, didn't you? Of course, you did. She is nothing without someone like you. All along, she's been your pu—"

Lord Armel gave a quick nod, and the executioner followed through with the order.

Malette's head rolled off the stump and fell onto the scaffold with a loud thunk. Blood stained the scaffold, yet the crowd cheered and jeered.

The duke's accusatory stare remained in place even after life bled out of his glassy eyes.

The air around Thessian cooled a few degrees, so he glanced at the Queen's dog.

Lord Armel's gloves became covered with frost. "A word of warning for you, sir. Should my master die, come what may, I will stop your beating heart." He produced a light nod to signal his departure. "Now, if you will excuse me, I must attend to other matters."

The Queen's dog seemed indifferent to the fact he had threatened the Hellion's Imperial Family. Oddly enough, Thessian knew Lord Armel would sacrifice his life to fulfil his dark promise.

# 27

# LOVE OR DUTY?

## LAURENCE

**Laurence stared blankly** at the cobweb-riddled ceiling of the inn's room. He could not move a muscle. Once again, Khaja's head rested on his chest, and her leg wrapped around his body as if he were some sort of sleeping aid for the beastwoman.

He huffed and tried for the last time to move her off him. Despite her slender appearance, she was as heavy as a bear.

Her leg peeled away from him, and he found himself staring right at her silver eyes.

She smiled.

The cut on her lip was a harsh reminder that she had no boundaries when it came to showing her affection for him.

Laurence turned his face away.

*"La-oo-ren-z ne heslich?"*

"Look, Khaja, I cannot understand you." He pushed at her

shoulder, and she shifted away from him.

Sitting on the bed beside him, she tilted her head to one side. *"Vosie ne kaiedes moin kadachek. Vosie ne kaiedes tsessen. Vosie ne kaiedes Khaja?"*

Laurence ignored her and clambered off the bed. He did not dare sleep undressed in her presence. All he had to do was wash up before meeting with the rest of the group.

*"Vosie ne kaiedes Khaja?"* Her voice quivered as she demanded an answer to the question he could not fathom.

Laurence glanced over his shoulder at her. He knew nothing of her culture, her language, or her beliefs. Fighting in wars for the Empire to escape his parents' stifling control was the only thing he did well.

"Whatever it is you want from me is not going to happen. I have someone I promised to marry. I cannot betray her trust."

Her eyes watered as if she understood him. *"Mir?"*

He shook his head.

Khaja hung her head, and her hands with protruding claws balled in her lap.

From where he stood, he could not make out her expression. Was she going to attack him? Kill him? Run off again? It was impossible to predict her behaviour, and he dared not attempt such a feat.

*"Jya otarkert vosie. Nare sier yast nur vibezn."* She hopped off the bed, wiped at her sniffling nose, and jumped through the window.

Laurence rubbed the back of his neck. He needed her cooperation to reach her tribe or whatever was left of it. Yet, acting as her mate was out of the question. He did not wish to deceive her heart in such a vile way. He may have spent a lot of his youth sleeping around, but he never once promised anything to anyone. Both parties knew what they were getting into—no lingering feelings or attachments.

A knock on the door told him that the group meeting was about to begin in Ian's room. He rolled his shoulders and proceeded to greet Eugene on the other side of the door with a weak smile.

Once everyone was present in Ian's room, Laurence rested his elbows on his knees. "Eugene, Sergey, what did you find out? You came back so late, I thought something serious had happened."

Eugene replied, "There was a cave-in. The entrance to the mine was sealed off, and we were trapped along with the miners. Thankfully, they had dug another tunnel in case something like that happened, which led up the mountain. Took us a while to get back down."

"That was dangerous," Laurence commented. "The Hollow Mountains are infested with monsters."

"That may be," Sergey added, "but none came out to greet us. It was so quiet, we thought we were on the wrong mountain."

Ian joined in, "That is unusual. We should investigate what happened to the monsters."

"I agree," Laurence piped in. "Let us all visit the mine today."

Sergey scratched his stubbly jaw. The fellow was beginning to lose his youthful appearance with his blond facial hair burgeoning. "We were told by the miners they found large lizard scales in the tunnels. Some even saw the monster's eyes glowing in the dark."

"Did you encounter the beast or see these scales?" Ian asked.

Eugene and Sergey shook their heads.

"Then the information could be a hoax to scare us off," Ian suggested.

Laurence had no idea what to expect. If the giant monster was real, they could be in danger when fighting in a tight space. Even worse, the tunnels could collapse on top of them.

"We will split into two teams," Laurence ordered. "Ian and I will enter through the main entrance if it has been cleared of rubble, and the rest will go in from the mountain. I will give you some healing potions His Highness provided in case of an emergency. They are hard to come by and cost a fortune, so use them only if one's life is in danger. Understood?"

The trio nodded.

"What about Khaja?" Yeland, their quietest member, asked.

Laurence tasted bile. "She has taken off."

"You do not make a good watchdog," Ian commented.

Glaring at the elf, Laurence countered, "Would you like to take care of her?"

"Why? I am not her chosen mate."

"Nor am I!" Laurence snapped.

Ian glanced at the squad leaders. "Leave."

The men wordlessly marched out of the room one at a time.

Once the door clicked shut, Ian continued, "A word of friendly advice for you, Sir Laurence. Beast folk are not known for their patience. A single night of copulating with the beastwoman may save your life, and we need her for the mission His Highness entrusted to us."

Laurence stared at him, aghast at such a foul suggestion. "Are you telling me to sleep with Khaja to appease her?"

"It is not as if Dame Cali does not know your record with the fairer sex."

"Leave Calithea out of this!"

"You hesitate because of your promise to Calithea, but don't you think she would agree with this if it meant we complete the mission and return early?"

Shooting upright, Laurence spat out, "I have heard enough!"

Ian did not get the hint. "Consider the situation where the beastwoman takes you by force or learns of Dame Calithea and attacks her. As we have discovered, Khaja is quite nimble, strong, and fast."

"You are extremely chatty since we left Newburn…"

"I speak when I must and am silent when needed."

"Then I suggest you speak of this no further."

Ian gave Laurence a pitying look. "Very well. I have spoken my mind. I will wait for you downstairs."

Laurence waited until Ian was gone and punched the nearest wall. A throbbing pain spread from his bleeding knuckles to his forearm.

*How can everything be so black and white to him?*

Deep down, Laurence knew that Calithea was not the type to hate him over a single night of unfaithfulness. She even agreed to become his mistress instead of his first wife if he wanted to remain a part of the Oswald family.

Heavy was his mind. *Do I prioritise my fiancée or the mission? Love or Duty?*

He cursed.

As Laurence climbed into the saddle, a familiar man approached.

Laurence sat back in his seat and steadied his horse. "What brings you here, Paul?"

Baron Lucy's guard inclined his head in greeting to Laurence. "Greetings. My lord wishes to invite you and your comrades to dinner this evening."

Laurence glanced at Ian, who nodded, and then back at the guard. "Tell Lord Lucy we happily accept his kind invitation."

Paul bobbed his head. The poor sod's leather boots looked so worn, Laurence could see his big toe poking out. Laurence pitied the guard who had such a cheap master.

"We must be off," Laurence informed Paul. "See you in the evening."

"Wait!" Paul shouted after them as the horses began to move.

Tugging on the reins, Laurence halted his horse. "What is it?"

The guard's lips pressed into a grim line. His dark circles were evidence that the man had not slept a wink the previous night. Whatever was eating away at him, Paul did not seem ready to release into the world. "I apologise. I misspoke."

Laurence gave a slow nod and urged the horse to a trot. He felt Paul's eyes burning holes in his back until they were out of the guard's line of sight.

# 28
# THE DRAGON'S HEART

## LAURENCE

**Laurence and Ian arrived** at the mine to witness the sight of hard-working miners, drenched in sweat and dirt, lugging boulders around. Fewer people were present than Laurence took note of in the wagons the previous day. A number must have been injured during the cave-in.

To his surprise, the opening was already half-cleared. Most of the miners probably worked through the night to clear the rubble.

Under the shade of a black tent, Baron Bald Lucy pointed his finger at the workers as he huffed orders. Instead of Paul, who delivered the message to them that morning, a man clad in mismatched leather armour and with a sword strapped to his hip stood behind the baron.

Laurence's eyes met with the stranger, and he felt a cold shiver creep down his back.

He nudged Ian in the side. "Who do you suppose that man with Bald Lucy is?"

Ian took a brief study of the man. "A mercenary."

"I thought so, too." It made sense for Baron Lucy to keep at least one guard around during his outings. The sentiment towards the Village Chief was not a positive one. Yet, the unpleasant feeling Laurence got from the man had him instantly on guard.

Putting forth his best smile, Laurence approached the Baron. "Good morning, Lord Lucy. Have you come to assess the damage to the mine?"

Bald Lucy peeled his eyes away from the exhausted miners. His expression brightened when he saw Laurence and Ian. "Yes. I came to help as soon as I heard there was trouble. These people would spend another decade clearing out the entrance if I did not come here to supervise them."

Despite Laurence's annoyance, he said, "You are doing a wonderful job, my lord. The tunnel is almost cleared. The miners will be able to return to work in no time."

Puffing out his chest, Bald Lucy boastfully replied, "I think so."

"Is this your new guard?" Laurence inquired.

Up close, the guard had several long scars on his left cheek as if a large cat scratched him there once. His upright posture reminded Laurence of a trained knight. That mercenary was no milk drinker.

The Baron glanced over his shoulder. "Oh, him? That's Ollie."

"Ollie?" Laurence repeated, half-believing that the name was a real one. It certainly did not match the blood-thirsty air around the guard.

"Yes," Lord Lucy replied readily. "He lives not far from the village. I often hire him when I come to inspect the mine. Are you here for your inspection, too?" He feigned sadness as he clasped his hands together. "As you can see, the mine is not accessible at this time."

Laurence beamed at the Baron. "That is quite alright. We have time before dinner."

The Baron smiled back. "Indeed..."

"I think we shall take a short walk around," Laurence informed with a curt bow.

Walking away from Bald Lucy, Laurence's unease grew with every step. He could not put his finger on why that foolish noble gave him such an unpleasant feeling.

"What do you make of Bald Lucy?" Laurence asked Ian in a low voice.

"He acts foolish on the surface."

"You think he is putting on a show?"

"I cannot be certain."

Laurence frowned. He had not considered the fact that Bald Lucy could be the cunning sort. After all, the noble's behaviour until now indicated otherwise.

*And yet, Bald Lucy keeps his accounting books well-hidden and knows to bring an intimidating guard with him to meet the commoners.*

The mine's entrance was cleared when the sun reached its peak position in the sky. After a long night and morning of hard labour, half a dozen workers had collapsed from exhaustion.

Eventually, Lord Lucy caved to the pressure from the miners and sent them back to the village in the wagons.

Not long after, the Baron had Ollie pack the tent, and they left in a carriage that was too fancy for the surroundings.

"Shall we go inside?" Ian asked as he toyed with one of his daggers.

"We should. We may even get to see the monster everyone has been talking about."

"Let us hope not."

Laurence picked up one of the hanging lanterns at the entrance to the mine.

Ian made quick work of lighting the wick with flint and his steel dagger.

A lonely, warm light began to glow in the glass case. Laurence closed the lantern and nodded to Ian.

They ventured into the mine, walking along the well-travelled paths of the miners. The footfall was heavy and easy to follow. The darkness that had swallowed them whole made Laurence thankful for the rusty lantern in his hand.

"I think I see something." Ian strode on ahead. His hand rested on the hilt of his dagger, making Laurence do the same.

"What is it?" Laurence tried peering past the elf but couldn't with the limited light. He wondered how Ian managed to see beyond the small light bubble they were in.

Ian paused in front of an object lodged in the wall. "Doesn't this Dragon's Heart gem look odd?"

Laurence stuck his head around Ian's shoulder. He brought the lantern closer to the wall to see it better. Amidst the dirt and stones embedded in it sat a dull brown rock that was almost no different to a garnet of poor quality.

"Are you certain this is the Dragon's Heart? Isn't it supposed to be blood-red?" Laurence rubbed his jaw in thought as he recalled one such eye-catching gem in the emperor's crown. There was no comparison.

"It is. I can feel this gem emitting faint mana."

"Then why does it look so—"

"Depleted?"

"Yes."

"Perhaps it has something to do with the monster the miners saw," Ian replied.

Laurence felt for his weapon out of instinct. "We should keep our guard up."

"Agreed." Ian used his dagger to chip away a piece of the gem, which he slipped into his pocket.

"I do not think it will fetch a good price on the market."

"I was going to study it when we return," Ian retorted.

Laurence could never win against the elf. "Let us get going. We have a date with Baron Lucy to keep."

They continued their journey to the sound of their boots hitting the rough ground and bouncing off the encasing walls. Yeland,

Sergey, and Eugene had to be in the mine somewhere—no doubt they would meet them along the way.

After an hour of travelling down several winding paths and dead-ends, Laurence was beginning to lose hope in finding any kind of monster. There were no beast tracks, no scales, no growling—nothing.

Deflated, Laurence finally said, "This is a fruitless endeavour. There is no monster here."

"We cannot be certain of that. There is still much to explore."

"It is too quiet for a lair of a beast. Monsters are territorial. If there was anything in this mine, it would have come to greet us when we set foot inside."

"The beast could be intelligent."

Laurence rolled his eyes. "I have not met many intelligent monsters in the Hollow Mountains. Have you?"

"The goblins are quite intelligent. They find a nest and lure victims there by kidnapping people."

"Goblins are pests, nothing more."

"We are all beasts, Laurence, only of a different kind."

Laurence let out a laugh. "Is that some elven wisdom?"

"No. It is simply my observation."

Stopping in his tracks, Laurence made Ian halt as well. There was too much bad blood between them, yet Laurence could not understand the reason behind it. He may have produced a little white lie to the elf to take him along for some fun in Newburn, and they may have caused a bit of trouble, but so what? Ian had never opened up to anyone. He never even attempted to get along with anyone else in Thessian's elite unit.

*Always alone. Always on guard.*

"I keep wondering, Ian, why did you save Prince Thessian's life?"

Even with the headscarf on, Laurence could tell the elf was furrowing his brows.

"I mean, your kind tends to avoid dealing with humans as much as possible. You keep to yourselves and only venture out into the world to form trade relationships. Someone like you, who has great fighting skills and smarts, to be rotting away in a remote village in Darkgate... Why?"

Ian looked around the passage. "This is not the best place—"

"There is no one here! We have nothing but time on our hands. May as well get to know one another. Although, you know everything about me."

"I suggest we leave such serious discussions for later."

Laurence ground his teeth and clenched the handle of the lantern. "Come now. What are you so fearful of? It is not as if you killed the King of Shaeban and ran away."

Ian's eyes flashed with fury at the mention of the former royal family of Shaeban. He slammed Laurence against the wall.

The glass of the lantern nearly smashed, but Laurence moved his arm just in time.

"I suggest you watch your words, Laurence. There is a limit to my patience."

Prince Thessian never revealed anything about Ian to anyone. It annoyed Laurence to no end, especially since he believed himself to be Thessian's closest confidant. Ian's presence in the elite unit was questionable at best. The elf may be a skilled warrior, but he had no idea how to work as part of a unit. There was no need for a lone wolf in the army.

"What happened to the honorifics?" Laurence asked with a smirk. "As for patience—" Laurence pushed Ian away and snarled at him, "—mine also has a limit. Not only were you openly telling me to cheat on my fiancée, but you also neglected your duties as a member of our team."

"I have completed every assignment given to me."

"You do not let anyone in! No one knows who you are and if you can watch their back when lives are at stake."

Ian's expression was hidden by his headscarf, but Laurence knew he had stumped the elf into silence.

Looking at the ground, Ian remained silent for a long time.

Laurence was about to apologise and move on when his comrade finally spoke. "I am the last member of the Wysaran Royal Family, Prince Iefyr Wysaran. We were betrayed by the elders, and our clan was destroyed overnight. Is that enough information about me, Sir Laurence?"

Laurence let out a slow whistle. "Well, colour me speechless, Your Royal Highness."

Ian glared at him.

"Very well." Laurence raised his hands in defence. "I will not prod the hornet's nest any longer."

"Thank you."

"Still, a prince serving a prince of another nation? Isn't that betrayal of some values?"

"The second my family were struck from history books in Shaeban and branded as traitors, I lost any claim to the throne."

"Are you seeking vengeance?"

Ian did not reply, which gave Laurence an answer regardless.

Squaring his shoulders, Laurence said, "Do not drag His Highness into your revenge plan. He is working hard to gain the position of Crown Prince. If you jeopardise—"

"I would never betray the man who took me in while knowing my true identity."

Laurence let out a sigh of relief. "Good. Feel free to ask me to help with whatever you need."

Ian stared at Laurence with wide eyes. "You would help me?"

With a cocky laugh, Laurence replied, "Of course. We are part of the same unit. May as well call us 'family'. I only wanted to get to know more about you, Iefyr."

His heart reached out to the elf who had been banished from his homeland and had his family slaughtered on the public square like some petty criminals. Stories of the downfall of the Wysaran Royal Family, who peacefully ruled Shaeban for over four centuries, were on the lips of every noble in the Empire ten years ago. Although their lifespans were on par with beastmen, this meant that for those ten years, Ian lived through his nightmare and stayed in it to plot his revenge. He even cooked for Thessian's men upon occasion, albeit giving them food poisoning in the process.

*Wait a second! According to the empress, Wysaran royalty were educated in poisons and antidotes since birth.*

"Did you purposefully poison the food to be taken off the cooking rota?"

"We should get moving." Ian snatched the lantern and walked off.

*You sneaky little—*

Two hours later, they came across their comrades at a fork near the entrance of the mine. They found nothing of note nor evidence of a beast residing in the mine. All that was left was their dinner with Bald Lucy.

Laurence spent the entire ride back to the village stewing in anger. He could not believe that Ian would dare to purposefully poison Thessian's men just to get out of doing chores. The next chance he got, he would write an angry letter to His Highness and reveal the truth.

*Who am I kidding?*

Thessian probably knew all along, which was why he never ate when it was Ian's turn to prepare a meal. Because of their backdoor camaraderie, Laurence and the rest of the knights had to suffer through explosive diarrhoea more than once.

"Sir Laurence, you are about to burst a vein in your forehead," Eugene joked.

"Oh, I wish I could burst some foreheads…" Laurence muttered under his breath and looked up, noting that they were not far from the village.

The sun had set beyond the mountains, and the remnants of the dying light gave the run-down Dragon Village an eerie appearance with sharp rooftops. No one dared to wander the streets after sunset due to a possible monster attack. Not like there were any well-trained guards to defend the villagers. Thankfully, the soldiers at the Northern Watchtower did a good job of keeping the monsters at bay.

A handful of lanterns provided spotted illumination of the main dirt road. Smoke rose from the chimneys as people lit the fires in their homes to stay warm at night.

After traipsing around the mine all day, Laurence wanted a nice hot bath and a comfortable bed to sleep in. Yet, he had to keep the dinner appointment with Bald Lucy. Hopefully, the guard from earlier had returned to his residence in the middle of nowhere.

Laurence got a bad feeling from Ollie. No doubt, the man had killed his fair share of men and regretted none of their deaths.

"We will head for the baron's home from here," Laurence announced when they reached the village.

"All of us?" Sergey inquired, yawning on his horse.

"Yes. All of us were invited," Laurence replied.

"He must really enjoy entertaining," Eugene commented with interest.

As a man of common birth from Darkgate, Eugene hardly ever attended any events where nobles were involved. At most, he had participated in a victory parade through the capital with the rest of the knights in Thessian's elite unit.

"Hopefully, there will be some good food." Sergey rubbed his belly. "I think I've lost weight with the slop they serve at the inn."

Laurence chuckled. "Baron Lucy enjoys showing off. We will sleep well sated tonight."

He noticed Ian glancing his way. They were too far apart for Laurence to ask what was on the elf's mind. At the same time, he once again recalled Ian's shenanigans with their rations and grumbled under his breath all the way to the baron's manor.

# 29
# LAST OF THE SMUGGLERS

## THESSIAN

**Another day had passed** without Emilia opening her eyes.

Sitting in the dining room, Thessian ate his breakfast without tasting it. The guilt he felt for letting her catch an arrow for him kept him up at night. He was drained from worry to the point where he considered negotiating with the Pope for another healing miracle.

*If one healed her wound, surely, the second miracle could awaken her.*

He banished the thought.

The Church of the Holy Light did nothing for free. Everyone of rank had an agenda and used their influence to meddle with foreign politics. Allowing Pope Valerian to make Thessian, a prince of the Empire, indebted to him would hurt his chances of becoming the Crown Prince. And, if Emilia's goal was to make him Emperor, Thessian was not about to jeopardise her plans.

*I have to believe in her ability and trust she knows what she is doing.*

Calithea cleared her throat, announcing her entry into the room. "Your Highness, I came to give you a report."

Thessian pushed his unfinished food away and crossed his arms. "Speak."

She swallowed nervously. "I have begun transferring my duties to Sir Jehan Wells—a man Her Majesty chose as my replacement as Guard Captain. He seems capable and knowledgeable in warfare—"

"Get to the point, Calithea!"

Cali winced and tightened her military stance. "I thought he would be useful as part of your military. He served King Gilebert as a general and knows his way around the battlefield. His strategizing is sound, too."

"He is Emilia's person. I am not about to deprive her of a Guard Captain. Is that everything?"

"Sir Jehan Wells is going to duel with Vice Captain Lacroix on the training grounds this afternoon. Would you care to see the fight?"

Thessian rubbed his jaw in thought. It could be an excellent opportunity to assess the skills of the men who would be in charge of guarding Emilia when she awakens. "I will observe the fight."

Cali gave a curt nod and bowed. "If you permit it, I shall take my leave."

"Dismissed."

Not a single cloud marred the perfectly blue sky above Newburn when the duel was about to begin.

Thessian took his seat on a bench, and Calithea stood beside him with her arms folded behind her back.

From his seat, he could see the factions that had formed within Dante's Royal Guard. Count Baudelaire's men were off to the left of the training grounds while Thessian's soldiers formed a group on the right. In the middle of the dirt field between them stood two men.

An older, bald gentleman—Sir Jehan Wells—whose appearance spoke of harsh years on the battlefield. He wore a shiny steel armour. Thessian assumed it was fresh out of the smithy.

Sir Jehan proudly patted his breastplate as if the kingdom's armour meant the world to him.

Opposite Jehan was a man Calithea identified as Sir Regis Lacroix. He seemed to be in his early twenties and a knight from Count Baudelaire's territory. Not a single scar marred Regis' passable face. From experience, Thessian could tell that Regis was cocky and believed himself to be the winner of the battle from the outset.

Since Emilia put her money on Sir Jehan's victory, Thessian expected the fight to be a good one.

Resting his back against the wall, Thessian asked Calithea, "Who do you think will win?"

"I have never seen Sir Jehan fight, so I cannot judge his proficiency with the sword. As for Sir Regis, he is quite competent for a man who learned his skills in fight arenas."

"Has he won against you?"

"No."

"Not that skilled then."

She let out a low laugh. "Sir Laurence spent many hours torturing us when we were recruits."

"All for a good reason. Otherwise, you would be dead the second you set foot on the battlefield."

Her expression grew grim.

Loss of comrades was inevitable during wartime. Thessian had lost plenty of men to unexpected enemy movements as a junior commander. Many years away from home and seeing death daily taught him that life could be cut short in a matter of seconds. The same could be said for his engagement to Lady Clarissa von Leutten, daughter of Marquess Leutten of the Empire.

Thessian spent his youth courting her every opportunity he got by gifting her flowers, exchanging letters, and attending events together. He was too blind to see the rift growing between them due to his busy schedule as a prince. Going to war at seventeen was the final nail in the coffin. When he was at his lowest, after losing two thousand men in an ambush, he received a letter asking for the annulment of their engagement. Little did he know she had never loved him. All along, Lady Clarissa had feelings for someone else. That was the terrible truth he realised upon receipt of a wedding invitation a mere month after his father officiated the annulment.

"Your Highness?" Dame Cali called, full of concern. "Is the duel boring you? Should I not have suggested you witness it?"

Thessian dispelled the longing he felt for his ex-fiancée. It happened over a decade ago. He needed to move on.

*Why am I still affected by her? It is not as if she is the only woman in the world.*

Lifting his gaze to the ongoing fight, he noticed that Sir Jehan Wells and Sir Regis Lacroix were evenly matched in strength when their swords collided. Jehan had fewer openings for attacks and a solid defence which the young knight had yet to master.

The men from both sides of the training grounds were shouting their support for their respective choices. Somehow, Thessian could not find it in him to be interested in the spectacle for much longer.

"I will leave the rest to you, Dame Cali," he said, getting up.

Loud cheers erupted from the gathered knights, drawing Thessian's attention.

On the ground lay Sir Regis, with Jehan's sword pointed at his throat.

Thessian chuckled. *Emilia chose her Guard Captain wisely.*

The next day, Thessian received a report from Cali that Lord Armel had captured the last of the smugglers. As he stormed over to the dungeon, his blood boiled with pent-up anger, which had no outlet for days.

He avoided dealing with Sara Sayeed and her company for fear he may kill them too soon. Every fibre of his being wished for them to pay for harming Emilia. So, for the time being, he was letting them enjoy the comforts of filthy prison cells.

Thessian passed the dungeon's guards, who sported a pallid complexion. After descending a flight of stairs and reaching the middle of a stretching corridor, he found Lord Armel standing in front of Sara's cell. In his hand, the Queen's dog held an ice dagger, and with the other, he squeezed a kneeling woman's shoulder.

"Speak. Who do you work for?" Lord Armel demanded in a tone as frosty as the air around him.

Thessian quietly approached them, feeling his skin stinging from the biting chill. He discovered that the ground had been covered with a sheet of black ice after almost slipping on it.

Sara banged against the metal bars of her prison. "How dare you touch my daughter? I'll kill you!"

Lord Armel let out a maniacal laugh.

Thessian halted his approach. *The man has lost it.*

"Kill me?" Clayton asked, full of mockery. "Worry not. You and your daughter will only find peace once I have my answers."

Sara spat in the assassin's direction and diverted her attention to the shaking girl on her knees. "Don't worry, Rose. We'll get out of here. I promise."

"Promises are for those who have the power to keep them," Clayton warned. "Do you not agree, smuggler?"

As if Rose weighed nothing, Lord Armel lifted her and plunged the ice dagger deep into her stomach.

Flailing mid-air, Rose cried out in agony. Tears streamed down her face. "Mother, it hurts!"

Thessian noticed something was wrong with the girl's arms. They weren't moving as much as her legs. Taking a few more steps, he realised that Rose's arms were at the wrong angle in their sleeves.

*Such torture of women is inhumane.*

Thankfully, the girl would pass away from the mortal wound inflicted on her soon enough.

"Rose! Rose?" Sara bellowed as she sank to her knees. "My darling daughter!"

Clayton asked one more time, "Who do you work for?"

Sara's tearful eyes filled with venom. "As if I would tell you!"

"I guess we shall repeat the process then."

Lord Armel dropped Rose onto the stone floor. He knelt next to the dying girl and placed his hand over the wound. A warm light emitted from the assassin's hand, and Thessian felt sick to his stomach.

*He is not planning to do this again, is he?*

To confirm Thessian's fears, Clayton brought Rose near death again, and again, and again.

With each healing, Clayton's complexion visibly worsened.

Finally, Sara abandoned her stubbornness. "I do not know who I work for! They kept their identity hidden during every meeting!"

Clayton discarded the numb girl on the floor.

Rose's eyes no longer responded to stimuli. She had to be in shock from constant near-death revivals.

"Do not take me for a fool, smuggler," Clayton replied. "Surely, you suspect who your client is."

"Fine! As long as you promise not to touch my daughter and heal her, I will tell you everything."

"Hmm."

Sara finally noticed Thessian's presence. "What are you doing here, traitor?"

Thessian closed the remaining distance, stopping a few steps away from the bars, and crossed his arms. "I came to see the ones responsible for hurting my friend."

Lord Armel said, "You should not be here, Your Highness."

"Dante has no living male royalty left..." As if answering her own question, Sara's eyes widened. "Ooooh! There is only one man who matches your description. You! You are Prince Thessian of the Hellion Empire, aren't you?" She did not give a chance for him to respond and continued talking with a growing sneer. "I got to fondle The Bloodthirsty Demon of Hellion. They were right when they said you have the buns of steel."

When Lord Armel raised a brow at the smuggler's provocative words, Thessian interjected, "You were about to tell us who you work for."

The assassin grabbed Sara's neck through the bars and slammed her face against them hard enough to make her nose bleed.

Sara tried to pull away and let out a grunt. "Y-you truly are a monster!"

"Says the woman who was ready to kill an entire city of innocent people," Clayton countered.

She ground her teeth. "It was King Araman Tiberius Cynan."

"The King of Reyniel?" Thessian and Clayton asked in unison.

She gave as much of a nod as she could in her predicament.

Clayton produced an eerie smile and let her go. He walked over to Rose, who had not moved an inch. In a matter of seconds, he created a new ice dagger above his palm and plunged the blade straight into Rose's heart.

The girl let out a cry which was echoed by Sara.

The leader of the smugglers yelled, "You promised to heal her!"

"Your daughter hurt my master," Lord Armel said as if that explained everything. "A fate much worse is awaiting you and your friends. See you tomorrow."

Lord Armel sauntered away.

Thessian stared at Rose's corpse. He had seen his fair share of dead bodies. The way Lord Armel killed her reminded Thessian of the war-hungry men who enjoyed slaughtering their enemies for the thrill.

He spared a glance at Sara, who wept into her palms, no longer interested in his presence.

*Death may truly be the easy way out for these smugglers.*

# 30

# WHISPERS OF WAR

## THESSIAN

**The memory of the cruelty** he had witnessed earlier lingered in Thessian's mind. On a certain level, he could relate to the Queen's dog. Emilia was Thessian's friend, and he was set on ensuring that those accountable for her current state paid the price. If Thessian's father were lying unconscious in that bed, he would also find it difficult to control his emotions.

Equipped with new information, he made his way to the spymaster's tower.

Scaling the stairs two at a time, the stale air and dreary walls made him feel as if time had frozen.

*How did Emilia survive here for seventeen years?*

He pushed away his stray thoughts. Thinking of her reminded him too much of his failure to protect her.

Shortly after, Thessian arrived in the spymaster's office and witnessed Lionhart sitting on a chair with his trousers down.

Lionhart finished adjusting the straps on his false leg and raised his eyes. "Has anyone ever told you, Your Highness, that it is rude to enter someone's office unannounced?"

"Your door was open." Thessian diverted his attention to the books Lionhart stacked atop a storage chest.

Thessian heard the shuffling of clothes and Lionhart's endless mutterings of how rude the nobles were.

A drawn-out silence followed before the spymaster asked, "What do you want? I am in no mood to entertain royalty."

"I came from the dungeon. Lord Armel captured and killed the smuggler who shot Emilia."

"I wish I was there to witness it." Lionhart's voice trembled with anger. "No. I should have killed that smuggler myself."

"The leader of the smugglers also admitted to working for the King of Reyniel."

The news did not seem to surprise the spymaster in the slightest. He sat on the edge of his desk and folded his arms over his chest. "I suspected he was involved. Even after a year-long war, his desire for the Dante Kingdom remains unquenched. The ceasefire was just an excuse for him to build up his forces again."

A war with the Reyniel Kingdom would be disastrous before Dante was integrated into the Empire. Thessian's standing army in Darkgate would take at least two weeks to reach Newburn, and another three to four weeks to arrive at the southern border. He needed eyes and ears planted next to King Araman.

Thessian smirked. *Who better to ask than the leader of an information guild?*

"Have you any spies in Araman's castle?"

Lionhart's hands shot up. "Do you think I am made of gold?" He pushed away from the desk and came to stand before Thessian. Grinning, he added, "But, yes, I have sent my men when I began to suspect the King's involvement with Malette."

"How soon can we know the situation?"

"No need to rush, Your Highness. King Araman will not openly attack Dante. He does not want to lose any more money, you see.

The war with the south of Dante has proven fruitless in the eyes of Reyniel's nobles. That is why he has been using the duke as a scapegoat for his plan to dethrone Emilia. If he could place a puppet on Dante's throne, Araman could take over the land without a fight. It is very similar to what has transpired in Dante already."

"Emilia is not a puppet!" Thessian fired back. "She has free rein as long as it benefits the Empire."

Lionhart chuckled. "Emilia would never allow herself to become someone's puppet. She is too smart for that. And should you ever consider making her a mere tool, I will not sit still."

"I owe her my life, Lionhart. I would not dare do that to my life's saviour."

"Good." Lionhart retreated to his desk and slipped behind it. "I have letters to write, spies to plant, and alcohol to drink. You may leave my office now, Your Highness. Thank you for the update, although I would have gotten the news from the guards in due time."

At the door, Thessian paused. "Are you confident in Lord Armel?"

Lionhart's mouth pressed into a tight line. His eyes reflected concern, but his words were simple and understanding. "Clayton would not dare hurt those dear to Emilia while she is still breathing."

The message was hard to miss: *The Queen's dog would only lose control if Emilia's heart stopped beating.*

# 31
# A TASTE OF GRAVY

## LAURENCE

The Baron welcomed Laurence and his group at the door of the manor. He rubbed his hands together in excitement as he smiled widely at Laurence.

"I am pleased you accepted my invitation, gentlemen."

Laurence grinned back. "As are we, Lord Lucy! We are famished after a long day."

Peering past the noble's head, Laurence found Ollie leaning against the wall.

*So, he didn't leave after his escort duties…*

Laurence looked around in case he could spot Paul, too. The guard wanted to tell him something in the morning, and Laurence could not shake the feeling it may be important.

Bald Lucy slapped Laurence on the back, pushing him deeper into the manor. "Come to the dining room, Sir Laurel. I believe we have much to discuss and celebrate."

*Celebrate? Certainly, putting you in prison would be reason enough to bring out festivities.*

The rest of Laurence's group trailed behind them.

Bald Lucy's mouth moved non-stop. "You have no idea how hard I work for the Crown, Sir Laurel. My hands have almost lost their softness from all of the reports I have to write to His Majesty — I mean — Her Majesty. I am beginning to feel as if I am the only one working in this kingdom!"

*If only Bald Lucy knew his days as a greedy tyrant were ending, he would not be so chatty.*

At some point, Laurence completely phased the Baron's nattering out. When his name got called multiple times, he realised they were all seated at the dining table.

Tasty-looking dishes covered every inch of the lacquered wood. Their plates seemed too empty when compared to the roasted hog at the centre.

"Sorry, I was thinking of how grand a meal you have prepared for us," Laurence said.

Baron Lucy's gleeful expression seemed frozen on his chubby face. "No matter, Sir Laurel. I simply wanted to know if you have found anything of note in the mine." With a wave of his hands, the Baron motioned to the food. "But I must not be rude to my guests. Dig in! Enjoy the supper!"

Laurence considered his words. "We found nothing of interest."

Sharing that much information would not affect their mission.

"We were almost looking forward to encountering the lizard monster the miners were talking about," Eugene said with a hint of disappointment.

The Baron's expression hardened. "Ah, the beast... The villagers have let their imaginations run wild in recent weeks. Their King's passing must have been the reason."

"Were they fond of King Gilebert?" Sergey asked, and Laurence nearly choked on his wine.

Drinking out of a wooden goblet reminded Laurence of taverns — a strange addition to the Baron's extravagant lifestyle.

"Everyone misses His Majesty, King Gilebert!" Bald Lucy proclaimed. He pointed at the mercenary, who was standing in the corner of the room like an intimidating pillar. "Wouldn't you agree, Ollie?"

"Sure," Ollie grumbled, unamused.

"See?" Bald Lucy let out a mirthful laugh. "The people in the Dragon Village *loved* their king."

Laurence felt his mouth straining to retain the smile he forced during the lengthy conversation. No one cared about the deceased King Gilebert or the two princes. They were old news.

The dinner continued with the Baron filling most of the conversation with banter about his struggles with the lazy miners and occasional crimes.

"...Ollie kicked the man in the chest and cut off his hand for stealing from me!" Bald Lucy said cheerfully.

"Dat's grewsum!" Sergey sluggishly shook his head with disapproval.

"I fink I am 'tuffed," Yeland whispered next to Laurence and hiccupped.

Poor lad did not seem to have a high alcohol tolerance. Three glasses of wine were enough to make him slur his speech.

Laurence's stomach ached as it stretched to full capacity from all the roast hog meat he had eaten. He patted his bulging belly and noted that Ian had, as usual, not eaten much. Well, if the elf wished to return to the inn and eat the swill the innkeeper made, Laurence had no mind to stop him.

Bald Lucy rested his elbows on the table and glanced at the clock on the mantel. "It's about time."

"Time fur 'at?" Laurence frowned. His tongue did not cooperate with him, and he made sure not to consume more than a glass of wine.

"I was talking to myself, Sir Laurel. Pay me no mind." Bald Lucy patted Laurence on the shoulder as he leaned in. "I hope you and your men enjoyed the meal. I had the servants pay close attention to it, especially that hog. Ollie caught it near the mountains. Now that the monsters have gone missing, the animals are finally returning."

"Wha you...bout?" Laurence's vision blurred. He tried to rub his eyes and missed his face the first time.

*What's happening?*

He lifted his gaze, only to have the world swimming around him. The Baron's face spun around Laurence's head like a couple engaged in a ballroom dance.

Yeland and Eugene face-planted into their plates.

Sergey yawned so loud, that Laurence's ears rang.

"Oi Bald, did oo poison mah food?" Laurence asked in a pitchy voice.

"Good night, Sir Laurel." Bald Lucy gripped the back of Laurence's head and slammed it into the plate.

Laurence's world grew dark as a final thought danced through his mind. *There's gravy up my nose...*

Each morning brought with it new troubles, and Laurence started hating waking up.

Today was no different.

He peeled his eyelids apart to a banging headache and a picturesque view of a prison cell. His hands and ankles were tightly bound with a rope.

He wiggled around, testing the weight of his clothes.

*All weapons got taken as well.* "Just great."

Somewhere beyond the wall of his confinement, he heard Sergey's voice. "Commander, is that you?"

"Yes. Who else is here?"

"That makes all of us, except for Sir Ian."

Yeland piped in from a distance, "I overheard the mercenaries talking. They found out he is an elf and plan to sell him on the slave market."

Seeing as no one came running when they began talking, there was a good chance they were not being monitored yet.

Laurence rolled to the bars and stretched his neck as far as he could to assess the layout. From his position, he could barely see three cells opposite him. In the last one, he could almost make out Eugene's dark hair against the wall.

"Any weapons?" Laurence asked.

"None," Sergey replied.

"All of mine got taken," Eugene added.

"I'm almost naked, Sir," Yeland commented with a touch of embarrassment.

Laurence put all of his authority into his voice. "Yeland, report your findings."

"While I was pretending to be asleep, two mercenaries walked in through the door on my left. They talked about Sir Ian, checked on our condition, and left."

"Was one of the mercenaries the man in the baron's mansion?"

"No, sir. I did not recognise them."

Laurence took note of the sole exit and moved on. "Sergey!"

"I woke up not long ago. Did not see anyone, but I believe we are beneath Baron Lucy's manor, Commander. There is nowhere else in the village where we could be located if we take in the size of this prison. And moving all of us long-distance would have drawn too much attention."

"Well spotted," Laurence commented. "Eugene!"

"I believe we were drugged with a variation of a drug called 'dwale'. It is commonly taken before surgery in Darkgate and the southern regions of the Empire. The reason we did not pick up on the smell of it had to be because of the array of foods that distracted our senses. We are lucky they did not use too much hemlock or morel, or we would not awaken."

*I doubt it's luck.* Not only were they defenceless, but the mercenaries also took their belongings, which meant the healing potions were taken, too.

Laurence heard the door to the underground prison swinging open.

Ollie's deep voice rumbled throughout the space. "Good

morning, ladies! I have come to help you loosen your tongues."

# 32

# A PRISONER'S LIFE

## LAURENCE

There could be many reasons why Ollie chose Laurence to be questioned first. It could be because he was jealous of Laurence's out-of-the-world handsomeness. Or because Laurence exuded leadership out of every pore of his being. Or perhaps the mercenary did not take kindly to being called 'the only man there who resembled a lady'.

Laurence pondered the possibilities as Ollie shoved him into a chair and secured Laurence's ankles with a rough rope.

They were in a room upstairs, close to the stairs that led to the prison. On his way there, Laurence noted his surroundings.

Sergey's guess had been spot on. They did not leave Baron Lucy's manor and were kept in an underground prison.

The mercenary checked the restraints one last time and straightened up. Placing his hands on his hips, he asked, "Not so lively anymore, are you?"

"I must admit, I awoke with a terrible headache and the foulest of moods. Not only did the cell you placed me in smell poorly, but my feelings were hurt. I thought Baron Lucy and I were getting along famously."

Ollie scowled. "Did the baron hit you too hard? Don't you see what's going on?"

Laurence tilted his head to one side. "I believe we are about to engage in some serious play. I must warn you, my good sir, I have a low pain tolerance. Now that I think about it, there is no need for torture at all. I will tell you all you wish to know."

The man produced a half-hearted laugh. "Who do you work for, and what is your real name?"

"I work for Her Majesty, Queen Emilia Valeria Dante," Laurence replied with a cheeky smile.

Ollie's fist collided with Laurence's left cheek.

*Ouch!*

The pain exploded from Laurence's jawline to his forehead. His banging headache from earlier could not compare in the slightest. A high-pitched ringing filled his ears, and he could taste blood on his tongue.

"I am not a patient man!" Ollie warned.

"I can see that." Laurence spat blood on the hardwood as the ringing subsided. "Very well, my name is Sir Laurel, and I work for Her Majes—"

Another punch flew in from the right this time.

Laurence saw it coming and kicked off, making the chair he sat on fall backwards. His body trembled and ached from the impact, but he spared his face another bruise.

Ollie grumbled under his breath as he righted the chair.

"My, Ollie, what strong arms you have!" Laurence commented. Smiling proved too difficult because of the punch earlier, so Laurence opted for a wink. "I now know you enjoy getting down to business all hot and heavy, but could you tone down on the violence? You see, I have a fiancée these days. I do not think she would appreciate me returning to her with a bruised face. They say she has quite the temper when she's angry."

The mercenary was about to punch Laurence in the gut when the door opened.

Baron Lucy waltzed in with a pleased look on his face when he saw Laurence's state. "Good afternoon, Sir Laurel. How are you finding my hospitality?"

Laurence let out a laugh. "I hate to disappoint you, my lord, but it is quite lacking. There are no beds to sleep on, the food you serve is drugged, and the mercenaries you hire stink worse than a horse's flatulence."

"You are quite a funny man." Bald Lucy chuckled. "Had you not tried to play me for a fool, I may have enjoyed your company a while longer."

"Whatever do you mean?" Laurence asked, aghast. "I am but a humble knight who serves Her Majesty the Queen. Yet, here you are, abusing said knight with boring speeches and lady-like fists."

"Who's got lady-like fists?" Ollie snarled.

Baron Lucy held up his hand, stopping his subordinate from throttling Laurence. "Take a walk, Oliver. I wish to speak with this one in private."

"I'll be outside." Ollie turned on his heel and departed with a huff.

Laurence called after him, "I would wave goodbye if I wasn't a tad tied up!"

Baron Lucy made a show of circling Laurence. The floorboards creaked slightly under his generous weight.

Laurence would have found it intimidating if it was Prince Thessian or Lord Armel or even Ambrose in the Baron's place. Lord Lucy could not hold a candle to them.

Although Laurence had initially misjudged the man's cunningness, he could tell that Lord Lucy did not like getting his hands dirty. Ollie acted as the Baron's hands—or fists—in this case.

Bald Lucy finally careened into Laurence's view. "Who do you work for? It cannot be the new queen. Your Hellion accent is impossible to miss. No Dante royal would hire an entire band of vagabonds from the Empire when there is plenty to choose from within the kingdom."

"That is where you are mistaken," Laurence said with confidence. "No one here measured up to us, and plenty of royal guards got killed during the attack on the king. Her Majesty could not trust the men there and their loyalties, so she looked elsewhere."

The Baron eyed Laurence with sharp interest. Long gone was the act of a foolish lord. "I suppose I could verify your identity through the servants in the palace. As for you going missing, there are plenty of treacherous roads and monsters in these regions. No one would question a group of rogues disappearing, even if they serve Her Majesty. A sheltered child like her is probably too scared to step outside her palace."

*Afraid? Emilia?* Laurence snorted.

"What is so amusing?"

"You should visit the palace one of these days. Her Majesty is not some weak noble lady who gets overwhelmed at the slightest pressure."

Bald Lucy let out a loud guffaw. "What else can she be? The girl grew up isolated in a tower. Her only value is in marrying a suitable man who can rule this kingdom."

A smile froze on the noble's face, and his eyes twinkled with excitement.

"Yes. The young lady *does* need a helping hand from a knowledgeable man." With a hand on Laurence's shoulder, Bald Lucy added, "Thank you for the suggestion. I think it would be prudent of me to visit the Queen once I have dealt with you."

*Is he planning to woo Emilia?*

Laurence gave Bald Lucy's appearance an in-depth assessment. The man resembled an apple. He possessed multiple chins and was old enough to be her father. He may have some riches, but Laurence wagered Emilia had mountains of gold stashed away somewhere. A woman with the power of foresight would not miss out on the opportunity to secure her independent wealth.

Now that he thought about it, Emilia could have warned him about Bald Lucy being a fox in sheep's clothing. It would have saved Laurence a cheek or two.

Lost in his world of schemes, Baron Lucy hummed on his way to the door. He slipped outside and motioned for Ollie to go in.

"Try to get the answers out of him, Oliver, but do not kill him. We can sell him and his friends for a good price to the Rouge Arena."

The mercenary grinned and closed the door behind him.

Laurence swallowed nervously. "So, about those lady-like fists of yours…"

"Commander? Did you need to antagonise him enough to return black and blue?" Sergey called from his cell.

Laurence grimaced and regretted it immediately. His busted lip stung at the slightest movement of his mouth. No matter how he lay on the cold ground, his body ached all over from the forming bruises.

"Best not to bother him," Eugene called from across the prison. "You could be next."

"I think it might be Yeland. He's so scrawny. A bit of pressure and his bones will snap," Sergey replied.

"I can hear you!" Yeland complained.

*A positive thing did come from getting beat up to a pulp.*

Laurence opened his clenched fist. There lay a jagged piece of ceramic. Ollie had to leave the questioning abruptly after breaking the baron's vase. The man had terrible anger issues.

"Did you tell them anything, sir?" Sergey asked.

"They believe we are vagabonds from the Empire. I cannot wait to see Bald Lucy's face when he learns we are, indeed, the Queen's royal knights."

"We may not live long enough to see the baron's face…"

"Eugene, no need to spoil the mood." Laurence adjusted the piece of the vase in his hands and began filing away at the rope restraints.

The piece he chose appeared to be on the fragile side and made of low-quality clay. Getting the ropes off would take longer than he had expected.

*All I have is time on my hands…*

Laurence's stomach rumbled.

*…And an empty stomach.*

"What about Sir Ian?" Yeland asked. "Did you see him?"

"No," Laurence admitted sourly. "They could have shipped him off to the slave market early or are keeping him elsewhere in the manor. Focus on our situation first, men. We cannot help Ian in our current state."

Laurence heard a bunch of reluctant grunts of approval from his men.

*Ian's resourcefulness will keep him alive.*

The elf possessed the smarts of royalty and the skills of an elite knight. A few mercenaries wouldn't put a dent in that smug visage. Even if Ian suffered from a handful of punches, his healing ability would bring him back to normal in no time.

*Unlike me, who is the true victim of looking like a raccoon.*

# 33

# RESTLESS

### THESSIAN

Thessian hopped off his horse at the campsite with Ronne following suit, ready to punish the men responsible for causing a ruckus within the ranks.

Fights among men were an inevitable outcome when the soldiers were on standby.

With no orders and nothing to do, not everyone got along, and as longing for their homeland increased with ennui, they would start to get irritable. Worse still, the absence of Laurence, Ian, or Calithea on-site disrupted the chain of command. It was Thessian's fault for not spending enough time there.

"Your Highness, should I gather the men involved?" Ronne asked behind him.

"Assemble them."

The darkness of the tents seemed to swallow Ronne as he briskly strode towards them.

Walking to his tent, Thessian sensed the nervousness of the soldiers. They knew he was not kind to those who made trouble in his army.

*The instigators of the fight must be sternly reminded of who holds the power.*

He peeled back the canvas and slipped inside his tent.

A sealed letter from Darkgate stood out like a sore thumb on his otherwise empty table.

*It must be a report from Ludwig.*

Thessian tore the envelope open and unfolded the parchment with neat handwriting.

*Your Imperial Highness, the Duke of Darkgate,*

*I wish to report that Renne has arrived safely. The luggage she brought with her caused quite a commotion.*

*We secured the item with great care, but it combusted by magic upon closer inspection. With deep regret, I wish to inform you that the item is not salvageable. We will take care of the disposal on our end.*

*P.S. Renne will provide you with a full report.*

*P.S.S. Please return as soon as possible. I am your secretary and cannot continue to manage the duchy in your stead.*

*P.S.S.S. Should you not return within three months, I will quit. This is not an idle threat!*

*Viscount Ludwig Esker Cressben*

Thessian read the report with care. The item Ludwig referred to had to be Marquess Walden.

*During the interrogation, Marquess Walden combusted? Was he affected by curse magic?*

Four hundred years ago, the kingdoms collectively agreed to ban curse magic, mind control, teleportation, necromancy, and dream weaving. Those practising forbidden magic were executed, particularly in the Empire.

*Of all things, did Walden get cursed by a dark mage?* It made no sense. The Marquess sought glory and political strength. He did not dabble with the unknown.

*Is it Kyros' doing?*

Thessian wondered if he knew anything about his younger brother at all. From the rumours, Kyros enjoyed spending his gold frivolously and selfishly. He kept up with the trends of the nobles and could not leave the Spiora duchy because of poor health in recent years.

*Are all those things a façade?*

*And what of Father's involvement with Julio Grande? Could someone have stolen the Imperial Seal to pardon the experiments on mage awakenings?*

*What has been going on at the palace in my absence these past ten years?*

Lost in thought, Thessian crumpled the letter in his hands without noticing.

He released the tight grip on his fists and exhaled slowly.

Once he had secured a hold on Dante, Thessian planned his next trip to Erehvin—the capital city of Hellion. With a possible uprising led by Duke Malette's family and King Araman of Reyniel, he put those plans on hold. Leaving Emilia alone to handle a war was not an option for him. She may scheme her way out of tough situations, but she did not possess any military experience.

"Your Highness," Ronne called from the other side of the tent.

Thessian slid the letter into the inner pocket of his coat and felt its weight against his chest as he stepped outside.

Two officers stood in front of him, with a straight row of about fifteen men standing at attention to the officers' left. The sight of the soldiers' battered faces and bandaged arms or heads showed the violence that had taken place.

He sucked in a long breath and eyed them in silence before walking down the length in front of them.

The soldiers did not dare raise their eyes. They knew better than that.

On the positive side, all the men involved were from the advance force and not his elite unit.

Stopping halfway down the line, Thessian turned on his heel and yelled out to one of the officers, "Lieutenant!"

One of the officers came over as fast as his gait would allow and stopped in front of Thessian with a salute. "Lieutenant Lyle Warren, Second Advanced Guard, Your Highness."

"Lieutenant Warren, why are my men dishevelled?"

"A disagreement over food rations, Your Highness."

"Are my soldiers starving?" Thessian momentary eyed Ronne over the lieutenant's shoulder, who was standing near the group, before returning his ire to the lieutenant.

"Are the storage tents empty?"

"They are not, sir!"

"Half rations for a week. If they complain, cut it further." Thessian was loud enough that the men involved could clearly hear the threat.

"Yes, Your Highness!"

"Dismissed."

The lieutenant dismissed his men who eagerly scurried away.

Thessian came over to Ronne and placed a hand on the boy's shoulder. "Have Leo and Verena return to camp. Calithea should finish her duties as Guard Captain soon, so they should take charge here until that happens. Inform them that I do not want any further incidents."

"Yes, my lord."

"You may wish to know that Renne arrived at Darkgate safe and sound and is on her way back."

Ronne made a face. "Ugh! That means she'll be testing her weird concoctions on me again. I barely got over the rash from the last one."

Thessian gave Ronne a reassuring pat on the back and headed back to his horse.

Sun peeked through the curtains in Emilia's bedchamber, pulling Thessian out of his sleep. Unable to rest in his room, he stayed with her, in case she woke up, albeit briefly.

He covered his yawn with his hand and found Ambrose still sleeping in a chair by the door.

The head maid had not left Emilia's side once. Her skin appeared pale compared to her usual rosy colour. If he had to guess, Ambrose also lost a bit of weight, as her cheekbones were more pronounced.

Almost silently, Thessian left his seat and approached Emilia's bedside. He looked at her sleeping face.

*She seems so peaceful.*

He tenderly took a hold of her hand and gave it a light squeeze.

*I hope you will awaken soon, my friend. There is much for us to do, so do not leave me for eternal rest.*

His ears picked up on the change in Ambrose's breathing, and he let go.

Thessian stepped away from the bed and pretended to stretch. "Good morning, Head Maid."

Half-asleep, Ambrose shot upright and curtsied. "I apologise for falling asleep in your presence, Your Highness."

"You must be tired. I do not blame you."

"I thank Your Highness for understanding."

His attention returned to the Queen. "Has the physician identified why Emilia remains in this state?"

"Benjamin tried every safe way of waking Her Majesty. She remains unresponsive to all stimuli."

"And what of Lord Armel? Has he used healing magic on her?"

"He has. Many times. According to him, it is not a matter of the flesh but a matter of the mind."

Thessian faced Ambrose. "What does he mean by that?"

"I am uncertain, Your Highness."

"The Queen cannot remain in this state. It has been over a week!"

Ambrose remained silent.

Thessian balled his hands at his sides as his shoulders shook with accumulated frustration. He had been patient and waited. With no progress being made after eight days, he felt useless. If Emilia did not open her eyes soon, the nobles would take notice and fight for control. Several factions could form and vie for the throne, fracturing the kingdom.

He clenched his jaw. *It may be time to have a word with Pope Valerian.*

That afternoon, Thessian found Calithea at the training grounds. He wrapped his coat tighter around himself as the frosty air crept under the thick layers.

The temperature in Dante fluctuated from warm to cold, as if the weather could not fully commit to the arrival of spring.

He took note of the two dozen knights involved in the training. They lay on the ground, arms wide, dripping with sweat and gasping for air.

Calithea had put them through quite a stern exercise regime.

He concluded that the nearly dead men likely belonged to Count Baudelaire.

She and Laurence made excellent trainers for the recruits.

"Cali," Thessian called on his approach.

She inclined her head in greeting. "What can I do for you, Your Highness?"

"We need to speak in private."

"Of course. Please come with me to the knights' quarters. There should be no one there."

It took less than five minutes to arrive in what appeared to be Calithea's office and bedroom. Although tempted to change their place of meeting, he had questions that needed answers.

Thessian rested his back against the wall and folded his arms over his chest. "Have you kept track of the Pope's movements?"

She adjusted her posture and folded her arms behind her back. "Someone saw Pope Valerian and his knight, Sir Erenel, visiting the garden, speaking with the servants, and even coming to the training grounds."

"What did he do at the training grounds?"

"He healed the injured knights, Your Highness."

Thessian tapped his index finger against his arm as he contemplated her words. "And the servants?"

"He merely greeted them and exchanged blessings."

"It cannot be that simple. Pope Valerian is fishing for information."

"Do you believe him to be a threat?"

He nodded. "We cannot know what he is plotting while trying to get on the good side of the palace staff. I will need to speak with him again. Emilia is still asleep despite the efforts made by Lord Armel and the royal physician."

"Then I shall accompany you, Your Highness."

"Not today. Find out as much as you can about Sir Erenel. I dismissed him the first time we met because of the urgency of the situation, but we cannot make a move without understanding the enemy first. Consider asking the Lionhart Guild for help."

Cali gave a curt nod.

He pushed away from the wall and sauntered to where the dame stood. "Any news from Laurence or Ian?"

She let a bit of disappointment show through her military mask. "None, sir."

"Keep me informed in case you hear something." Thessian flashed her a reassuring smile. "Laurence will be back from his mission before you know it."

Cali returned his smile. "Thank you for your kind words."

"I want what is best for those under my command. No matter your origins, you are a woman worthy of your position and have gotten to where you are today through skill and perseverance. If you can keep Laurence in check, that is a boon to all of us."

Her face flushed.

"I believe it is time for me to leave. You may return to your duties, Cali."

"Yes, sir!"

On his way back to the palace, Thessian discovered Lady Riga sitting on the bench in the courtyard and staring into space.

She did not notice his approach and retained a blank expression until he was right in front of her.

Riga blinked and lifted her head. Her eyes widened in surprise, causing her to jump out of her seat.

With a deep curtsy, she said, "Greetings, Your Grace. Forgive me for not taking notice of you!"

He chuckled. This child's demeanour was more ladylike than that of Lady Diane Walden, who was imprisoned in the palace. Not that he cared to find out where. Lady Diane's advances were beyond uncomfortable to tolerate. With Marquess Walden dead, her mental state may completely deteriorate should she stumble upon the news.

"May I ask, how is Her Majesty faring?" Lady Riga asked.

Thessian motioned to the seat next to her. "May I?"

"Yes, of course!"

He sat down on the stone bench, all the while contemplating how much to divulge. "The Queen is in a deep sleep."

"Is her life in danger?"

"Not that I am aware."

"Then when will she wake up?"

Resting his elbows on his knees, he leaned forward. "I do not have an answer for you, Lady Riga."

The girl sighed and fidgeted with her gloves. "Her Majesty promised to introduce me to a magic tutor. Papa told me not to use magic until I have a proper teacher."

"What about when you fought the dragon?"

"That was an emergency!"

"Indeed, it was. The magic tutor you wish to meet is on the palace grounds. His name is Viscount Clayton Armel. I suggest you wait until the Queen is awake to approach him."

Riga's unruly blonde curls fell off her shoulder as she tilted her head. "Why?"

"He is in a terrible mood because his master has been hurt."

"Is Queen Emilia his master?"

"You catch on quick, my lady."

She giggled. "My sisters usually tell me how slow I am at picking up social cues. Thank you for the warning."

"As I understand, you and Her Majesty were involved with helping Calithea get together with Laurence."

Riga's jaw dropped. "How did Your Grace find out?"

"The clues were hard to miss."

"I promise, I only told Dame Calithea what Mama once said: 'Men are more controllable when they are intoxicated' and 'Marriage is the surest way to capturing a man.'"

Thessian scowled as he sat upright. "Hold on a second! What do you mean by controlling an inebriated man? I thought Laurence made the first move."

She clammed up.

Rising to his full, intimidating height, he scowled at her. "Lady Riga, I demand an answer!"

She squeezed her eyes shut and folded in on herself. "I-I suggested to Dame Calithea to get Sir Laurence drunk and then spend the night with him."

"And the Queen?"

"Her Majesty told us we were wrong in using such an approach on Sir Laurence. She told us to right the wrong through conversation."

He relaxed a little after hearing that Emilia did not take part in the entrapment of his best friend. Yet two of his subordinates dared to manipulate Laurence and play him for a fool.

Thessian recalled Laurence's giddiness and excitement before his departure. The man even asked for a raise and was willing to abandon the Oswald name to be with Calithea.

*Did Laurence have feelings for Calithea all along and refused to make a move? And Calithea is not the type to resort to dirty tricks.*

*In the first place, Calithea never held a great understanding of the ways of nobility. At the last Imperial Ball, after the victory parade, Calithea kissed the hands of every lady like a gentleman would. She may have truly thought Riga's suggestion was a custom.*

*Then the culprit is obvious...*

"A word of warning," he began in a harsh tone he used on his soldiers. "Never use such tactics on decent men unless you wish to be the subject of their ire."

"But Sir Laurence and Dame Calithea seem happy."

"Did you not understand me?"

"I apologise! I will do as you command, Your Grace."

"Only time will tell if this event helps or hinders their relationship. Do not get involved and, I implore you, do not listen to your mother's advice about men."

She bobbed her head so much that he thought it would come off her neck.

Thessian ran a hand over his face and excused himself.

Plenty of noblewomen in the Empire tricked men into marriage. The noblemen who trapped innocent women in engagements through their wealth or political power could be described in a similar fashion.

In the end, Thessian thought it best not to intervene unless Laurence showed signs of unhappiness.

# 34

# A BARD AT HEART

## LAURENCE

Two days went by. Or so Laurence assumed, based on the amount of shift changes between the guards that were stationed at the door. His stomach rumbled with dissatisfaction. The stale bread and water provided by Bald Lucy tasted as bad as they looked.

Bored and wanting to annoy the guards, Laurence had produced multiple self-composed songs in his head.

In a hoarse voice, he sang:

> *There goes a fairy maiden*
> *Along the riverside.*
> *Her friendly fairy sisters*
> *Told her not to go out at night.*

*She came across a sailor.*
*His face grew a little paler,*
*For he left all his clothes*
*Along the riverside.*

*She came across a sailor.*
*His face grew a little paler,*
*For he left all his clothes*
*Along the riverside.*

*And so the fairy maiden*
*Donned the garments of a sailor,*
*And went to tell her sisters*
*Of her ventures in the night.*

"Oi, you!" a mercenary shouted, storming towards Laurence's cell. "Keep it down, will ya?"

After Laurence's engaging chat with his new best friend, Ollie—the leader of the mercenary band—his face was a bit messed up. He could barely make out the guard's disgruntled expression as one of his eyes had swollen shut.

*Fortunately, no women are here to see my appearance.*

"Is it my singing?" Laurence asked. "Or the lyrics? I made that one up myself. For you see, I always wanted to be a bard. My parents forbade it, of course. Something about 'the dignity and reputation of the clan being at stake'. Shall I sing you another?"

The guard spat out curses as he rummaged in his pocket for the keys. "When I get in there, I'm going to—"

"Korhyn, get back here!" the second guard yelled. "Oliver warned us against approaching the merchandise."

"He's beaten up, anyway!" Korhyn fired back. "Another bruise or two won't be noticed."

"I said, get back here!"

Korhyn slammed his palm against the metal bars and hissed, "Yer one lucky sod."

"That I am." Laurence blew the guard a parting kiss. "Now

scurry off, little mouse."

That finally seemed to snap the last string of reason in Korhyn. He whipped out the keys, slotted one into the keyhole, and unlocked the cell.

"I'm gonna murder ya!" Korhyn's body vibrated with anger, and his face turned bright red.

Laurence shed the loose ropes on his wrists. Jumping up, he grasped the guard by the lapels and drove his knee into Korhyn's gut with all of his suppressed frustration.

Toppling over to one side, the mercenary gasped for air. His body convulsed from the lack of oxygen reaching his lungs.

"Korhyn!" the second guard's voice drew closer with each heavy step.

Laurence secured a dagger from the suffocating man and waited for the second guard to approach before leaping out of the cell.

Blade first, Laurence rammed the dagger into the neck of the enemy. Without delay, he returned to the cell and made certain Korhyn met the same fate as his colleague.

"Commander, did you get them?" Sergey asked.

Laurence grinned, which tugged on his busted lip. "Ouch! Indeed, I have."

In a rush, he picked up the iron keys off the mercenary's body. As he tested different keys on Sergey's door, a creak of the stairs made his head turn.

"Someone is coming!" Yeland whispered against the bars.

Laurence tossed the keys to Sergey, whose arms remained bound. "I will deal with whoever is coming."

Light on his feet, Laurence approached the ajar door. Despite his calm breaths, he could feel his heart fluttering with nerves. He pressed his body flush against the wall and readied his weapon.

The door creaked open.

In the middle of his strike, he stilled when a familiar head of red hair came into view.

Laurence nearly fell over from relief. "Khaja?"

She turned her head. Seeing him there, she hugged him so tight, that he thought his ribs would crumble. "La-ooo-ren-z!"

"Commander, this is not a good time for a lovers' reunion!" Sergey called as he unlocked Eugene's cell.

Laurence gasped for air. "Can't...breathe!"

Khaja pouted at him and pulled back. "*Jya naveren vosie.*"

"How did you get past the mercenaries?" Laurence paused when a realisation dawned on him.

Khaja came down the only set of stairs that led to the prison, and those stairs were at the core of the manor. He lifted her hands to check for any blood stains. The shirt and trousers she wore were the same ones he gave her.

*At least she did not slaughter them on her way in.*

The beastwoman looked at him with confusion, so he let go. "Sorry, I did not mean to be rude."

Separating from her, Laurence joined the others, who grouped together.

Yeland and Sergey sported bruises on their faces, and Eugene cradled his right arm.

"Are you hurt, Eugene?" Laurence asked.

"I may not be able to hold a weapon, Commander."

"Yeland, take Eugene back to the tavern to retrieve our belongings and horses. Sergey, we are going to find Ian and repay the kind hospitality we received during our stay here."

Sergey's mouth stretched into a wide grin. "I cannot wait!"

Laurence turned to Khaja, who raised a brow at him. He sighed and took a hold of her hand. "Come along, Khaja."

"Think we should tell Dame Cali?" Yeland whispered to Eugene.

Laurence spoke over his shoulder. "Should this get back to Calithea…"

"I saw nothing!" Eugene replied stiffly.

Yeland groaned. "Saw what?"

"Wonderful." Laurence then said to Sergey, "Ian is our priority. Once we find him, we can deal with the rest."

"I can take care of the search while you and the lady take care of Baron Lucy," Sergey offered.

"Good," Laurence said, striding towards the exit. "Let us meet up west of the village."

"Yes, sir!"

They scaled the stairs and split off into groups.

The manor appeared eerily quiet. There were no guards at the top of the stairs or down the lengthy corridor. Once Laurence and Khaja emerged near the dining room, he picked up on the sounds of the Baron's merriment.

Laurence ground his teeth. *Is Bald Lucy poisoning some other unsuspecting victim?*

He could not act rashly. Although Khaja possessed great strength, speed, and fighting abilities, she could not understand a single thing he said. A comrade who could not take orders only amounted to a hindrance. Yet, he dared not leave her unattended for fear of what she might do.

Creeping past the door, they arrived at the corner that led to the entrance hall.

Laurence briefly stuck his head around to check on their surroundings.

Paul stood at the front door with the maid, Maria. They were having a deep conversation in hushed tones.

Gripping the handle of his dagger, Laurence waited until their conversation ended.

Maria pinched Paul's shoulder. "How can a softie such as you work for the Baron? You need to keep quiet," she cautioned, "or you'll be sold off to some unknown place."

She turned on her heels and left towards the kitchen.

Paul bit his nails as he eyed Maria's retreating form. He slumped against the wall, slid down, and covered his face with his hands.

Laurence placed a hand on Khaja's shoulder and whispered, "Wait here."

Whether she understood him did not matter. He snuck over to Paul and pointed the dagger at the guard's neck.

With a growl, Laurence said, "Make a noise, and you die."

Paul's hands slid away from his face. A look of relief washed over the man's face, and he smiled.

In a low voice, Paul replied, "It's you, Sir Laurel! I am happy you are alive."

Laurence frowned. *This could all be an act.*

"Where are Oliver and the rest of the mercenaries?"

Paul looked around nervously. "Should we move? I will answer all of your questions, but we are out in the open…"

*Is this a trap?* One glimpse at Paul's sorry expression relieved some of Laurence's doubts. "Lead the way."

Paul scrambled to his feet and brought Laurence and Khaja to the empty drawing room on the first floor.

The door closed behind them, and Paul blew out a breath. "Sir Laurel, you must leave here. Your lady friend, too. If Baron Lucy finds out you've escaped, he will be furious!"

"I bet he will." Laurence pointed his dagger at the man again. "Answer me. Where are the mercenaries and their leader?"

"Baron Lucy suddenly had a visit from Count Fournier and Marquess Carrell. He sent Oliver and his men away, all except for the prison guards."

A slow smile stretched Laurence's lips. "Did you just say Count Fournier and Marquess Carrell?"

"Yes."

"Great. We are well acquainted."

It had been over six months since Laurence accompanied Thessian to the negotiations with the supporters of the coup. Thankfully, Laurence spent most of his time getting to know the lords who were eager to betray their dreadful king. They were an interesting bunch, but Laurence liked Count Fournier the most. The man exuded power, and his stories about his hunting trips and fights with the monsters were never dull.

"And what of Sir Ian? He's an elf from our party."

"I am not aware of his whereabouts, Sir Laurel. My lord assigns all tasks related to the kidnapped people to Oliver."

"And how many people is that, exactly?"

"Enough to make my conscience heavy."

"You will have your chance to atone soon, Paul."

The guard's face paled. "You are not planning on staying, are you?"

"If you do not wish to help, I suggest you leave and wait in the village. We are about to turn this place upside down."

Paul gnawed on his lower lip. The internal struggle with which the guard grappled was clear on his face. He would be betraying his lord and losing his job. He would also end up going to prison for his deeds. No man would willingly jump into a jail cell.

"I will help," Paul admitted after a long minute. "If I may ask for a favour, could you spare Maria? She did nothing wrong. She needs to support her family in the village, so she doesn't want to lose her position."

Laurence nodded. He did not care whether or not Maria was trialled alongside the baron. She did not make it to Laurence's shortlist of those who needed capturing.

Relief washed over Paul's face. "Then, I will distract Maria and Tolik. They are ordinary servants."

Laurence waited until Paul left the drawing room. He turned to Khaja, who was busy sniffing one of the cushy chairs.

"Do you like chairs?" he asked with a raised brow.

She growled. "*Jya zadech arikesh weto pishgen iya.*"

"I am starting to think we need to use a children's learning aid to communicate..." He motioned for her to come back to him. "We need to hurry. Cannot let the baron and his guests wait too long for our entrance."

Khaja snarled at the chair one last time and took his hand.

On the way to the dining room, Laurence stopped at a glass window. He saw his reflection and groaned. His left eye resembled a plum, his lower lip was swollen on one side, and a bath would have been great to settle the mess his hair had become.

*I hope the lords recognise me...*

Count Fournier and Marquess Carrell couldn't smell him like Khaja. He grimaced at the image of the lords strutting over for a sniff.

*One wolf-like beastwoman is enough.*

Arriving at the doors that led to his destination, Laurence grabbed the handles and sucked in a deep breath. With a wide, crooked smile on his face, he flung the doors open.

Bald Lucy's eyes nearly jumped out of their sockets as he leapt out of his seat at the head of the table. "You should not be here!"

Laurence ignored him. "Lord Carrell, Lord Fournier, long time no see. I hope your treatment here is better than mine is."

Lord Fournier slowly rose from his seat. "Is that you, Sir Laurence?"

"The one and only!"

The Count directed his glare at Bald Lucy. "What is the meaning of this, Baron?"

"T-that m-man is a criminal. Y-yes..." Bald Lucy stammered over his words in a shaky voice. "He pretended to be one of the Queen's royal knights!"

"At present, I am one of Her Majesty's knights," Laurence commented with a shrug.

"What an amusing situation!" Lord Carrell wiped his mouth with a napkin. "I believe you have some explaining to do, Baron Lucy."

Bald Lucy shuffled backwards until his back hit the wall. He lifted his hands in defence. "I c-can explain, my lords."

Laurence heard Khaja's warning growl behind him.

"*I arikesh weto ankota iya!*" The beastwoman pushed her way into the room and pounced on Lord Fournier.

# 35
# A DEN OF SLAVERS

## LAURENCE

Laurence ran after Khaja in an attempt to get to her before she could rip the throat off the Count. "Lord Carrell, please restrain Baron Lucy!"

While on his back, Lord Fournier grabbed the beastwoman's wrists and kept her claws an inch away from his face with sheer strength.

A flurry of snarls left Khaja's lips. *"Jya fera werst vosie, arikesh!"*

"Sir Laurence, where did you find this violent beastwoman?" Lord Fournier managed to ask.

Laurence wrapped his arms around her waist and pulled with all his might. "She is not usually this violent."

Khaja did not budge. At least, she could not get any closer to the count.

"She does resemble a beastchild that attacked me in the Hollow

Mountains about three months ago," Lord Fournier added.

Laurence shifted his grip from her waist to her neck. He wound his arm around it and squeezed her throat enough to reduce the air going in.

She struggled to push Laurence away and, eventually, collapsed into his arms.

Sweat beaded on Laurence's forehead. He wiped it away with his free hand. "We found her in a brothel in Newburn. She was a beastchild then and had a control collar around her neck."

Lord Fournier climbed to his full height and adjusted his dishevelled clothes. "The slave traders must have gotten to her after she fled from our fight."

"You need not look further for the slavers, sir, for Baron Bald Lucy here appears to be involved with them."

Everyone's attention turned to the baron.

Lord Carrell twisted Bald Lucy's arm and pressed the baron's round face into a plate of unfinished sea bass. "Care to explain, Baron?"

"I do not know what that scoundrel is talking about!" Bald Lucy wailed. "Release me! Paul! Paul! Get in here this instant!"

"With a heavy heart, I must inform you that Paul decided to come clean about your crimes," Laurence said and lifted Khaja into his arms.

Lord Fournier came over to Laurence and stared at the woman's face briefly. "We must discuss this lady's existence in more detail. For now, Lenard, let us escort the Baron to the dungeon in Redford for questioning."

Lord Carrell adjusted his grip and pointed a dagger at Bald Lucy's throat. "I will hand him over to our men outside. Come along!"

With a reluctant shuffle, Bald Lucy followed Lord Carrell's instructions, and they left the room.

"Lord Fournier, I do apologise for Khaja attacking you," Laurence added with a bow of his head.

"Why are you defending her?"

"I am acting as her guardian while on a mission for Prince

Thessian."

"That does not mean you must defend her actions."

*Why did I need to stand up for her? She has been nothing but a distraction...*

Lord Fournier, who towered over Laurence, let out a light-hearted laugh. "This is not meant to be an interrogation. Be at ease and let us get you treated at my castle. My daughters would love to meet another one of Prince Thessian's knights."

---

Late that evening, after everyone had been gathered, Laurence's party bundled into different carriages or rode their horses.

Sergey had informed Laurence that Ian had escaped a day prior. The elf assumed they would get away and did not plan on risking his neck for a pointless rescue mission.

For some reason, Laurence was not surprised.

An hour into the journey in Lord Fournier's carriage, Laurence glanced at the beastwoman sleeping next to him. Khaja had not stirred since her fight, which made Laurence assume she had not slept for days.

"If I may ask, what made you visit the baron's home?" Laurence inquired to break the silence.

Lord Carrell replied first, "Prince Thessian asked us to track a young dragon for him. Our investigation led us to the Dragon's Heart Mine and the Hollow Mountains."

"All those stories of a lizard monster are starting to make sense now," Laurence muttered.

Lord Carrell continued, "Before we left, our knights searched Bald Lucy's manor. They found an abundance of evidence of the beast stashed away in a vault alongside some terribly-kept accounting."

Laurence ran a hand through his hair. "Could you send those accounts to Her Majesty?"

"Were you serious when you admitted to working for her?" Lord Fournier inquired.

"Only for this mission. We did not expect to stumble upon a slave trader." *They must be left unchecked in Dante...*

"Bald Lucy is a cunning fox. He used to be good friends with King Gilebert," Lord Fournier said with a sour expression. "I did not expect him to be capturing and selling travellers. Had I known, I would have—"

Lord Carrell patted his friend on the shoulder. "We will know who is behind him soon enough, Edgar."

"Just thinking that it could have been Riga or Volga or my wife who ended up in the hands of Bald Lucy." Lord Fournier clenched his massive fists. "I think it best you do the questioning, Lenard. I may throttle him before he breathes a word."

"I will see to it he sings us a song of truth." Lord Carrell's gaze travelled to Khaja's sleeping form, but he remained silent.

"Is there something on your mind, Lord Carrell?" Laurence asked.

"It is quite marvellous seeing one of the beastmen in the flesh. She managed to topple Edgar in a flash. Strong, fast, and long-living—it is a pity their kind suffered such injustice in the past."

Laurence shifted in his seat. He felt uncomfortable with the dissecting stare Lord Carrell used on Khaja. "Have you come across any more of their kind or a village, perhaps?"

Lord Fournier finally relaxed and stroked his long beard. "Lenard and I take turns keeping the monsters in the Hollow Mountains in check. During my last expedition, I met her along the less-travelled path. As I mentioned before, she attacked me, and I had no choice but to defend myself. I was forced to slash one of her sides, causing her to flee. Riga also sent a letter recently, admitting she killed the Grey Wolf, who was an adult beastman."

"Do you think they could be related?" Laurence asked, leaning in.

"Possibly. I do not believe their numbers are great, otherwise, they would have been discovered much sooner."

"What about you, Lord Carrell? Did you see anything in the

Hollow Mountains?"

"I did notice some areas had monster corpses lying around. I thought the monsters were fighting each other over a territorial dispute."

*At last, a clue!* "Could you show me on the map where those areas were?"

"I will do so when we arrive in Edgar's castle. In the meantime, I advise you to take a rest, Sir Laurence. You are a bit worse for wear."

Laurence laughed. "Yes, if Lord Fournier permits, I will make full use of his hospitality and bathe for an entire day. Prison life is not for me, it seems."

They all laughed and immediately stopped when Khaja let out a disgruntled noise.

---

The next morning, after a hot bath and a meal, Laurence waited in his room for the others. He worried Khaja would go on a Fournier killing spree if he left her unattended.

A knock on the door had him launching out of his seat by the window to open the door for his comrades.

One by one, Yeland, Sergey, and Eugene sauntered into the room.

Ian did not wear his headscarf, letting his long white hair rest on his shoulders, and he carried the satchel the baron had taken from Laurence.

At the door, the elf handed it to Laurence without a word and waltzed inside.

Laurence glimpsed the contents, noting the two healing potions were still there.

He closed the door and assessed everyone's state. A couple of days of torture and starvation did not look well on them.

Yeland, who was on the slim side, had an ashen complexion and bruises all over. Eugene's arm was bandaged by Lord Fournier's physician with a prognosis of a broken wrist. Without a boost from a healing potion, it could take three to four months to heal. Sergey sported some developing bruising on his face and neck, where Laurence assumed someone choked the lad. Even Ian, who healed faster than the rest, was not left untouched by a brutal fist to the face.

Laurence looked and felt no better. *So much for a quick mission for Queen Emilia...*

"What do we do now, Commander?" Sergey asked.

"We take a break," Laurence announced. "I have to write His Highness on our progress, and we need to rest and heal. Especially you, Eugene."

Eugene gave a lopsided smile. "I have to admit, I thought the worst of us would be you, sir."

Yeland and Sergey nodded.

Pointing to his face, Laurence replied, "Does this look like I got away unscathed? My identity as a handsome bachelor is at stake here."

He peered past the men at Khaja. She sat on his bed, legs crossed, in a pink frilly dress the countess dropped off the night prior. He tried not to laugh. The colour and the overblown decorations did not suit the beastwoman.

"There is not much time left," Ian warned. "We have wasted nearly two weeks on a side mission."

"I know." Laurence's humour waned. "We have another two weeks to get back on our feet, find the remaining beastmen, and return to Newburn. I wanted everyone to know where we are at. So, take a few days to rest and recover. See you all at dinner."

The men waved or nodded their goodbyes.

All except for Ian.

The elf folded his arms over his chest. "We should leave the injured here, Sir Laurence. Drink a healing potion to recover and let us search the Hollow Mountains for traces of beastmen."

"I think there are more pressing matters to discuss." Laurence dropped the satchel on the bed and turned around. Placing his hands on his hips, he questioned Ian, "For example, why did you abandon us?"

The elf shrugged one shoulder. "I knew you would find a way to escape without needing me."

"And if we did not?"

"Then you would be unworthy of serving Thessian."

Laurence scowled and did his best not to grab Ian by the collar. "Just because you were royalty once does not give you the right to discard His Highness' people!"

"I did not 'discard' you, Laurence. I had faith in your abilities. After I left the manor, I spent my time keeping a sizeable portion of the mercenaries on my tail to make your getaway easier."

*Arguing with Ian is the same as having a meaningful conversation with a mule. Is it the difference between our races or station?*

Ian did help in his own way and retrieved the healing potions. He had plenty of time to use one on himself but chose not to.

Laurence ran a hand over his face. "Why did you not say that in the first place?"

"It would not have changed the outcome."

*He is certainly a mule.* "Take some time off, Ian. Enjoy yourself. Mingle with the common folk. It would do you good."

"Are you going to delay the mission?" Ian asked, unamused.

"We all need a break. This is non-negotiable."

Ian grumbled and left with a slam of the door.

Khaja crawled off the bed and walked over. She eyed Laurence with those strange, molten-silver eyes of hers.

"La-oo-ren-z, sad?"

Laurence let out a bitter laugh. Of all the words of the common language, she knew his name and the term for sadness.

Well, she was not wrong. Playing the role of a cheerful friend or a foolish third son was beginning to get tiring. As Thessian's second-in-command, Laurence had to act approachable. The soldiers had to feel comfortable reaching out to him, while Thessian wore the armour of ultimate authority. There were plenty of days when his position felt like heavy chains. Yet, he did it to remain by the prince's side.

Laurence rolled up his sleeves and pointed to a table full of blank parchments and an ink pot. "Come here, Khaja. Let me teach you better words than 'sad'."

# 36

# THE PALADIN

## THESSIAN

**After two days of silence** from Calithea, Thessian decided to take matters into his own hands.

Once he finished his breakfast, he headed to the training grounds. When he did not find his subordinate there, he inquired about her with the servants and guards around the palace.

An hour into his search, he stumbled upon a maid often seen reporting to Ambrose.

The young blonde dropped her bucket of water by the well in the courtyard, splashing the hem of her dress and shoes. In her panic, she ducked down and hurriedly wiped at her dress with an embroidered handkerchief she pulled out of her pocket.

Thessian approached her. "Maid, have you seen the Guard Captain?"

The young girl let out a yelp and fell on her buttocks. Lifting her eyes to see him, she quickly seemed to regret her decision and scrambled into a kneeling position before burying her face in the muddy ground. "M-milord, I-I apologise for showing y-you such a s-sight. P-please forgive this incompetent m-maid and s-spare my life…"

He sighed. "You are forgiven. Now will you answer my question?"

"Y-yes, milord. I have s-seen her going in the direction of the relief tents set up for those affected by the fire. S-she visits there every morning."

Thessian stepped back to appear less intimidating. She must have witnessed the slaughter of the king's guards or the king himself to act with such fright.

"I bid you a good day." He inclined his head and turned on his heel in the direction of the castle's gates.

Fifteen minutes later, he came to the large patch of grass that had neatly arranged rows of grey tents erected on it. Thessian was once more reminded of Emilia's generous soul. She sent supplies through the servants and provided protection with the palace guards. Although it was a temporary measure, Thessian could tell by the occasional smiles of those displaced by the fire that Emilia's heart reached her people. Hopefully, in due time, they would come to see her as more than just a Cursed Queen.

In one of the tents, he spotted Calithea chatting with a woman who was cradling her infant.

Cali smiled brightly and offered the woman a small leather pouch.

He furrowed his brows. *Is Calithea giving her coin away?*

Walking away from the woman, Cali saw Thessian. The dame's expression turned serious, and she approached the prince. "Sir, is there anything I can help you with?"

"Follow me outside."

With long strides, Thessian led them to a secluded area by the castle's wall. He turned around and narrowed his eyes on his subordinate. "Calithea, what were you doing there?"

Her posture stiffened to match his harsh tone. "I was gathering information and helping the townspeople, Your Highness."

He relaxed a little. Paying for information was not uncommon. "Did you learn anything?"

"Pope Valerian and Sir Erenel often visit those less fortunate to heal them and spread the word of Luminos. The woman I spoke with said the Pope healed her sickly baby with a miracle."

"The way you speak sounds as if you are beginning to respect the members of the Church."

She lowered her head. "I-I was not able to uncover anything dark or sinister about Pope Valerian. According to my sources, he and his holy knight are working separately from the cardinals of the Church. They have removed a sizeable number of priests and high priests from power over corruption charges and embezzlement."

"Did you hear this from the commoners, too?"

"No. The Lionhart Guild provided a report. They also gave me information on Sir Klaus von Erenel. He is said to be the first-born son of Marquess Erenel, from the Drovia Kingdom. When his powers awakened at the age of fifteen, Sir Erenel gave up his right to succeed the title and became a knight of the Church. Apparently, he is the leader of the Order of the Holy Knights and the sole knight with the power to heal, which gained him the rare title of 'Paladin of Luminos'."

"Sir Erenel must be a devout man, quite strong too to be able to serve as the Pope's only protection detail."

Cali took a step closer and spoke low. "Mister Lionhart said there are rumours that the cardinals of the Church tried to assassinate Pope Valerian on many occasions and failed."

"Why would they wish to assassinate the man they chose?"

"He was not selected by the twelve cardinals. The followers of Luminos chose him as they flocked in droves to the City of Light on the day of the vote, overshadowing the decision of the cardinals who opposed the new pope."

Thessian's brows rose with his astonishment. Pope Valerian and his paladin were a mysterious bunch. It was unheard of for a Pope to travel the land, mingle with the commoners, and be hated by the cardinals.

*That is if any of this information is true.*

The City of Light kept a tight leash on their information leaks. Even the spies from the Empire had a tough time getting out alive and most managed to only report on the day-to-day life of a cardinal or two. The Pope's chambers were unreachable. Only the most devout to the Pope worked there, and they could not be bought. The selection process was based on their faith in Luminos and the Church's teachings. The deeper the faith ran, the higher the position they held. So, it made sense that Valerian Knox was protected by the most powerful holy knight in existence.

"We should not underestimate Sir Erenel," Thessian voiced his thoughts out loud. "As for Pope Valerian, I believe I should pay him a visit. I have been cautious because of the political implications, but Emilia remains unconscious. If I wait any longer, we will have an uprising on our hands."

"Would you like for me to escort you, Your Highness?"

Thessian nodded and started walking towards the palace. "Where do you think the Pope is right now?"

Cali thought for a long second and replied, "Around this time, he is often seen by the guards in the inner courtyard."

"Is he still gathering information from the servants and the guards?"

"It would appear so."

Thessian clenched his jaw. Valerian Knox was no simple man. He had the power of a king in his hands, and the harmless act he put on in front of people drew others to him. But, Thessian was not blind. He could see a venomous snake behind a mask of servility and kindness in Valerian. After Marquess Walden's betrayal, Thessian was not about to put his trust in just anyone. Not even those who served the Empire for decades.

Beyond another set of castle gates, they walked along a winding road uphill. Thessian's mind was overwhelmed with the tough decisions he needed to make. After all, his younger brother could be plotting against him, and his father may be entangled in atrocious mage research. He needed answers, and they would not come falling out of the sky.

Thessian said over his shoulder, "I want information on anyone of note at the Empire's palace and the Spiora duchy."

"I will send a raven, Your Highness."

"No. Someone trusted who can defend themselves. I want a return from Ludwig, and I don't want it left to chance."

His heart ached at the thought of his father sanctioning Julio Grande's research. Yet, the evidence Thessian found at Julio's research station under Emilia's palace was hard to ignore. No matter what excuses he came up with, no one but the Emperor of the Empire had the Imperial Seal.

*Is Mother unaware? Or is she involved too?*

"This is a matter of utmost importance, Calithea. Deal with it accordingly."

"Yes, Your Highness!"

Not long after, they arrived in the inner courtyard.

The Pope was hard to miss.

Valerian was kneeling on the damp grass with his hands clasped together. With closed eyes, he muttered something under his breath as Thessian approached.

The prince did not get too close.

Sir Erenel stepped in Thessian's way and raised his arm enough to stop the prince and Calithea. "Forgive me, Your Highness. His Holiness is in prayer and interrupting him is an affront to Luminos."

"How long is his prayer?" Thessian asked.

"That is known only to His Holiness and Luminos."

Thessian felt the threatening aura of the paladin, who would readily attack anyone who disturbed his master. Perhaps, Sir Erenel served the Pope out of free will rather than as a forced assignment.

Upon observing the man closer, Thessian concluded that Sir Erenel was older than him, yet it was hard to pinpoint the knight's exact age.

Valerian finished his mutterings, and, rising to his feet, he gently brushed the dirt and grass off his knees. "Greetings, Your Highness. May the blessings of Luminos guide you."

Peering past the paladin, Thessian did not return the religious greeting. Instead, he waited until the Pope joined them.

"There is a matter I wish to discuss with you in private, Your Holiness."

The Pope smiled cryptically. It was hard to tell what went on in his head.

"It must be related to the Queen. Let us speak near the fountain. Our escorts can keep prying eyes and ears at bay," Valerian suggested.

"Very well." Thessian gave a curt nod to Cali, who moved away to give them space.

Sir Erenel bowed low to his master and followed suit.

Trailing after Valerian to the central fountain, Thessian could not feel any hostility from the Pope. On the contrary, the man outwardly displayed the best of manners and the patience of a saint.

Thessian decided to skip the needless political pleasantries and got straight to the point. "What do you know of Emilia's condition?"

Valerian sat on the edge of the fountain and lowered his hand into the water. While toying with the flow, he replied, "The Queen has received a blessing from Luminos. There is no need to worry. She will awaken soon."

"What makes you so certain?"

"I pray to God every day on the Queen's behalf. My certainty lies in my faith."

Thessian rolled his eyes. "Faith cannot fix everything."

The Pope took his hand out of the water and wiped it with a handkerchief he kept in his pocket. "Your Imperial Highness does not believe in God?"

"I do not believe in *your* god."

Valerian chuckled and lifted his eyes to meet the prince's. A hint of dislike was embedded in the Pope's green gaze.

"What is it you want from me? If it is another miracle for Her Majesty, then there is no need for it. The miracle Luminos provided for the Queen was the grandest and strongest one I have ever felt.

She is completely healed of any mortal wounds, and all thanks to the god you do not believe in."

"Then why is she not waking from her slumber?"

"Wouldn't it be prudent to ask the royal physician that question?"

Thessian scowled. "Do not play games with me, Your Holiness. I do not know what it is you are planning to achieve here, but if you cannot help Emilia, I suggest you leave this kingdom."

"Oh, but help her I shall. After all, she needs me to ascend the throne with the least resistance from the people and the nobles. With the support of the Church of the Holy Light, her coronation will proceed smoothly."

"And what do you get out of helping her?"

Valerian smirked. "That is between Her Majesty and I."

Thessian held back from punching the Pope, feeling his nails digging into his palms. Whatever plans Valerian had, he wanted Emilia for some reason.

*Emilia is no fool. She will not allow herself to be manipulated by such a snake.* At that thought, Thessian blew out a breath.

"Since you are of no help, I will excuse myself," Thessian added, his emotions back under control.

Valerian stood and offered his hand to the prince. "Would you care for a blessing, Your Imperial Highness?"

"The Hellion Imperial Family bows before no man," Thessian retorted.

The Pope laughed. "Do not forget that the emperor is ordained by God. One day, you or your brothers will end up bowing before God to take the Empire's crown. I will eagerly await the day your proud family is on their knees."

"We have our own priests to conduct the succession ceremony. There is no need for His Holiness to get involved."

"For now, perhaps." Valerian smiled and inclined his head slightly. "Until we meet again. May the blessings of Luminos guide you."

*Hopefully, it will not be anytime soon.*

Thessian stormed off.

## QUEEN OF HOPE

After almost two weeks of debating whether he should broach the subject of Emilia's healing with the Pope, it turned out to be a complete waste of time on his part.

*The miracle to heal Emilia was the grandest? What a load of tosh.*

As an afterthought, Thessian visited the spymaster's tower. He scaled the stairs and stopped in front of the door. This time, he paused and knocked.

"Antonio, I told you to go and find someone else to listen to your romantic failures. I am not interested!" Lionhart barked.

"I am not Antonio," Thessian replied loudly through the door.

On the other side, he heard a lot of shuffling and moving of furniture before a door swung open, and Lionhart studied the prince from under his dark brows.

Blowing his dark curls hair out of his eyes, Lionhart asked, "What brings you here, Your Highness?"

"I wanted to know if there are any updates on the Reyniel Kingdom or the smugglers."

Opening the door wide, Lionhart permitted the prince entry into his office and limped back to his desk where he sat down in his chair. A half-empty bottle of wine stood out amidst the mounds of paperwork. With Emilia asleep, the spymaster appeared to be drinking his anxiety away behind closed doors.

"There is nothing concrete on King Araman yet. I heard whispers that he is frequently visited by a sage, so I've asked the guild to look into this. As for the smugglers..." The spymaster shuddered. "I pity them for being alive."

Lord Armel waltzed into the room as if he owned the place. "Why would you pity those who hurt our master?"

"Emilia is not my master, boy," Lionhart grumbled. "She is my friend and employer. I do not plan on ever sacrificing for another master."

*Did Lionhart give up his leg for his master?*

Lord Armel rested his back against a bookcase and folded his arms over his chest. His black attire and raven-coloured hair made his skin seem unnaturally pasty. "You will be pleased to know, Lionhart, that the smugglers are dead."

Lionhart blew out a breath of relief. "Thank the gods!" He wagged his finger at Lord Armel. "You should have killed them sooner. Because of you, I had to deal with endless reports of dungeon guards on duty vomiting from listening to horrible screams."

Lord Armel shrugged one shoulder. "I did what I could to extract information out of them."

The assassin, who lacked compassion, only seemed to care for Emilia. The memory of how Clayton tortured Sara's daughter was still fresh in his mind. As someone who killed thousands of people over the years, Thessian was not new to death or slaughter, but he did not enjoy pointless torture. He preferred to dispense a swift death upon his enemies over a drawn-out one.

"Did you learn anything new?" Lionhart asked, resting his elbows on the table.

"I did. The chemists told me they were taught how to mix the serpentine powder by a sage from the Reyniel Kingdom. The name may surprise you."

"Get on with it!" Lionhart pressed.

"It is Lina Galleran."

Thessian frowned. "The sage is a woman?"

Lionhart's expression turned sour at the mention of the sage's name. "She is a wretched soul who is willing to sell her services for the things that pique her interest. It seems King Araman has met her needs."

"What do you know about her?" Thessian asked.

"Lina is nothing short of a genius in matters of the natural world. She may not be a mage of the Mage Assembly, but the contraptions she creates would have the best researchers in the Empire questioning their credentials."

"Is she dangerous?"

Lionhart raked his fingers through his messy hair. "She is a disaster waiting to happen. First, she created a poison that could not be detected even by silver. Now, it's an explosive powder that can wipe out cities... To answer your question, Your Highness, yes, she is very dangerous."

"Then she must be dealt with." Thessian's unease grew. He could not allow an individual like Lina to roam the land with the possibility that her knowledge would be used against the Empire or its people. "Lord Armel, are you not planning on pursuing this woman?"

The Queen's dog raised a brow. "Not unless my master wants me to."

Lionhart added, "It would not be a good idea to send a band of assassins after Lina when she is under the protection of King Araman. Best to play the fool until we know enough about her deal with the king."

"Are you saying it could be something other than gold?" Thessian asked.

"Lina can't be bought with money. Whatever Araman has, it must be interesting enough for Lina to stick around and offer her services over a long period of time."

Thessian pinched the bridge of his nose. The more he learned about King Araman and his kingdom, the more of a threat they appeared to be. Sooner or later, a war with Reyniel was inevitable. But, until there was a clearer picture of Araman's plans, he had to proceed with caution.

"Worry not, Your Highness." Lionhart broke through Thessian's train of thought. "I will deal with the information gathering. It is what I am paid for, after all." He got up and pointed to Lord Armel. "See me outside for a moment."

Thessian held up his hand. "Lord Armel, the head maid said you told her of Emilia's condition being a matter of the mind. What did you mean by that?"

"I see no reason why I must report to you." Lord Armel pushed away from the bookcase and walked out of the office.

Lionhart followed after the assassin, leaving Thessian stunned and alone.

They were not gone long as the spymaster returned a minute later.

Unable to contain his curiosity, Thessian asked, "What did you say to him?"

"I told him that he should not overstep his bounds with the Queen. After all, Clayton must never forget that he is a pawn of a monarch and nothing else."

"Even though Emilia sees you and the rest as her friends?"

A look of sadness swept over the spymaster's face as he picked up his bottle of wine and uncorked it. "There may come a day when even Emilia will need to harden her resolve and make great sacrifices."

# 37
# HOPELESS

## EMILIA

**Emilia sat up in bed and yawned** as she stretched her arms. No doubt the day would be filled with more paperwork. After the Great Newburn Fire, she vowed to organise a proper fire department or even hire a group of men to be on the lookout for fires. Then, she planned to find out what happened to Thessian after the fight with the smugglers and deal with Pope Valerian.

She opened her eyes and instantly froze.

The sight before her wasn't her bedchambers.

She rubbed her eyes and pinched her cheeks.

*Ouch! Well, that didn't work...*

Her heart raced at the sight of her bedroom from her previous world. The walls were grey and almost bare. Emilia cared more about books than the living. As such, her room had three floor-to-ceiling bookcases of novels she had read over and over again despite knowing every single line in them, a bed, a wardrobe, and a desk where she neatly arranged her notebooks, stationery, and laptop.

Even the poster of the book cover for The Cruel Empire was hanging on the wall by the door with the author's flashy signature.

How many times she had used the memory of that image to soothe her pain and fall asleep in the cold and silent tower she found herself in? Emilia had lost count.

"No... This cannot be happening! I died!" She clutched her hair and pulled on it. The pain of her strained roots told her she was, indeed, back in her old world and the straw-coloured locks she clung to proved it.

"Emily!" her mum called from downstairs. "Get moving!"

Her heart sank at the sound of her mother's voice. Sucking in a deep breath, she tried to focus and get out of bed, but her hands shook with nerves, and her limbs did not obey.

Even after all those years in Dante, Emilia still dreaded the sight of the woman who pushed her to her limits and asked for nothing but perfection.

"I'm hallucinating..."

"Don't make me call for you again!" her mum hollered from downstairs.

The threat made her shiver, but the last thing she wanted was to see her mum and return to that lonely and unfair world.

"I want to go back to Dante. I miss Ambrose and Lionhart. How is Thessian going to survive if I'm not there? And Clayton—"

Panic began to wash over her. *Was my life in Dante only a long and weird dream?*

"Emily! You have to apologise to the dean and your professor today!"

*Wait...What?* Emilia shuddered at those words. *Apologise?*

"Is today the day I die?"

Her body began to move on its own as if someone wrapped her limbs with invisible strings. She climbed out of bed and slipped her feet into a pair of grey slippers that matched the rest of the dull furniture in her room. Or maybe, the entire world was a grey mass of objects without distinct flavour or soul.

With limbs as heavy as steel, she put on her jeans and a green T-shirt with her university's logo. Her mind filled with a fog of thoughts from the old Emily, pushing away Emilia's consciousness beyond an invisible wall.

*I can't believe they want me to apologise to him! He stole my work!*
*Why won't anyone believe me?*

She gnawed on her lip. It stung from the open cut that formed there since she learned Professor Olsen published her thesis on National Economic Disparity in Middle-Class Households under his name for peer review.

*What did I do so wrong?*
*Why me?*

After tying her greasy hair into a ponytail, she splashed some water on her face in the bathroom and forced herself to brush her teeth.

Emily fought back tears upon seeing her reflection. She must have gotten two or three hours of sleep last night. Dark half-moons rimmed her sunken grey eyes. Her skin was dry from a lack of facial treatments and moisturisers, and her eyebrows needed a good plucking.

*Not like I have anyone to impress or look pretty for…*

Upon returning to her room, she picked up her rucksack and shoved her laptop and a book on Macroeconomics inside. Sealing the bag, she blew out a breath.

"I just need to get him to confess. A few words of admission from him will do."

Making her way downstairs, she braced herself for her mum's reaction. Last night, they had another fight. As always, it ended with Emily being a terrible disappointment to her parents.

*What use is eidetic memory when everyone only cares about appearances?*

Inching past her mother's office, the floor under her feet let out a groan.

"Emily?" A second later, her mum swung the door open.

Emily's mother was a beautiful woman in her late fifties. She stood a few inches taller than her daughter and never went anywhere without having her grey hair pinned in a perfect updo and expensive makeup to match her outfit for the day.

To her mother's dismay, Emily took on more of her father's facial features. Her jawline was square, her nose long and straight, and her lips were on the thin side.

After letting out a deep sigh, her mum folded her arms under her ample breasts. "You better come back home only after properly apologising. Get down on your knees if you have to. Do you know how embarrassing it is to have a daughter who got into a top university only to slack off and spend her time reading trashy books?"

"I didn't slack off, Mum! Professor Olsen *stole* my work! How many times do I have to say it?"

Her mother raised her hand. "Enough!" She checked her golden watch. "I have a video conference with my clients in five minutes and will be gone for the rest of the day. Go, apologise, and come back home. Got it?"

"What about Dad?"

"He left this morning for a business trip to Morocco. Don't bother him with your excuses."

Emily gritted her teeth and nodded once.

"Good." Her mother returned to her office and shut the door.

The tension in Emily's body did not dissolve. Feeling her mother's indifference to her situation hurt more than the betrayal she felt from her mentor. Even her dad did not care to check in on her once in the past two weeks. He claimed to be busy with work, but Emily knew better. Expecting love or affection from her family was a pointless gamble. The only person who truly enjoyed spending time with Emily was her grandmother, who had passed away two years ago.

She sniffled and wiped at her runny nose with the back of her hand. "I miss you, Nana."

Emily left her house, which was located in a quiet cul-de-sac. A few days ago, her stomach began to ache, and she stopped feeling the pangs of hunger. This gave her more time to do her research into how to get her professor to confess. He wouldn't let anything slip with the dean present, so she needed to visit Professor Olsen in his office before the meeting.

She peered over her shoulder to the front door of her house.

*There is no going back.*

Emily's hand trembled over the door handle to her professor's office. She nearly spat at the silver plaque with his name on it as it stared back at her.

*Remember control. Controlling my emotions means controlling everything. I have my phone set to record. I just need his admission...*

Blowing out a breath to steady her shaking, she lifted her hand and knocked twice.

"Come in," came Professor Olsen's gruff voice.

She swallowed her nerves and turned the handle with her sweaty hand.

The professor's bright smile faded when he saw her. Wrinkles creased his large forehead that went up to his receding hairline. Turning in his office chair and away from his desk, his round belly came into view, tightly wrapped in a white shirt and brown cardigan.

"Isn't our meeting scheduled for twelve?" he asked in a harsh tone. "Miss Grace, I believe you have got the time and place wrong for your apology. Unless...you wished to apologise to me in private beforehand." He smirked and nodded to himself as if that made sense in his head.

"I'm not here to apologise for you stealing my work, Professor!" she snapped back.

*No. No! Get a hold of yourself, Emily! You need to be calm for this to work!*

He let out a harsh laugh. "Miss Grace, I don't know what you have imagined in that head of yours..."

Emily clutched the hem of her T-shirt to stop herself from lunging at him. "Sir, how could you do this to me? I gave you all the files of my work and research on a USB drive for feedback, not for you to publish them under your name."

"Young lady, I think it's time for you to leave." He reached for his phone.

She took a step towards him and fell on her knees. "Please, Professor, tell the truth! Why did you do this to me? Why did you steal my work?"

At that moment, through blurry vision marred by tears, she saw a wide grin on his face.

Professor Olsen knew what she was trying to do.

Her plan was a complete failure.

He dialled a code on his desk's phone and picked up the receiver. "Mary, could you call for security? There's a troubled student here causing a ruckus."

Emily hung her head and stared blankly at the stained carpet under her palms. Her tears wet the scratchy textile as her plan came apart.

*Is this it? Do I have to apologise to everyone for the wrong I didn't do? Do I carry the brand of a college failure, a useless daughter, and a friendless weirdo for the rest of my life?*

Sometime later, she felt strong hands grasping her by the arm and pulling her upright.

"I'll take her outside," the security guard told the professor.

"Be careful with her, Sean. She's in denial and a bit too emotional."

Emily glared at him from under her brows. "Too emotional? You stole my work!"

When she tried to get close to her professor to land a punch on his smug face, Sean wrapped his arms around her waist and carried her kicking and screaming out of the office.

"You better calm down before I call the police on you!" Sean warned.

A laugh of defeat left her lips. She sagged in his arms, and he dropped her in the hallway. Covering her face with her hands, she cried her eyes out on the spot to the judging eyes of other students.

The school's secretary, Mary, came over and placed a hand on Emily's shoulder. With the other, she offered a handful of tissues. "Here. Take this and clean yourself up in the bathroom. You will feel quite silly later if you keep crying in the hallway like this."

Emily grabbed the tissues, wiped her snot with them, and sluggishly picked herself up.

Sean stood nearby, close to the professor's door, most likely in case she tried to go back.

"Do you want me to accompany you to the toilets?" Mary asked in a kind voice.

"I can get there by myself."

*One step...*

*Two steps...*

*Three steps...*

*Four...*

Emily kept counting the steps to the nearest toilets and hid in the last cubicle. Behind the closed door, she slid down and used her rucksack to muffle her screams which quickly turned into more tears.

The door to the bathroom clicked shut, and two girly voices filled the room.

"Did you see the videos?" the first girl asked with a laugh. "Some idiot tried to attack our Economics professor!"

"I heard she's not all there in the head," her friend replied. "What's her name? Elly Cade? Emma Grace?"

"It's Emily Grace! She was in one of my electives last year. You should have seen her. She walked around all self-important and didn't bother talking to anyone. She sailed through the class because she has an amazing memory, apparently."

"How unfair! I would kill for a good memory. I have to cram everything before every test."

The first girl replied, "Wanna know my guess? She got lazy and didn't do the work, so when her parents found out, she blamed her mentor."

Her friend gasped. "That's horrible!"

"Yeah, those rich kids from elite private schools always get in on their parents' money. Poor Professor Olsen got the short end of the stick."

Emily shrunk in on herself. *I can't go out there.*

*Do I quit uni? They said there are videos of me out there.*

She buried her hands in her hair. "What if my parents find out? Mum and Dad will never forgive me for embarrassing them like this…"

"Did you hear something?" the first girl asked.

"It's probably someone filming themselves. Let's go."

Evening fell over the city.

Emily dragged her feet to the bus stop. She spent hours in that toilet cubicle, crying her eyes out, and no one cared. Eventually, she was kicked out by the cleaning lady and had to leave the empty premises.

Heavy rain came crashing down on the busy street she walked on.

The people around her scrambled for shelter. A few of them bumped into her, almost sending her flying onto the road full of traffic.

By the time she was drenched like a rat, she thought, "My laptop's probably dead."

*Does it even matter anymore?*

Emily could already envision her parents' disappointment and anger at her failure. But her tears no longer came out. It was as if a hole had opened up in her chest and swallowed all of her emotions.

She felt cold.

Numb.

Useless.

*Is this all I amount to? Is there any point in continuing only to be hated and misunderstood by those around me?*

Before she knew it, she was home, sitting on the living room sofa in the dark.

Her phone vibrated in her pocket. She peeked at the caller ID to find it was her mum calling.

Emily cringed and answered the call. "Mum, I—"

"Can't you do anything right? I just got out of a difficult meeting and had multiple voicemails from your dean and professor. How could you attack your mentor? Are you insane? Should we admit you to a mental facility?" Her mother groaned. "Emily, when I get back tomorrow, I am dragging you back there to apologise!"

Emily did not reply.

"Did you hear me, young lady? You better write a letter of apology in the meantime. I don't care if it takes you all night. You just need to read it once to memorise it anyway."

"Alright, Mum. I'll do that."

Her mother blew out a heavy breath. "Good. We can still salvage the situation. You will need to repeat a year, but it's not the end of the world. Just keep your head down and get it over with."

"Okay."

"You're suddenly compliant. Good. See you in the morning." Her mother ended the call.

The phone slipped from Emily's hands onto the floor with a soft thud. Without realising it, she was once more overwhelmed with pain that cut so deep, she thought her racing heart would rupture. She gasped for air as her shaking hands reached for her throat.

Huddling on the floor in a ball, she wished for it all to end—her torment, her misery, and her suffering.

But God was not on her side that day.

Perhaps, He abandoned her long ago, because once her lungs took in oxygen again, and her breathing, eventually, evened out, she was left in the same bottomless pit of wretchedness as before.

*I can't do this anymore...*

*I'm not strong like Thessian, who was also betrayed by his family.*

*I'm not strong like Mother.*

*I'm a failure...*

As Emilia relived the day of her death, she banged on the

invisible wall that separated her from controlling her former body.

"Don't do it, you idiot!" she screamed at her past self. "Don't do it, Emily! Not again!"

Quitting university and starting all over wasn't the worst thing that could happen. She could find a job and move out of her family's home. She had her whole life ahead of her.

*How many times have I wished to redo this day while I was trapped in that tower? How many other ways had I found to keep on living in this world?*

*Too many to count.*

Dying wasn't the answer. She knew that. That was why she fought so hard to survive Thessian's coup of her kingdom. She wanted to live, away from pain and uncaring parents.

She wanted to love and be loved.

Emilia wept as she hollered between her tears for Emily to stop taking the sleeping pills.

How many she took? Emilia lost count.

And all that remained was an embrace of the cold and unwelcoming darkness.

# 38

# OVERCOME WITH SORROW

## LAURENCE

**After four days of rest** at Lord Fournier's castle, the bruises on Laurence's body and face had gotten lighter. He felt even better when he learned that Ollie and his mercenaries were caught.

The next day, he planned on visiting Ollie in prison for an affectionate reunion. After all, Laurence owed that man a few punches to the face.

However, even as the night had long since claimed Redford, sleep eluded him.

Meanwhile, Khaja draped her milky leg over his middle, making him glance down. Nothing had changed since they reunited. She slept on top of him and refused to stay in the room alone. At least, her affection for him did not push the boundaries past sleeping on the same bed. She no longer pinned him down or attempted to ravage him, for which he was thankful.

As if sensing he was looking at her, she burrowed her face in his neck and inhaled deeply. Her ample breasts pressed against his arm, and the smell of lavender and thyme oil in her hair filled his nostrils.

A shiver travelled down Laurence's body, and he slapped himself on the forehead.

*I will not think inappropriate thoughts. I will not!*

He peeked at his lower half and groaned.

*Too late.*

Laurence ran a hand over his face and attempted to sit up. To his surprise, he managed to separate from Khaja without trouble unlike all of his previous attempts.

Taking this God-given opportunity, he scrambled off the bed and made his way to the window with the view of the moon-bathed Hollow Mountains in the distance.

*This is a natural reaction to a beautiful woman lying on top of me.*
*I do not find her attractive. I will not find her attractive!*

Once they found Khaja's tribe and the mark was removed, he would be able to return to Calithea and live out the rest of his life in sacred matrimony.

*Just a bit longer, Laurence. You can do it.*

"Laurenz?" Khaja called as she sat up and rubbed her sleepy face.

Since she began learning the common language, she got a lot better at pronouncing his name. To his surprise, she consumed knowledge at an incredible rate and, in a matter of days, was able to memorise multiple words from the common language.

He waved for her to go back to sleep. "I am fine, Khaja. Rest up. I plan to take you to see the town tomorrow."

Her wolf ears wiggled, and she started to crawl towards him on all fours.

He raised his hands and said in a stern voice. "Sleep."

Khaja hesitated and sat back on her haunches. "Laurenz no sleep?"

"Yes."

"Khaja no sleep."

He shook his head and approached the edge of the bed. "You know, you are quite stubborn."

The beastwoman smiled and caught his wrist. She pulled him down onto the bed before wrapping her limbs protectively around him.

*This is going to be another long night...*

---

In the early hours of the morning, Laurence penned his reports to His Highness and Queen Emilia. He kept them short and sweet, with a dash of frustration in Emilia's letter. She could have warned him about Baron Bald Lucy being a conniving slave trader.

After handing the letters to Lord Fournier's butler, Laurence's stomach rumbled.

"Breakfast will be served in the dining hall shortly, Sir Laurence. Please head there with your lady," the butler said with a bow.

"She's not my—" The butler walked off faster than Laurence could finish his sentence. "I hope this does not get back to Calithea..."

On their way to the dining hall, Laurence spotted Countess Fournier sitting on a lonely bench in the inner courtyard. Her long blonde hair was loose around her slim shoulders, and her pretty face was displaying a deep-set frown for all to see.

Laurence studied Khaja's reaction for a moment. When the beastwoman did not pounce on the lady, he assumed the beastwoman was fine with the countess' presence.

Taking this chance, Laurence sauntered over to her ladyship and bowed his head in greeting. "Good morning, Countess Fournier."

Lady Estelle blinked away her tears and wiped at her face with a handkerchief she was holding.

Rising off the bench, she replied, "Good morning, Sir Laurence.

I do apologise for allowing you to see such a terrible sight."

He waved his hands in the air. "I would never think the sight of a beautiful woman is offensive."

Lady Estelle let out a gentle laugh, which she covered with her gloved hand. "Thank you for your kind words. Is there anything wrong with your stay?"

"Your hospitality is perfection itself, your ladyship. If I may, what is causing you such upset?"

The countess looked down at the letter she was clutching under her handkerchief. "I received word from Riga. It appears she has caused a bit of trouble for Prince Thessian."

Suddenly, Laurence was all ears. "What happened?"

"She got involved in a relationship between two of the prince's subordinates and gave them awful advice. I told her, time and again, that I often jest and not to take everything I say seriously. But that child...Riga is not very good at reading social cues and has been like that since she was little. Every time I or Edgar would say something, no matter what it is, she would quote us as if it were gospel. A part of me hoped she would get better if she saw the world outside the castle walls..."

Laurence pitied the unlucky souls who wound up listening to a twelve-year-old for romantic advice. Just how desperate did they need to be to ask Riga out of all the knights in Prince Thessian's army?

"Worry not, I am certain things will work out. Lady Riga is in good hands at the palace."

Lady Estelle pressed her lips into a grim line. She inched closer to Laurence, making him lean in. "Riga told me that the Queen is in deep sleep and has not woken for almost two weeks."

"What?" Laurence's yell startled the birds in the trees. He looked around, noting that no one else was there. "How did that happen?"

"Queen Emilia took an arrow for the prince."

Laurence barely stopped his mouth from hanging open. Emilia possessed the bravery of a veteran knight, and even they might not willingly give their lives for His Highness at a critical moment. His respect for the young queen grew tenfold.

"Riga also wrote that the Pope came to Newburn and healed the Queen with a miracle, but it did not help."

"The Pope is there, too?" Laurence paused and furrowed his brows. "Wait, that is not the biggest problem here. I ask that you tell Lady Riga not to share such sensitive information in her letters. If this gets into the wrong hands, who knows what our enemies might do?"

Lady Estelle waved his worry away. "There is no need to fret over this. Riga has devised her own cryptic language when she was six. We have been using it at the castle for communication for years. That is how we confirm our identity in these letters."

"Lady Riga is a clever young lady."

"That she is!" Lady Estelle gushed and went on to tell him more stories about her daughters.

Laurence tried to recall his childhood. Most of it revolved around hiding away during his mother's tea parties to avoid the old ladies and sword training with a hired tutor. On the occasions when his father took him to the palace, Laurence got a chance to spend time with Prince Thessian, who was two years older. They bonded over their love for the sword, and Laurence quickly became friends with most of the Imperial Knights in the order.

They slowly made their way to the dining hall, and Lady Estelle excused herself.

Khaja tapped him on his shoulder and pouted.

"What is it?" he asked.

"Laurenz, happy?"

He tried to wrap his head around the meaning behind her words. *Happy about what?*

She pointed at the shrinking back of Lady Estelle. "Pretty?"

*Is she jealous of Lady Estelle?*

He shook his head. "No. Not pretty."

Khaja smiled widely and linked her arm with his. It was something she picked up after seeing Lord Fournier and his wife doing so through the window of their room.

Laurence cleared his throat and nodded to the guard on duty to open the doors to the dining hall. Khaja might have changed her approach in wooing him, but she did not give up on their mate bond.

At the long table, Laurence sat between Khaja and Sergey. Across from him were Eugene and Yeland. As always, Ian was nowhere to be found. Not that Laurence could fault the elf. The last meal they partook in ended up in them getting poisoned and thrown in a dungeon.

Lord Fournier along with his wife and daughters were at the head of the table. The only other person who was missing out on food was Marquess Carrell.

"Sir Laurence, how are you and your men finding your lodgings?" Lord Fournier asked, drawing everyone's attention.

Laurence put on his best smile, which was a bit difficult as it tugged on his bruised face. "We have no complaints. Everything is perfect, Lord Fournier."

The lord stroked his lengthy beard. "That's good. Should you need anything, let my servants know. We would not want to treat His Grace's people with disrespect."

Laurence set his cutlery aside and wiped his mouth with a napkin. "My lord, may I ask why is it you refer to His Highness by his ducal title?"

"The answer is simple. Although Prince Thessian was born into the Hellion's Imperial Family, he earned the title of Duke of Darkgate through his achievements in war. As a man of the sword myself, along with our allies, we use his new title to show our respect."

"I am certain His Highness appreciates the gesture," Laurence replied.

Lord Fournier chuckled. "I have not noticed a change in him. His Grace is difficult to read. Ah, I do apologise, I interrupted your meal. Enjoy the food, gentlemen!"

The knights nodded, and Sergey nudged Laurence in the side with his elbow. "Commander, how did you manage to tame the beastwoman?"

"What do you mean 'tame her'?" Laurence looked at Khaja, who was trying to mimic the way the nobles ate their food. After a struggle with trying to cut the hard cheese with a knife, she tossed the utensil over her shoulder and dug in with her hands.

Laurence turned back to Sergey with a quirked brow.

"I mean, she behaves herself. She hasn't attacked or tried to kill anyone since we arrived at the castle."

Taking a sip of his ale, Laurence pondered on how to answer his comrade. He did nothing special other than spend all of his time with her and sleep beside her. Although, he did teach her a little over two dozen words.

Thinking about that, Laurence's lips tugged into a wide grin. "Khaja." He pointed at his face. "What do you think of me?"

She smiled back at him. "Laurenz pretty."

Sergey gasped.

Yeland and Eugene burst out laughing across from them.

"Sir, I never took you for a pretty man." Eugene stroked his smooth jawline with his good hand. "Handsome on a good day, maybe."

Yeland nearly choked on his food.

Laurence sat back in his seat and crossed his arms. "I tried to teach her to say 'handsome', but it proved to be too difficult for her as I could not show her an example."

"Then how did you teach her to say pretty?"

"I showed her some shiny gems."

Sergey burst out laughing. "She must think our commander is a pretty gem!"

The other men joined in on the joke.

Rubbing the back of his neck, Laurence glanced at the beastwoman. *Who knows what goes on in Khaja's head?*

She finished her meal and licked her fingers.

Laurence grabbed his napkin and started to wipe her hands. "You should learn to eat properly, Khaja."

"Sir, you would make a good mother," Eugene piped in.

"Gentlemen," Laurence began with an edge of warning, "one more word out of you, and you will resume His Highness' training regime after this meal. You're included, Eugene. Injury or no."

The men shifted in their seats and returned to their food, some still struggling not to laugh.

*I may not make a good mother, but I certainly would be a handsome father.*

As promised, after breakfast, Laurence headed to see the town with Khaja. He had pulled a hood over her head to hide her ears and took her hand, in case she decided to make a run for it.

Experience taught him that she could escape his sight at any moment, which would not bode well for the residents of Redford.

Laurence breathed in the coal-infused air. Although most of the snow around Redford had melted, giving way to life beneath, the cold whips of the wind did not let up. It was his first time visiting Lord Fournier's town. During the negotiations for the coup, His Highness and the Dante nobles met in a border village up north, which was a part of Marquess Walden's territory. With Walden's betrayal, it would be difficult to move any more troops into Dante unless they took the treacherous paths through the Hollow Mountains. Thessian would need to rely on the willingness of the local nobles to provide their soldiers. And not many nobles would sacrifice their armies without receiving something of equal value in return.

Khaja stopped in the middle of the street which had stalls set up by the local farmers, weapon smiths, and butchers. She sniffed the air and turned to the butcher's stall.

Laurence sighed. "You just ate…"

She pulled him over to a wooden stall that had different cuts of meat hanging from sturdy hooks.

The butcher smiled at her and rested his elbow on the counter. "How can aye help ye, miss?"

Khaja sniffed the air again and frowned.

Laurence cleared his throat. "I apologise, good sir. My friend does not speak the language well."

The butcher stared at their linked hands. "Yer friend?"

"She gets lost easily," Laurence clarified with a charming smile.

"No matta. Yer tha guests of Lord Fournier. If ye need any help, ask."

Laurence waved goodbye and pulled Khaja back. "Come along. We have much more to see."

Khaja mimicked his wave and followed along.

*So, it wasn't the meat she was after? Did she fancy the butcher?*

Laurence peered over his shoulder at the well-built man who could probably lift a horse. The butcher had a lot of facial hair and seemed to be in his late thirties, but perhaps Khaja liked older men. Or younger... After all, Laurence had no idea what her true age was.

They followed the dirt path to the outer wall, passing pointed wooden houses on either side of them. After an hour-long walk, she did not show any signs of tiring.

At the gates, Laurence spied Ian who was asking the guard something.

Picking up the pace, Laurence waltzed over. "Where are you headed, Ian?"

"There is a place I wish to—" the elf's eyes settled on Khaja, and his speech faltered, "—visit."

"Can we come along? We have seen everything there is to see..."

Ian seemed uncomfortable. "It may not be a good idea to bring her along."

"Why not?"

The elf sighed. "Never mind. She should know what happened."

Laurence tilted his head to one side. "What are you talking about?"

"Come with me," Ian instructed and nodded to the guard.

The guard said something to the others, and the gate was lifted for them to pass.

While following Ian into the forest not far from Redford, he could not shake the trepidation that tugged on his nerves. The more he thought about Ian, the beastwoman, and His Highness, the more he felt his unease growing. Whatever secret they shared, it could not be anything good, and the elf was too tight-lipped to give anything away before it was too late.

"Mind telling me why you are leading us into a forest? Are you going to pick some more poisoned mushrooms?"

Ian spoke over his shoulders but did not slow his stride. "I was not planning on poisoning your food anymore."

"Thank the gods for that!" Laurence let out a nervous chuckle. "Then why are we here?"

Ian did not reply.

Eventually, the elf came to a stop.

Encased by ancient trees on all sides, Laurence looked around. Streams of sunlight pushed through the thick branches and growing foliage, illuminating patches of the forest bed.

Khaja pushed away from Laurence.

He tried to hold on to her hand, but she shook him off and ran over to one of the tree trunks.

Once again, Laurence felt his unease rearing its head. In a stern voice, he demanded, "Where are we, Ian?"

"This is the place where the Grey Wolf died, according to Lord Fournier."

"The beastman who attacked His Highness?"

Ian gave a curt nod. "We need to know if Khaja is related to him. This is our best chance to find out."

A soul-crushing howl startled Laurence. He turned his head in the direction of the sound to find Khaja touching the claw marks on a tree.

The beastwoman released another howl that shook him to the core. He had never heard anyone produce such an agonised cry.

When she looked at him, with tears streaming down her face, his heart sank.

"It seems, they were acquainted…" Ian muttered.

Laurence glared at the elf. "What exactly happened? Report!"

"I am no longer your subordinate, but I will tell you. His Highness and Lady Riga killed the Grey Wolf to protect Redford. You can see the burn marks on the ground here." Ian pointed to a charred circle not far from where Khaja stood.

Khaja sank to her knees, and her entire being folded in on itself. She wiped at the endless rivers of tears that covered her lovely face. Her next howl turned into a shaky whimper.

Gingerly, Laurence approached her and pulled her into a tight hug. When they first met, she was a child trapped in slavery. Who knew what the clients of that underground brothel managed to do to her before they rescued her? Now, she lost someone precious to her.

*A father? A brother? A lover?*

At that moment, his heart reached out to her. All he could do was let her cling to him while she let out the overwhelming grief in her heart.

# 39

# NAMELESS

**Surrounded by stone walls** that dwarfed her, a four-year-old child stood on a wobbly stool.

In desperation, she tried to peek at the world outside through a high window, but her foot slipped, sending her falling onto the cold, hard floor.

She raised her head and stared at the window that seemed to always be just out of reach. It was the only source of light during the days. At night, her world was mostly painted black. It was a time when the darkest of shadows came out with their scuffling, scratching, and often flapping sounds.

Her bony hand reached for the ray of light that could not be captured. Specks of dust danced through it, and she sneezed.

Stomp.

Stomp.

Stomp.

Nameless scrambled to her feet and hid in the farthest corner of the room. Squeezing her body tight against the bone-chilling walls, she waited as the heavy footsteps approached.

Stomp.

Stomp.

Stomp.

Lowering her body, she hugged her knees close to her chest. Her panicking heart pounded in her tiny body with the sound of the guard's booted feet drawing closer.

A minute later, the noise stopped in front of the wooden door to her room. The handle rattled, making the child cover her ears.

"Where're those blasted keys!" the guard snarled from the other side.

A jingle of metal was followed by the sound of the lock to the child's room being unlocked.

Swinging the door open, a huge man entered and scanned the space with a scowl. "Where's dat rat hidin'?"

"Are you daft? How hard can it be to find her in a single room?" An older boy spoke behind the guard. He peered around the man's back and spotted the child in an instant. His wicked smile grew. "There she is! Are you trying to hide from me, Nameless?"

The child chewed her lower lip as the boy approached her and slapped his hands to his hips.

"Don't get too close, Yer Highness," the guard warned. "What if ye catch her curse?"

The boy let out a mirthful laugh. "You think a curse scares me? It's her fleas that would be of greater inconvenience."

"Forgive me, Yer Highness," the guard replied with a bow of his head.

The young prince, with shiny black hair and eyes as blue as the clear skies the child sometimes glimpsed through her window, pulled something out of his pocket. He hid the item in his fist and held it out in front of Nameless.

"What do you think it is this time?" the prince asked with a gleam in his eyes.

Nameless shuddered against the wall.

The boy let out another laugh. "Instead of cursed, they should have called you an imbecile."

He opened his fist. And there, on the palm of his hand, were three red berries with black stems. He offered them to her. "Eat it!"

The child reached out with a shaking hand and took a hold of a round berry. She felt the strange, smooth texture between her fingers. The berry popped with a light squeeze, spreading sticky juice all over her hand.

"I said, eat!" The prince grew impatient and shoved the berries into Nameless' mouth.

In her struggle, she bit his invasive fingers, and he yelped.

Backing away, the boy pointed at her and yelled, "She dared to harm royalty! Guard, teach her a lesson."

Nameless spat the berries out and turned into a ball as a mountain of a man rolled up his sleeves and stormed over.

She squeezed her eyes shut in the hopes she would be spared.

Grabbed by her long black hair, she was swung out of her corner and into the centre of the mostly empty room.

The guard secured her by the neck and forced her face into the dirty floor. "Grovel and apologise ta His Highness, ye cursed child!"

She screamed and fought out of his hold. Her nails scratched at the hard wood beneath her, but the guard's hand held fast.

"Yer Highness, what would ye have me do with 'er?"

The prince rubbed his chin in thought. "Since she refused my kindness, have her starve for another day. If she dies, the curse might die with her."

"I'll inform Lady Hester. It'll save her a trip ta this tower." The guard let go and straightened up. He walked over to the prince and motioned to the door. "Would ye like ta return ta tha main palace? This is not a place for tha Crown Prince of the Dante Kingdom."

The child's head perked up at the name. She stared at the prince and the guard through a mess of black hair that blocked her vision.

"Yes," the prince replied with distaste. "My fun here is ruined…"

They walked to the door when the prince spoke over his shoulder in a grim tone. "Today is the late queen's death anniversary, Nameless. The queen you murdered by being born into this world. My mother!" His glare grew strong enough to burn. "Although, you are no longer Nameless. Thank Luminos or whomever is smiling upon you today for His Majesty has gifted you a name fit for a princess of this land, probably to sell you later." His hands balled at his sides, and he spat the rest of the words out, "I will be seeing you, *Emilia Valeria Dante.*"

They left, and the guard locked the door behind them.

That night, a harsh fever riddled the child's tiny body. Yet, no one came to check on her.

No one ever did.

Consumed by shivers that violently shook her entire frame, she wrapped a brown woolly blanket around her as she lay on the floor. Her teeth chattered, and her bones hurt as if ready to break. Countless images of places and people she had never seen fleeted through her mind's eye.

Beyond the pain of the fever, overwhelming sorrow claimed her heart. Tears stung her eyes as the feelings of betrayal and sadness grew stronger within her. Then, as if a switch was flipped, she sat up and blankly stared at her small hands in the murky moonlight that peeked in through the window.

"Didn't I die?" Emily turned her hands every which way and pinched her sunken cheeks. "Is this the punishment I get for ending my life? Is this Hell?"

She looked around. Dark stone walls of what seemed to be a Medieval castle encased her. The more she tried to make sense of her situation, the harder it became to think. Her mind was crammed with memories of two miserable existences.

No joy. No love. Not even a sliver of affection was ever spared to Nameless.

No. Not Nameless.

"Emilia. Valeria. Dante," she muttered under her breath. "This is impossible…"

Getting up, Emily swayed on her feet. A pounding headache felt like a hammer to the head, making it difficult to think. She shuffled to the lopsided stool and stepped on it. Just like before, she was too short and frail to see out of the window.

"What happened to my body in the real world? Is this a dream? Am I in a coma?" She shuddered at the possibility. She didn't want to see her mum's disappointed face yet again or her father's disdain.

Emily retrieved the blanket off the floor and crawled onto the bed Nameless was terrified of as she once encountered a rat on it. Wrapping the harsh material, that smelled of wee and sweat, around her, she turned into a ball and cried herself to sleep.

*Reality or delirium, what did I do so wrong to suffer so much?*

A week went by, and nothing had changed. Emily didn't magically wake from a terrible nightmare, and the room she was trapped in was starting to get claustrophobic. So, she pushed the bed against the window, which took all day, and peered out of the dusty windowpane.

As expected, she was in a tower of a huge castle. She could see a sizeable city past the castle walls and beyond that was terrain and mountains she had never seen before. The truth was hard to swallow, much like the bread the maids left for her to eat every morning.

Emily leant back enough to see a faint reflection of the child's face in the thin glass. She had black hair instead of blonde. Her eyes were a startling blue like the Crown Prince's and the second prince's, who often accompanied his older brother. Her cheeks were so sunken, she no doubt was closer to a skeleton than a child.

She didn't bother lifting the filthy dress she wore to study her malnourished body.

Her stomach let out a loud rumble, and she sighed.

"What am I supposed to do with a body of a child?"

The door handle started to turn, and Emily nearly fell off the bed as she scrambled to the corner of the room. The child's habits were hard to override when the body was filled with dread.

The door opened, and a maid stuck her head in.

"It is hiding in the corner over there..." the maid with deep brown hair said after spotting the child.

"Do you think its curse can pass on to others?" the second maid asked from beyond the door.

The brunette inched into the room and pulled a younger fair-faired maid inside, who clutched a bucket of sloshing water.

Sucking in a deep breath, the brunette stepped closer to the child. "We are here to wash you, so do not make a fuss."

When the maid reached out, Emily jerked away. "Don't touch me!"

Stunned, the young women stared at her in disbelief.

The blonde nearly dropped the bucket. "It can talk... I heard it doesn't know how to."

"I'm not an 'it'," Emily countered and glared at the young maids. They were more than twice her height. "I'm a person."

The maids looked at each other and burst out laughing.

Emily's hands formed small fists at her sides. She was hungry, filthy, and no one had taken out the chamber pot in over a week. If she died a second time, who knew what kind of torment awaited her in the next life?

She couldn't let that happen.

No matter what, she would survive. She had knowledge of the world and the story's plot. All she had to do was find a way to get out of her room.

Sucking in a deep breath, Emily forcefully straightened her hunched-over posture. Even at her tallest, she was only as high as the maids' thighs. "I am a princess of this kingdom. How dare you refer to me as if I am an object?"

"I think it might be possessed by the demons!" The blonde lost her grip on the bucket as she jumped back.

The water splashed their legs, making the maids shuffle away some more.

"Let's inform the head maid," the brunette replied eagerly.

The maids scurried out of the room, forgetting to lock the door behind them.

Seizing her chance, Emily launched for the exit only to bump into the legs of the tower's guard.

"Where do ya think yer going?" he snarled.

Emily fell back on her buttocks and scrambled away on all fours. Her body shook in response to memories of countless times Nameless was held down or hit by the guard to please the princes. "No-nowhere..."

"So tha maids weren't making up a tall tale?" he muttered to himself. "Ya can speak? Tha princes will surely find this interestin'."

He slammed the door shut, and she heard the lock falling into place.

Emily trembled and whispered, "I think I made a big mistake..."

# 40
# GOD OF THE WORLD

## EMILIA

**After observing a series of beatings** Emilia once received as a child from Lady Hester, she finally managed to break through the invisible wall that forced her to witness the hardships she wanted to put behind her.

The images faded into nothingness but did not leave her unscathed. Her heart ached, her eyes stung, and most of all, she once again was filled with hatred towards the late king, the princes, and everyone else involved in the years of her suffering.

The only thing that soothed her burning soul was the knowledge that most of them were food for worms beneath their gravestones.

Their deaths—a soothing lullaby.

Silence.

As if her eyes were opened for her, Emilia appeared on the summit of a mountain, surrounded by never-ending mounds of snow and scattered evergreen trees. Despite being in such a cold and windy place, she felt warm and comfortable.

Looking down at her clothes, she could not believe her eyes. Gone were her queenly garments. She was dressed in jeans and a T-shirt with the logo of her favourite band. Instead of ankle boots, she sported a pair of sneakers.

"Am I dead again?" she voiced her thoughts.

"Not yet," came a humorous, feminine reply.

Emilia rapidly scrutinised the area for the source of the voice. It seemed to come from everywhere, but there was nothing in sight.

"Up here!" This time, the voice came from above.

Lifting her gaze, Emilia spotted a football-sized glowing ball of light dancing above her head. "Where am I?"

The ball of light descended until it was directly in front of Emilia's face. "I wanted to visit you, Emily."

"I think you misspoke. My name is Emilia Dante."

"Not so."

Emilia's chest grew stuffy. She had only barely surfaced from a series of memories she wished would forever disappear, and yet, here she was again, being reminded of who she once was. "Who are you?"

"I am many things, but you would call me a goddess." The ball of light bounced up and down excitedly. "Emilia lives within one of our many worlds."

The Queen crossed her arms. "*You* are the author of the novel?"

The goddess laughed. "I whisper stories to many prophets, some become legends, for your world it became a story, written down for many to enjoy, which you did."

"Right..." For a higher being, the goddess sounded more like a naughty child who got her hands on superpowers. "So why am I in this novel? I ended my life as Emily Grace and, all this time, thought I was being punished for killing myself..."

"This is not punishment. It is a gift!"

Restraining her welling anger, Emilia spoke through gritted teeth. "You call becoming a trapped and hated princess a gift?"

"Emily had to endure, to become that which you are today."

"You talk in riddles. Why am I here?"

"Now who speaks in riddles? Here in this world or here with me?"

"Both?" Emilia squinted as her eyes began to burn from staring at the goddess' bright light.

"I watched you read my prophecy again and again," the goddess replied in a saddened tone. "You resonated with the people we created so much that I thought it fun for you to meet them. You decided to leave your world behind, so I brought you here."

Emilia felt her nails biting into her bare arms. "All this misery I've lived through was at your whim?"

"But you are no longer unhappy!" the goddess protested. "Look at what you have achieved! You met your favourite Thessian—"

"No offence, *Goddess*, but when I died, I had hoped that was it. I didn't want to become some tortured side character in a story you got someone to write. Honestly, if you were going to drag me into a book, you could have at least given me some magical powers or an actual ability to see the future."

"Had you been born a mage, Emilia's life would have been worse, and you would not survive the prophecy. I gave you a royal status and kept your perfect memory." The goddess paused and grumbled, "Actually, how dare you be rude to me? Those I help revere me and are thankful for another chance."

"I am *sooo* thankful," Emilia replied with sarcasm dripping off every word.

The ball of light glided away as if pouting.

Emilia sighed. Not only was the whole scenario of meeting a

goddess ridiculous, but she also didn't want to be cursed or hated by said goddess. "I'm sorry. I overreacted."

The ball of light didn't move.

*I guess, she's still pouting.* "I am thankful for the opportunity you have created for me to live again. Please can you tell me your name?"

Finally, the ball of light floated back. "Those in this world call me Luminae or Luminos. If you pray to me daily, I may even grant you a blessing now and again."

"Daily?" Emilia gaped. "Isn't that a tad excessive? Do you know how much paperwork I have to read through in a day?"

"How will you communicate with me if not through prayer?"

*I don't think I want to communicate with you…* "How about I pray every time something major happens in my life?"

The goddess' harsh tone had a warning to it. "Are you attempting to negotiate with a god?"

"Is that a bad thing?"

Luminos swayed from side to side. "Very well. I will be generous and accept one prayer a month."

"Thank you." Emilia looked around, wondering how long she had to hang out with an emotionally unstable higher being. "When can I go back? As nice as this meeting is, I think the others will worry."

"Ah, of course. Time as you understand it is different here." The goddess' giggle unsettled Emilia. "You can go, but you must do me a favour."

"What would that be?"

"Ask my servant, Valerian Knox, to stop praying every chance he gets. He talks so much, that I have no time to listen to anyone else. She may have made him handsome, but he is too devout. I can't even rest because of him."

Emilia raised a brow. "I have a feeling I'm here just for that."

Luminos went completely still mid-air. "Well…you are the only one in this world with whom I can speak directly."

*Ah, so I am now the unlucky messenger of God. Great…*

"I am going to send you back. Remember to pray once a month!

If you do it in a temple, you can see me in my true form."

Emilia's body started to become transparent. She looked at her hands in amazement as they slowly disappeared. Sparing one last glance at Luminos, she finally asked what had been bothering her for a while. "What happened to the dragon?"

"Oh, that's easy. He's hiding in—"

TO BE CONTINUED …

# LANGUAGE OF THE BEASTMEN

**Here are some of the phrases Khaja has used in this book:**
*"Jya naveren vosie."* - I find/found you.
*"Jya zadech arikesh weto zaregh iya."* - I smell hindwalker who captured me.
*"I arikesh weto ankota iya!"* - The hindwalker who hurt me!
*"Jya otarkert vosie. Nare sier yast nur vibezn."* - I marked you. Our bond is for life.
*"La-ooo-ren-z ne heslich?"* - Laurence not happy?
*"Vosie ne kaiedes moin kadachek. Vosie ne kaiedes tsessen. Vosie ne kaiedes Khaja?"* - You no like my gift. You no like kissing. You no like Khaja?
*"Vosie ntes ukiy kur deche heslich."* - You are hard to make happy.
*"Khaja zaregh golnad oin."* - Khaja capture big one.
*"Vosie ntes mir, arikesh. Jya otarkert vosie."* - You are mine, hindwalker. I marked you.
*"Jya zadech arikesh weto pishgen iya."* – I smell the hindwalker who stole/took against will me.
*"I arikesh weto ankota iya!"* - the hindwalker who attacked me!

# QUEEN OF HOPE

# BEASTMEN DICTIONARY (TO DATE)

**Words and their meaning:**

Jya - I
Vosie – (singular) You
Vas – (plural) You
Wo – we
Osie – they
Mir – mine
Moin – my
Nare – our
Vast – is
Ntes – are
Eund – and
I – the
Kur – to
Ne – not/no
Da – yes
Mopeca – can
Delte – should
Deche – make
Emberh – take
Kablenen - seem\appear
Oin - one
Dei – two
Ointes – first
Deites – second
Hedu - today
Redu - yesterday
Indu – tomorrow
Kaiedes – like (similar to, hold affection for)
Tietna – animals
Aunen – the rest, others
Zaotuo – pointed, sharp, protruding

Yille – ear
Arikeshe – (plural) hindwalkers, a term used for humans
Arikesh – (singular) hindwalker
Werst – kill
Ukiy – hard
Ankota – attack
Heslich – happy
Fabise – weak
Sohen – go, go out, leave through
Raci – here
Paci – there
Fera – will, planning to do something
Ne fera – not will (won't)
Otarkert – marked
Zaregh – capture
Golnad – big, large
Kadachek – gift
Tsessen – kiss, kissing
Sier – bond
Nur – for
Vibezn – life
Varetz - Father

# ABOUT THE AUTHOR

May Freighter is an award-winning, internationally bestselling author from Ireland. She writes Fantasy, Urban Fantasy, Paranormal Romance, and Sci-Fi Mysteries that will keep you entertained, mystified, and hopefully craving more. Currently, she's attempting to parent two little monsters and hasn't slept in over 4 years.

Who needs sleep these days, anyway?

On days when May can join her fictional characters on an adventure, stars must align in the sky and meteors will probably rain down. So, keep an eye out.

Her hobbies are photography, drawing, plotting different ways of characters' demise, and picking up toys after her kids. Not exactly in that order, either.

For more information about the author and their work, visit their website: www.authormayfreighter.com

# FIND OUT WHAT HAPPENS NEXT IN: